the
book
of
franza

&

requiem
for
fanny
goldmann

the
book
of
franza

&

requiem
for
fanny
goldmann

INGEBORG BACHMANN

TRANSLATED FROM THE GERMAN AND
WITH AN INTRODUCTION BY PETER FILKINS

**hydra
books**

NORTHWESTERN UNIVERSITY PRESS
EVANSTON, ILLINOIS

Hydra Books
Northwestern University Press
www.nupress.northwestern.edu

The Book of Franza and *Requiem for Fanny Goldmann* originally published in German
as part of *"Todesarten"-Projekt.* Copyright © 1995 by R. Piper GmbH & Co., Munich.
English translation copyright © 1999 by Hydra Books/Northwestern University Press.
Introduction and compilation copyright © 1999 by Hydra Books/Northwestern
University Press. Published 1999. All rights reserved.

10 9 8 7 6 5 4 3 2 1

Printed in the United States of America

ISBN 978-0-8101-2754-8

The Library of Congress has cataloged the original, hardcover edition as follows:

Bachmann, Ingeborg, 1926–1973.
    [Fall Franza. English]
    The book of Franza & Requiem for Fanny Goldmann / Ingeborg Bachmann ;
translated from the German and with an introduction by Peter Filkins.
        p. cm.
    "Hydra books"—T.p. verso.
    "The book of Franza and Requiem for Fanny Goldmann originally published in
German as part of 'Todesarten'-Projekt"—T.p. verso.
    ISBN 0-8101-1204-3 (alk. paper)
    I. Filkins, Peter. II. Bachmann, Ingeborg, 1926–1973. Requiem fur Fanny
Goldmann. English. III. Title: Requiem for Fanny Goldmann. IV. Title. V. Title:
Book of Franza and Requiem for Fanny Goldmann. VI. Title: Book of Franza. VII.
Title: Requiem for Fanny Goldmann.
    PT2603.A147F313 1999
    833'.914—dc21
                                                                    99-35468
                                                                         CIP

contents

introduction: darkness spoken

When Ingeborg Bachmann traveled to Egypt and the Sudan in the spring of 1964, little did she know it would be a journey that would inspire her life's central achievement. Having worked since the 1950s on drafts for a series of novels about postwar Austria, Bachmann returned from Egypt with an entirely new conception for them. Soon her work on several drafts of what she called her "Desert Book," as well as on her acceptance speech for the Georg Büchner Prize, led to extended drafts of *The Book of Franza* and *Requiem for Fanny Goldmann* during the fall and winter of 1965–66. Out of these crucial writings Bachmann developed her idea of a novel cycle to be titled "Todesarten" ("Ways of Dying") that would chronicle the multitudinous ways in which individuals, particularly women, are "murdered" by a society that she felt erased and silenced them. Though Bachmann set aside both of these novels in order to complete *Malina*, the cycle's "overture," published in 1971, only her tragic early death in 1973 prevented her from completing them as the second and third installments in what would have likely become a novel cycle to rival that of Balzac.[1]

Given the number of twists and turns in Bachmann's writing career, it's remarkable how singular and unmistakable her voice remained throughout it. Poet, short-story writer, author of radio plays and opera libretti, essayist, and novelist, Bachmann developed through an array of genres over time in her unflagging effort to give voice to the unspoken.[2] Just where the self begins and the power of history ends is the central predicament at the heart of her work, the reason why having much to do with her own life and times. Born in Klagenfurt, Austria, in 1926, Bachmann came of age with the onslaught of World War II and the annexation of Austria by Germany in 1938. Though she suffered no immediate loss of family members or severe physical duress herself, Bachmann would later cite the march of Hitler's troops through Klagenfurt as the end of her childhood.[3] In the years to come, the slaughter of innocence by historical might also became the dilemma that she would explore over and over again in her writing.

"War is no longer declared, / but rather continued," writes Bachmann in "Every Day," a poem from her first collection, *Borrowed Time*, published in 1953. What is significant about the statement is both when it was made and the implications it still holds today, for no author in the latter half of this century has been more intensely concerned with "the manifestation and expression of the destructive effects of war within the individual self"[4] than was Bachmann. Deeply devastated by the hysteria and horror manifested by the war, she never felt that the violence and atrocities ceased with Germany's surrender. Rather, as a member of the postwar generation, she was just as deeply disturbed by the greed and corruption of Germany's "miraculous" recovery in the 1950s, as well as by the lack of recognition and remembrance for the victims who had truly suffered.

Memory and history, then, were Bachmann's twin muses. What sets her apart from other writers of the era is how she saw the manifestation of fascism as not being limited to the specific context of the war but also existing within everyday life, particularly in relationships between men and women. As she noted in an interview just a few months before her death in 1973, "Fascism begins in relations between people. Fascism is the primary element in the relationship between a man and a woman."[5]

Noting that there was no "war and peace" in contemporary society, but rather "only war," Bachmann wished to trace the evolution of fascism within intimate relationships, as well as within single individuals, rather than sweeping historical events.

Nowhere is this more true than in Bachmann's "Todesarten" novels. As we learn in *Malina*, "people don't die here, they are murdered."[6] The setting, however, is not a battlefield, but rather the haunted peacetime of postwar Vienna. More specifically, the real battlefield is that laid out between three individuals: the nameless female persona, or "I-figure," who narrates the novel; her Hungarian lover, Ivan; and Malina, a shadowy male figure who shares an apartment with the "I-figure" and is present at her "murder" when she disappears into a crack in the wall. However, it is questionable whether Malina exists as a real person at all, for as the "I-figure" comes to realize that "I have lived in Ivan and die in Malina,"[7] both Ivan and Malina can be seen as forces struggling for control of the life and mind of the "I-figure."

This, however, makes the consequences of the power that Ivan and Malina hold over the narrator no less real as "crimes." Indeed, as Bachmann writes in the introductory remarks she prepared for *The Book of Franza* during a 1966 reading tour, "[T]hese crimes are so subtle that we can hardly perceive or comprehend them, though all around us, in our neighborhoods, they are committed daily." Just what these crimes involve is harder to pin down, for by their very nature "they require greater refinement, another level of intelligence, and are themselves dreadful."[8] Suffice it to say that their sources can be broken down to two basic yet intertwined categories, namely how "the whole approach of men toward women is diseased" and the fact that "language is punishment. It must encompass all things and in it all things must again transpire according to guilt and the degree of guilt."[9]

What informs the first category are the many ways that men have historically held sway over and silenced women. The second category involves something more subtle, which also serves to complicate the first, for it speaks to a problem inherent to the very medium through which Bachmann's women attempt to give voice to their inner lives. For the question that is the impetus for Bachmann's investigation of "Ways of Dying" within everyday society is a double one. On the one hand she asks why men silence women; on the other hand she wonders about the root causes that lead women to silence themselves. While the former involves the clear manipulation of power structures that deny or determine the place and role of women in society, the latter touches on an issue that involves both genders, namely the way in which language corrupts those who unconsciously succumb to its "letters, syllables, lines, the signs, the setting down, this inhuman fixing, this insanity which flows from people and is frozen into expression."[10]

In other words, the central problem for the women in Bachmann's "Todesarten" cycle is not so much that they cannot speak, but rather that they cannot find a *means* through which to speak. Because their memories are enslaved to either the history of the war or its residue found within destructive relationships, any expression that does not transform these experiences only perpetuates them. As a result, the inner reality of these women remains largely unspoken, particularly when language represents a logocentric prison that posits their being as whole and comprehensible. Meanwhile, the experience of the postwar generation is one of fragmentation, Bachmann's own attitude toward language having been shaped early on by the philosophy of Ludwig Wittgenstein and his by now famous statement that "[t]he limits of my language are the limits of my world."[11] Within this formulation, and in the face of the fragmentary nature of history's transformation into memory, the true essence of human beings, as well as the atrocities by which their essence is negated, becomes unspeakable. Thus, without a language to name the ineffable or the memory of it, it becomes impossible to name the self. But rather than simply choose despair and silence in the face of language's inherent limitations ("And I despair in the face of despair," she writes in her last published poem, "No Delicacies"), Bachmann seeks a "new language" that will posit a "new world,"[12] one in which, for all its duality of horror and beauty, "[t]he unspeakable passes, barely spoken, over the land."[13]

This effort to find a medium with which to voice the inner reality of the self in terms that do not objectify or violate the self is also the focus of *The Book of Franza*. Written for the most part in late 1965 and early 1966, *The Book of Franza* develops many of the narrative techniques that would later serve Bachmann in *Malina*, which was to have been followed by *Requiem for Fanny Goldmann* as the second novel in the cycle and *The Book of Franza* as the third. Bachmann's posthumous papers also contain extensive drafts for a fourth "Todesarten" novel about a woman named Eka Rottwitz, though these drafts are even more fragmentary and do not hold together as a consistent narrative. However, despite eventually being set aside in order to complete *Malina* and the stories of *Three Paths to the Lake* (published in German as *Simultan* in 1972), both *Requiem for Fanny Goldmann* and *The Book of Franza* were substantial enough drafts to be published posthumously, as well as to become the subject of intense critical interest in the years since Bachmann's death.

This is particularly true of *The Book of Franza*. Within it critics and scholars have not only found a kind of "Ur-text" for *Malina*, but also a compelling and complex narrative in its own right. For instance, whereas the female "I-figure" in *Malina* "wants to illuminate its own dark history in order to make it its own,"[14] Franza Jordan suffers from "the sickness of the past" and attempts to flee it. Indeed, as the novel opens, we learn that much like the female persona's disappearance into a wall in *Malina*, Franza has been hidden away in a sanatorium outside of Vienna after long suffering in an abusive marriage with the prominent Viennese psychiatrist Dr. Leopold Jordan. Franza, however, escapes and flees to her childhood home of Galicien, a fictional town in southern Austria, as she sends a cryptic telegram to her brother, Martin Ranner, that she needs his help.

Martin, who is a geologist, but whom Bachmann says in her introductory remarks will later become a historian, meets up with Franza in Galicien and helps to nurse her "dissected soul" through a complete collapse. As she regains her bearings, Franza thinks back more and more to her childhood and how it represented a magical realm of innocence and adventure, the heraldic ancestry of her family's farm still encoded by "signs and names" that held meaning despite the war. Though she wishes to submerge herself again in this realm, she realizes that the names represent "something that no longer was," just as Martin wishes to "extract himself, having no need to dwell on the memory of the past." Meanwhile, with a research grant and tickets in hand, Martin is also on his way to Egypt, Franza convincing him to take her along despite her still shaky condition.

The sea journey to Egypt, however, is a rough one, and in more ways than one. Along the way Franza undergoes a relapse and begins to ramble on about the horrors of her marriage to Jordan. From these ravings we learn that Jordan had made a "case study" of his wife in connection with his book on female concentration-camp inmates experimented on by Nazi doctors, and that it was the discovery of Jordan's "notes" that led to her breakdown. Feeling herself violated, her own psyche imprisoned by "the cage of his notes," Franza realizes that "he tried to break me, my instincts, . . . setting off the war within me" by stealing "[m]y laughter, my tenderness, my capacity for joy, my compassion, my ability to help, my animal nature." Thus Franza must travel into the "Egyptian darkness" in order to find a space that is empty of the history that haunts her, the desert providing just such a realm where "[t]he eyes and the desert meet, the desert settling upon the retina, sweeping away everything" that has come before.

Suffice it to say that Franza's journey into the "unspoken" quality of the desert's void in order to escape the "unspeakable" nature of her marriage to Jordan ends in mortal failure. Though she identifies with an array of victims that includes a butchered camel, a bound woman, Jews in the Third Reich, the Papuas, and the ancient Egyptian Queen Hatshepsut, Franza still ends up a victim of male violence, her long journey having led to nothing more than the physical manifestation of the psychological "murder" perpetrated against her long before by Leo Jordan, if not by history itself.

Yet one could argue that Franza's downfall lies not so much in her past as in the fact that she can find no means by which to assimilate the past. She herself ponders this when she asks, "My story and the story of all those who make up the larger history, how do these find a place within the whole of history?" Though on one level this does indicate a kind of identity formed through identification with others, such a sweeping construct allows no place for Franza's individual self to evolve. Instead, her "sickness" remains, as Angelika Rauch points out, tied up in her inability to "come to terms with the past through memory and the process of assimilation," thus making "the construction of an identity . . . impossible."[15]

But not the writing of a novel. For what we must also remember is that at the end of *The Book of Franza* Martin Ranner survives. Like the shadowy Malina, he is figure of rationality, a scientist who will turn to history upon his return from

Egypt. In addition, he will also be the one to tell Franza's story, for though he is unable to do so at first, he is the only one who will be able to say what really happened. Extrapolating even further, it may even be possible that Martin is the narrator of this story, his journey with Franza helping him to appreciate how "the facts that make the world real . . . depend on the unreal in order to be recognized by it." From the very start, in fact, Bachmann reminds us that Franza's journey and search for identity is one made *through* words as Martin rides a train through the Semmering tunnel on his way to Franza in the opening pages.[16] For though he is on his way to Vienna, "the Vienna here cannot be a Vienna, for there are only words that allude to and insist that something exists." Still the train rolls on, emerging from the tunnel, "brought along out of the darkness of the through journey," during which the "words line up together" as, presumably, we read them.

The demand for this kind of engagement on the part of the reader also occurs in *Requiem for Fanny Goldmann*. There "the failed mourning on the surface of the text contrasts with the memorial depth experienced in the reading process,"[17] as Bachmann relates the tragic story of Fanny Goldmann, a once-successful actress in Vienna who suffers a miserable and lonely death from pneumonia brought on by heavy drinking. Born into the Wischnewski family, her father, a colonel in the Austrian army, having committed suicide under dubious circumstances surrounding the murder of Austria's prime minister during the German annexation, after the war Fanny marries Harry Goldmann, an American Jew born in Vienna who has returned as a soldier. This marriage lasts but three years, after which Harry emigrates to Israel and Fanny begins an affair with Anton Marek, a second-rate writer ten years her junior. When Marek jilts her for the German Karin Krause, Fanny falls into a tailspin from which she cannot recover. Adding to this despair is the fact that Marek writes a novel about her, as she, like Franza, feels dissected and "slaughtered" by the imprisonment of her being in language controlled by others, herself "robbed, stripped of all her sentences and judgments."

Fanny, however, makes no effort to escape, but instead suffers in total obscurity as she resigns herself to the idea that she has "no future." Whereas the "I-figure" of *Malina* struggles to uncover her past and Franza tries to flee it, Fanny remains caught in a perpetual stasis, unable to embrace her father as a Nazi suicide and incapable of establishing anything more than a surface presence as "the most beautiful woman in Vienna," or Marek's former lover, or merely the figure pressed into the pages of his book. As Karen Remmler points out, "Like the violence depicted in the other two *Todesarten* novels, *Requiem* describes the inability of a complicitous victim to mourn her own loss of resistance."[18] Hers, then, is a "long and dark and untellable story," but also, as Bachmann points out, "untellable as all stories are." Nonetheless, Fanny's "funerary mass takes place in the act of reading."[19] For though Bachmann provides an "external" setting for the novel at the Frankfurt Book Fair with a conversation between Malina (that same shadowy figure of the novel and here a writer) and Jörg Maleta, a young "genius" from Austria, the irony is that we are compelled to concentrate on the "internal" story of Fanny Goldmann in order that we learn "what really happened," even after the fact and despite all of the gossip and menace that threatens to obscure it.[20]

By reading, then, we participate in Fanny's interior life and help her to give voice to "something incredibly important," though she cannot "hear herself speak," just as we complete Franza's journey for her by ourselves having to journey through her "puzzle of days, the undetectable chaos of reality that tries to articulate itself in a dream, which sometimes in a composition brilliantly reveals to you who you are." As readers we must travel this path by ourselves, but it is Bachmann who charts its hidden course for us, since she is the one responsible for its "composition." As a result, these novels grant us a distance that Franza and Fanny cannot discover for themselves. What we also gain is an understanding of how "[w]ar is no longer declared, / but rather continued"[21] in numerous subterranean ways within contemporary life, as well as an assertion of our ability to break out of the plight of the victim buried beneath the rubble of postwar fragmentation by seizing hold of the fragmentary as a constructive tool for our reading.

There is then a sad irony to the fact that all we have are unfinished "fragments" of *The Book of Franza* and *Requiem for Fanny Goldmann*. Like ancient lost texts, they raise many questions about the true intent behind them, but it is also their very fragmentation that helps us to read them in ways closely aligned with the narrative breakthroughs Bachmann was able to bring to full fruition in *Malina*. As Irmela von der Lühe writes, "Bachmann's poetry, language and thought require that they be pondered in a new way; that they be 'thought along' [*Mitdenken*] how person and fiction, author and work belong together in view of these texts."[22] The difficulty of such a process is that we must fill in the elisions at the center of Bachmann's characters for ourselves. Yet the accomplishment and demand of this is very much part of what Bachmann writes about in her poem "Of a Land, a River and Lakes," namely the urge to "speak across borders / even if borders pass through every word."[23]

As Hans Höller writes, "*Malina, The Book of Franza*, and *Requiem for Fanny Goldmann* illustrate that it is not only through death that the victim confronts ultimate truth, but rather through the experience of the fear and sorrow of our time."[24] It is a testament to Ingeborg Bachmann's genius that despite what she saw as the pervasive menace of the "unspeakable" in the postwar world, she herself never stopped searching for a way to evoke the ineffable and unspoken qualities of our inner nature in order that such fear and sorrow be given true expression rather than be converted into oppression and silence. That she did not live longer to tell us even more about such "Ways of Dying" is the real tragedy of her life and work.

Peter Filkins
January 15, 1999

notes

1. For a discussion of the history of Bachmann's work on the "Todesarten" novels from the 1950s until her death, see the critical overview written by Monika Albrecht and Dirk Göttsche in their indispensable five-volume edition of the *"Todesarten"-Projekt* (Munich: Piper, 1995), 1:489–647.

2. For a discussion of Bachmann's life and early work as a poet, see my introduction to *Songs in Flight: The Collected Poems of Ingeborg Bachmann* (New York: Marsilio, 1994), xvii–xxxiii. All of the translations of Bachmann's poems used here are from this edition.

3. See Bachmann's 1971 interview with Greda Bödefeld in *Ingeborg Bachmann. Wir müssen wahre Sätze finden: Gespräche und Interviews,* ed. Christine Koschel and Inge von Weidenbaum (Munich: Piper, 1983), 111–15.

4. Hans Höller, *Ingeborg Bachmann: Das Werk — Von den frühesten Gedichten bis zum "Todesarten"-Zyklus* (Frankfurt: Athenäum, 1987), 289 (my translation).

5. Bachmann, *Gespräche und Interviews,* 144 (my translation).

6. Bachmann, *Malina,* trans. Philip Boehm (New York: Holmes and Meier, 1990), 155.

7. Ibid., 223.

8. Bachmann paraphrases here from the opening passage of J. A. Barbey d'Aurevilly's 1874 story "La vengeance d'une femme," a central source for Bachmann's conceptual breakthrough for the "Todesarten" cycle. See Dirk Göttsche, "'Die Schwarzkunst der Worte'—Zur Barbey-und Rimbaud-Rezeption in Ingeborg Bachmann's 'Todesarten'-Zyklus," *Jahrbuch der Grillparzer Gesellschaft*, 3d ser. 17 (1987–90): 127–62.

9. Bachmann, *Malina*, 177, 60. Also see Karen Achberger's *Understanding Ingeborg Bachmann* (Columbia: University of South Carolina Press, 1995), 118, for a further discussion of gender-specific versus linguistic inexpressibility in Bachmann's work.

10. Bachmann, *Malina*, 57.

11. Ludwig Wittgenstein, *Tractatus Logico-Philosophicus*, trans. D. F. Pears and B. F. McGuinness (London: Routledge, 1961), 115. Bachmann quotes this line several times in her writing.

12. "No new world without a new language," writes Bachmann in the title story to her volume *The Thirtieth Year*, trans. Michael Bullock (New York: Holmes and Meier, 1987), 50.

13. Bachmann, "Early Noon," *Songs in Flight*, 39.

14. Christa Bürger, "'I and We': Ingeborg Bachmann's Emergence from Aesthetic Modernism," *New German Critique* 47 (1989): 26.

15. Angelika Rauch, "Die Über(be)setzung der Vergangenheit: Ingeborg Bachmann's *Der Fall Franza*," *The German Quarterly* 65 (1992): 44 (my translation).

16. Ibid., 48.

17. Karen Remmler, "Silent Slaughter and Dismemberment in Ingeborg Bachmann's *Requiem für Fanny Goldmann*," in

Ingeborg Bachmann: Neue Richtungen in der Forschung? *Beiträge zur Robert-Musil-Forschung und neueren österreichischen Literatur*, Bd. 8, ed. Gudrun Brokoph-Mauch and Annette Daigger (St. Ingbert: Röhrig, 1995), 160.

18. Ibid., 167.

19. Ibid., 160.

20. See Sandra Frieden, "Bachmann's *Malina* and *Todesarten*: Subliminal Crimes," *The German Quarterly* 56 (1983): 70.

21. Bachmann, "Every Day," *Songs in Flight*, 41.

22. Irmela von der Lühe, "'I Without Guarantees'— Ingeborg Bachmann's Frankfurt Lectures on Poetics," trans. Maureen T. Kraus, *New German Critique* 27 (1982): 49.

23. Bachmann, "Of a Land, a River and Lakes," *Songs in Flight*, 125.

24. Höller, *Ingeborg Bachmann*, 273 (my translation).

translator's note and acknowledgments

Because it is an unfinished novel fragment, the history and question of what Ingeborg Bachmann intended as the final shape of *The Book of Franza* remains somewhat vexed. Published posthumously in 1978 as part of the four-volume *Werke* edited by Christine Koschel, Inge von Weidenbaum, and Clemens Münster, for many years the novel was titled *Der Fall Franza,* or *The Franza Case.* However, Monika Albrecht and Dirk Göttsche's research for their five-volume *"Todesarten"-Projekt,* published in 1995, revealed that the last title favored by Bachmann was *Das Buch Franza,* or *The Book of Franza.* Given the "biblical" setting of the novel and its intended function as a kind of spiritual text for feminine consciousness, the latter seems indeed more fitting than the more menacing notion of "The Franza Case" composed by Franza's husband.

But unfortunately the questions about the text do not end here. Written in 1965–66 before being set aside sometime in late 1966 or early 1967, it was planned as the third novel of the "Todesarten" cycle, even though it was the first to reach substantial length after the several other drafts and attempts that Bachmann had worked on since the early 1950s. Indeed, Bachmann progressed far enough on *The Book of Franza* to give four readings from it in March 1966, which is the reason she wrote what has come to be known as the "Foreword" to the book, if not to the entire "Todesarten" cycle. These readings were from drafts of the first and third chapters of the present edition, "Return to Galicien" and "The Egyptian Darkness," respectively, both of which were very advanced as drafts, though Bachmann only completed two of the three sections planned for the latter chapter.

However, "Jordanian Time," the second chapter, was never completed by Bachmann and still stands in a good deal of disarray. A version of it was put together for the 1978 publication of Bachmann's *Werke*, but the work of Albrecht and Göttsche reveals many other possible directions in which Bachmann could have headed with the chapter. Many of these directions, however, remain only that, their narrative journey broken off long before arriving at a final culmination. Still, such drafts provide a great deal of interest for scholars, as well as a window onto what Bachmann might have done to complete the novel if given the chance, so the question then becomes what to include and how to do it in a way that helps the novel to remain readable as well as a faithful "reading" of Bachmann's intent.

In such a case, the translator must take on the additional roles of editor and critic. Given that this is the first translation of *The Book of Franza* into English, readability is of primary importance, for I see my job as very much involving the effort to make more readers familiar with Bachmann's work. Hence, I've taken a kind of middle-of-the-road approach, one that taps the compelling texts revealed by Albrecht and Göttsche, but also slightly rearranges them in order to attain a more readable text that represents a good number of the directions Bachmann took. The result is that the "Jordanian Time" printed here is longer than the 1978 version and also less fragmentary in its shape and feel. In addition, at both the beginning and end of this version, Franza is slightly more lucid and detailed about her relationship with Jordan, while the inclusion of earlier sections where Franza talks about fascism, finding her file, the nature of fear, and her own "erasure" from Jordan's manuscript link up very well with the "crimes" Bachmann writes about in her "Foreword" to the novel.

As for what has been lost, there is an extended passage about

Franza's failed relationship with the Hungarian pianist Ödön Csobaldi, who quite possibly is the same person as Ödön Patacki in *Malina*. This passage also leads to her first meeting with Jordan after being in a taxi accident, but ultimately the scene arrives at no closure, nor is there enough about the intervening years between her meeting Jordan and her eventual breakdown. As with two other brief passages, one concerning a fight Franza and Jordan have about Martin, another that touches on a brief affair Franza has with a man named Ulrich, the chapter seemed to me to maintain a sharper focus if I stayed more with what seemed consistent with Franza's thought process while on the boat to Egypt, rather than extensive and incomplete background narratives that confused the narrative voice.

Requiem for Fanny Goldmann, on the other hand, is even more difficult to pin down as a consistent text. Though its narrative technique is more straightforward and traditional than the other "Todesarten" novels, it's not as clear just what its final shape would have been, primarily because Bachmann worked on drafts that strongly connect it to the even more unfinished "Eka Rottwitz" novel. As with *The Book of Franza,* a version of *Requiem for Fanny Goldmann* was published in the posthumous *Werke* of 1978. I have chosen to include the bulk of that text here, but I have framed it with excerpts from the "Eka Rottwitz" fragment that became very much intertwined with the Goldmann narrative as time went on. The first of these inclusions involves a brief portrait of Malina as a writer who wants to avenge his sister Maria's death by working on a novel that is clearly a version of *The Book of Franza.* Though this creates a discrepancy when Martin Ranner, Franza's brother, also shows up as a friend of Fanny's in the narrative to follow, in which Malina also appears as a writer at the Frankfurt Book Fair, I've chosen the passage to highlight the possibility that Malina is the "real" narrator of all of the "Todesarten" novels, something that Bachmann continued to toy with herself.

My selection from the 1978 version begins with the story of Fanny's life and ends with the belated news of her death passed on to Toni Marek and Karin Krause as they return from Munich. That previous version includes a later scene at the Frankfurt Book Fair in which Marek and Karin relate Fanny's death from pneumonia as mere gossip, the idea being that her real suffering has passed into obscurity in much the same way that the publication of Marek's book "slaughters" her life. However, instead of this scene I have included the very last scene that Bachmann worked on for the novel, one that reflects back on Fanny's life and her marriage with Harry Goldmann, "the only man who had been good to her." What I like about it is how the passage very much works as a kind of "requiem" for Fanny's life at the same time that it acknowledges her "untellable story." Hence, as with *The Book of Franza*, my effort here is to touch on as many facets of Bachmann's ongoing narrative process as possible while also maintaining a narrative coherence that serves the author's prevailing urge to tell "what really happened."

There is no way to know, of course, just what Bachmann would have done with either of these novels had she lived. As with any writer, it is just as possible that she would have returned to earlier versions and discarded later attempts as it is that she would have scrapped everything and found entirely different solutions. We simply cannot know. Hence, any translation that does not include every single draft, no matter how incomplete, is itself incomplete, and as a translator, all one can do is try to strike a devil's bargain between faithfulness to the unknown intent of the author and the demands involved in trying to arrive at a successful artistic work. Indeed, in trying to serve the latter, I can admit to one additional sin. Often I have split up Bachmann's extremely lengthy paragraphs into smaller ones in order to again increase the accessibility of the novel to readers in English. The same holds true for some of Bachmann's page-long sentences, though such truncation is very common when translating from German. Neither effort, however, is intended to make the novel any "easier," but rather to engage readers more readily with the inherent complexity of Bachmann's thought and vision. In order to further facilitate the reader's ability to experience as much of Bachmann's meaning as possible, notes to the novels appear in the back of this volume and are indicated by small asterisks in the text.

Finally, I would also like to acknowledge several institutions and individuals who have made this translation possible. I am very grateful to Simon's Rock College of Bard for a sabbatical and leave that allowed me to devote my full time to the project, as well as to the Bundesministerium für Wissenschaft, Verkehr und Kunst and the Österreichische Gesellschaft für Literatur for travel stipends and research grants that allowed me to work in Bachmann's archives in Vienna. My thanks as well to Dr. Eva Irblich and Professor Robert Pichl for their assistance and permission to use the archives, and to Hans Stockenreitner for all of his kindness and hospitality during my stay. I am also indebted to Susan Harris at Northwestern University Press for her longstanding patience and support throughout the project, to Nick Weir-Williams for the chance to take it on, and to Monika Albrecht for putting up with my slight undoing of her and Dirk Göttsche's tireless and invaluable editing of Bachmann's unpublished manuscripts. Finally, and most important, I owe my deepest gratitude to Dr. Heinz Bachmann, the writer's brother, who not only read through every word, commented at length, and made countless useful suggestions, but also continues to provide an inspired model of care and intelligence in shepherding his sister's work.

the book of franza

foreword

Ladies and Gentlemen:

I have with me parts of a novel to read to you. . . .

Because you are always asked at such readings to grasp the entire whole from just a fragment, I feel that I must furnish you with a summary of its contents, though you know quite well that it is difficult today to describe a book's content.

Hence the contents, which are not the content, look like this: a young man, an assistant at a Vienna institute, a geologist who eventually will have a change of heart and give up the ancient for the sake of the contemporary when he becomes a historian, a man of twenty-eight years, living in Vienna, born in Carinthia, and who by mistake has been awarded a stipend to finance the journey he is about to make together with his sister, who has disappeared from a Baden clinic outside of Vienna despite being seriously ill. This older sister, her dying, is in the book, as well as how the brother tends to her, though by the end he is freed of all bonds.

The book, however, is not simply a journey through an illness. Ways of dying also include crimes. This is a book about a crime.

I've often wondered, and perhaps it has passed through your minds as well, just where the virus of crime escaped to—it cannot have simply disappeared from our world twenty years ago just because murder is no longer praised, desired, decorated with medals, and promoted. The massacres are indeed over, the murderers still among us often being attested to and their guilt established, some of them, not all, even sentenced in court. The existence of these murderers has been made known to all of us, not only through more or less discreet statements, but also through literature.

Yet this book has little, only very little, to do with this. It seeks to reveal something, to seek out something, namely something that has not disappeared from the world. For today it is infinitely more difficult to commit crimes, and thus these crimes are so subtle that we can hardly perceive or comprehend them, though all around us, in our neighborhoods, they are committed daily. Indeed, I maintain and will only attempt to produce the first evidence that still today many people do not die but are murdered. For nothing is—if not perhaps more powerful—more monstrous than man, if I may remind you of what you learned in school. Crimes that require a sharp mind, that tap our minds and less so our senses, those that most deeply affect us—there no blood flows, but rather the slaughter is granted a place within the morals and customs of a society whose fragile nerves quake in the face of any such beastliness. Yet the crimes did not diminish, but rather they require greater refinement, another level of intelligence, and are themselves dreadful.

The settings then are Vienna, the village of Galicien, Carinthia, and the Arabian, Libyan, and Sudanese deserts. The real settings, the interior ones laboriously concealed by the external, are elsewhere—at times within the thinking that leads to a crime, and at times in that which leads to dying. For it is this interior in which all dramas take place, in the power of a dimension in which we or imagined characters can grasp the nature of pain and suffering. It is simply not true that we live in a time without drama, an assertion that is untenable, like so many others, perhaps mine as well. But I am afraid, given what my book is about and because I worry about this book, that the opposite assertion and other theories are even less true.

chapter one
return to galicien

The Professor, the Fossil, had dug his sister's grave. He had already arrived at this hypothesis before he had the least proof in hand. Already on the way to Vienna, as the train rumbled through Bruck-an-der-Mur, then on through Mürzzuschlag, and was about to enter the Semmering tunnel, which he once thought the longest in the world, he felt that he had understood Franza's message. That is, if one could even call it a message, himself feeling like Champollion,˙ the first to shed light on a forgotten form of writing, an occupation he would have much preferred.

Before the tunnel, before he had to cease studying the cartouche of a king on the one side ("The Concise Dictionary of Egyptology") and a telegram from the Austrian postal system on the other, he felt certain. He tucked Franza's three-page telegram into his coat pocket and readied himself for the through journey. For one thing was still the same, namely that the railway still scrimped on electricity for its day trains. The blue lamp indeed was lit, but it shed hardly any light in the compartment where he sat thinking, How typical of Franza to send a telegram. She couldn't simply write a letter, and it must have been at least a couple of years, no, more like ten years since she and the Fossil—by whose holy will indeed?—since she decidedly was not the same as before and went out of his life, not only disappearing from Baden, just outside Vienna, but also from the mind, in which it is truly possible for things to disappear, escaping just as she had from Galicien, just as she had run away from him in Vienna and retreated from him, ever since she. . . .

But who had she become? A woman, his sister, who, though that word made him think of someone, no longer was what she used to be and no longer the same woman. And how typical, he said to himself: Although she had sent him only a few telegrams, this one perhaps the second or third in ten years, it was still typical, or at least that's what he felt as he sat in the dark and no longer enjoyed the taste of his cigarette and stubbed it out in the broken ashtray as he thought to himself, How typical.

When a train travels through the Semmering tunnel, when the story goes that it travels to Vienna, something is named, a city called Vienna and a village called Galicien when the story is about a young man who could be identified as Martin Ranner, but who could also just as well be called Gasparin, though it remains to be seen, if nothing changes entirely—if, in fact. . . . And though it's proven that Vienna exists, one cannot comprehend it through a single word, for Vienna exists here on paper and the city of Vienna completely elsewhere, namely at 48°14'54" north latitude and 16°21'42" east longitude. Thus the Vienna here cannot be Vienna, for here there are only words that allude to and insist that something exists, and that something else does not exist, though it is not this specific train that travels through the tunnel named above, nor the young man who sits in the train that travels through the tunnel.

What is it then? The train schedule might confirm that here (where?) trains travel daily through the tunnel, and also at night, but it cannot confirm this particular train, nor what is on this piece of paper; therefore no train can be traveling and no one can be sitting inside it, meaning that none of it exists, not even this: He thought, read, smoked, gazed, saw, strolled, tucked away a telegram, then later said—therefore no one can be speaking if none of it exists. Only the rubble of words that tumbles, only the paper that turns over with a rustle, otherwise nothing happens, nothing is turned, no one turns and says something.

Who then will say something and out of words construct something—everything, that is, and much else that is not? Yet the paper wants to travel through the tunnel, and before it enters (but indeed it has already entered!), before it does, it is still not covered with words, and when it emerges, it is covered and its pages numbered and divided up. The words line up together, and brought along out of the darkness of the through journey (lit only by the blue lamp) the originals and the copies roll on, the illusions and the true conceptions rolling into the light, rolling down through the head, emerging from the mouth that speaks of them and asserts them and distinguishes them from the tunnel inside of one's head, although this tunnel in fact does not exist, itself only an image appearing from time to time inside a certain cranium, which if split open would reveal little, for there would be nothing there as well, neither of the tunnels.

What does it mean then? Such a digression, during which a train travels through the Semmering tunnel, would have to conclude that in relation to the train, just as with all else, a confusion exists. Yet as far as we're concerned the train can travel on, for what is written about it will be spoken, the train will travel on, since it is asserted that it exists. For the facts that make the world real—these depend on the unreal in order to be recognized by it.

Also the Semmering tunnel has an end and always had one. He was then eighteen and she was twenty-three, about to give up her studies, allegedly having fainted in a hall of anatomy, or in an equally romantic tale she fell into the Fossil's arms. Meanwhile, the Semmering mountain, its slopes almost completely covered in snow right down to the area around the tracks, hung there without a word, reflected in his eyes. He had misplaced his ticket, so when the conductor approached he handed him the telegram absentmindedly, then stuffed it back into his pocket with an apology as he rummaged through all of his pockets, looking twice in his wallet amid the bills and scraps of paper, all because of Franza, and at last found the damned ticket. All because of this telegram, stop and stop and stop, as she put it, as if without those traffic signs he would have to hypothesize and ponder and imagine once more another conclusion (how many had it been?) arrived at amid these stops.

In the end one word stood there: Franza. She must have come to her senses, for the last time she had clearly signed it "Your Franziska" or "Your old Franziska." Nonetheless, she was to blame for his low spirits, for it occurred to him for the first time what he could have done: pretend not to have received this telegram and later sent a postcard while under way, best of all one from Alexandria, something he could imagine vividly, Alexandria. So why in fact didn't he ignore the telegram? If there was ever something that did not fit into his plans, into his time so carefully divided up, it was indeed this telegram. And here he was traveling to Vienna after he had so meticulously prepared to leave Vienna, paying ahead on his rent, saying good-bye, setting things in order at the institute. Now he was traveling back to where he had come from already. Wiener Neustadt in all of its modern ugliness, after that Baden, then Vienna again, the South Train Station. The southern train. That was in fact the train that would always be their own, his and Franza's train. For just as one travels along one track in life and back again on the same, together they had really known only the southern train, all other railways of the world having been second class in comparison, and once experienced, forgotten for good.

Martin walked into the station and up to a telephone booth, having already counted out the coins in his hand. As he leafed through the telephone book and dialed, it would have pleased him to see the entire tasteless station once more leveled to a ruin. It then struck him just how the building must have once really been—somewhat windy, drafty, dark, somehow threatening, taking one's breath away as one entered, just as it must have been during the school term when Franza had allowed him to visit her for a few days. This South Train Station in which one no longer froze and was afraid naturally was not the real South Train Station.

He got through to the clinic. His repeated sentences, pressed through the crackling on the line, were then passed on further by one woman's voice to another. The first voice was sterile and empty, having said the name of the clinic a hundred times over and that it indeed was the clinic, while the second voice revealed an overly anxious devotion, for it was the secretary in the waiting room, the Fossil's right hand, if indeed there was a waiting room. Then the Fossil himself was on the line, rattling off his name, aware of his importance, pronouncing it with the slightly nasal tone that only those Viennese of the highest echelons and formerly of the imperial-royal order could still practice, though in the Fossil's case it was a special mixture of a cultured tone and a tone of authority, whereas Martin had settled into a younger, purified form of German, one full of coyness which was laced with soggy consonants, always a bit too soft, this softness never leaving the speech, even when one spoke curtly or was angry or wished to speak with precision as Martin did at this moment.

The Fossil attended to him like a welfare case or someone with an imaginary illness who had grown to perturb him, dishing out a precisely mixed dose of professional kindness and sharpness. If Martin understood anything in having only once interrupted him with a question, which was immediately ignored, it was that he should not get mixed up in the divorce (what? proceedings, contingencies?) being handled by a lawyer. And as he hung up it occurred to him that he understood less than he had before, when he had understood nothing, because earlier he was not involved in anything and had known nothing about a divorce.

He had come in search of his sister who had disappeared, and even now he still did not know where his sister was, or even why he had come when he had not received any information about her whereabouts. He threw another coin in and got the first voice again as well as the crackling. He hung up. He wanted nothing more to do with the second and third voice, for his ears couldn't stand it. He hailed a taxi and gave the driver the address in Hietzing. He rode along, having been defeated. Yes, if he really faced it, he had been defeated, banished beyond the borders of this world in which a brother obviously had no right to ask a question that could cause embarrassment to such an authority. If there was one thing he had to do it was to at least find the person who had sent the SOS to him, even if it required force and no further questions, and it had to be done right away, whether he got involved or not.

He couldn't figure out if the "Jesus, the Herr Doctor" that the cook let slip in all honesty, but also diplomatically, meant that his arrival disturbed her or pleased her, nor was he certain whether she would allow him to step into the apartment, though he did enter and close the door behind him. Luckily he remembered that she must be "Frau Rosi," and as he began to turn her name over in his mind, he realized that as she muttered a "Mary and Joseph" it meant Franza was not here. When Frau Rosi spoke it always involved an agonizing translation of her Viennese dialect into high German, such that one had to think of the words she wished to say, "Jesusmaryandjoseph" probably meaning that she felt her guardianship of the house was in question. Naturally she didn't feel she was employed as a guardian, nor as a servant, referring to herself instead as an employee who had insurance and benefits, and in no way the soul of the house, as the Professor referred to her among others, nor the foolish person who often bore the brunt of his tiresome, oppressive anger. She honestly did not know that the lady was no longer at a spa in Baden, though behind her brow she worked it out that she had been left in the dark about nearly everything. One morning she had found a cheap pair of panties, but certainly they did not belong to the lady. And once in the bathroom there had been a plastic bag and a hair comb, but naturally such things never occur in the best houses, and she was only in the best of houses and had always been, and whatever was known she would not elaborate upon in front of the lady's brother.

Martin, who noted her consternation, was not interested in such an inquiry, but rather took a further step into the apartment, as if he were a police officer with orders to conduct a search as he headed directly into the sitting room with her behind him. He recognized everything, though the curtains were open now and a broom leaned in the corner and there was a sense of things having been tidied up that had little to do with the usual evening arrangement. Here the evenings had taken place, the last one more than six months ago, during which he had looked at her without being disappointed at all, but rather with complete indifference, looking on like an automaton who had been invited by accident. He made it a point to chat with Mahler, who had lost the position of Surgeon General and informed Martin of the complicated events behind the scenes. Meanwhile, Martin had stood there looking like a detective about to set down chalk marks or track down footprints or pieces of glass in order to remember precisely where each person had stood, or who had sat where and with whom, including the two most famous psychiatrists in Vienna, and the three not quite so famous, and the minions and invited clowns, and the writer whom he didn't know, and a globetrotter who used to market his slides to the public. There had also been Frau Gebauer in the middle, a pianist, and of course all the spouses of important men, as well as the head of the Ministry of Education. Yet it wasn't enough to simply observe who had been there, for he had also wanted to record the tangled web of rivalries and animosities that stretched between them. As he stood with Mahler outside the library, he had been amused at how such a tensely preserved harmony could be so easily disturbed by the slightest petty remark. Only later, on the journey home, did the usual forms of snobbery come out, as well as the contempt for all others felt by everyone there. And so he stood there in the salon whose walls, if they could talk, would have endless stories to tell, though they could say nothing about Franza as she had carried glasses back and forth, circulated, and was everywhere, asking him, Would you like a whiskey, Martin?—those being her last words to him and practically the only ones he could remember.

Meanwhile, Frau Rosi stood there with a dust cloth in her hand, holding it like a weapon, as if to prevent him from doing something. But what could that be? He walked further into a side room and she followed him. Then he opened the door to the bedroom he had never entered before, not even knowing its location. He then opened the wardrobe and took out a couple of dresses that had to be Franza's, and with a couple of dresses hanging over his arm he said offhandedly that he had to make a call. That seemed to disturb Frau Rosi more than the fact that he had taken Franza's clothes, for she said that wasn't possible, because, as you know, the telephone is in the office. So he walked into the office with the dresses still draped over his arm and sat down at the desk, though he didn't open a telephone book since there was none in sight.

Instead, there was a private directory with an unlisted number, the clinic number, the number for the Surgeon General, and the Baden number scribbled in the margin. He first called Baden again in order to assure himself that she was still missing as before, with only her things left behind, with the exception of the clothes she was wearing, the coat, and the accessories any female would need to go out into the street, though no one had been informed except the Professor, who didn't see the need to inform anyone. Obviously the police were not in the picture, for the matter concerned a Jordan. It trickled into Martin's consciousness that the "honorable lady" they kept referring to was also Frau Jordan, and he wondered how much of his sister was still his sister. He didn't worry about the fact that Frau Rosi still stood in the doorway "like a painted Turk," as she would later tell the Professor. Instead, what occurred to him was that this was the desk of the great shepherd of human souls. This caused Martin to feel further spite, for he thought he had read something in an article about theological foundations of the ministry and psychotherapy and the overarching relationship between them, though it was all the same to him, especially given how much better Herr Jordan had formulated it, Sickness and time and the sickness of the times, and in which areas natural science and the question of its domain in regard to religion needed to be explored. In his unrelenting anger, with his arm beginning to stiffen, he thought of how Franza would need entirely different clothes at this time of year, himself not an expert in such matters. Taking her clothes had only been a futile gesture, for he simply wished to take something of hers with him.

Then Frau Rosi took the dresses from his arm, if only to try to do something, saying that she would like to wrap them in a plastic cover. Since the special suitcase wasn't there, she would put them into a different case. That was fine with him and didn't matter, for he had to call Frau Nemec and say . . . what should he say to Elfi Nemec? He didn't know, for he couldn't call and tell her that he was in Vienna, sitting in a stranger's house at a desk he had no right to open. Besides that, his arm still hurt, and Nemec's number naturally was not in the Fossil's directory, and he didn't know Elfi's number by heart. Of course, he could call the Professor again and inform him in a cold, chilly manner that he was at his house and was debating whether to inform the police in the name of (indeed, which name?), on behalf of the family (but which family?), but the Fossil knew that there was no family, and that only Martin could claim in his own name to be missing an older, and on top of that, only sister, thus causing Martin to dismiss the idea.

As Frau Rosi was packing in the bedroom, he ripped open the desk drawers and quickly rifled through the folders, tax receipts, more folders, case histories, manuscript pages, and vouchers, all of them neatly written out in Franza's childlike hand, folder after folder, until finally he came to the bottom right-hand drawer, where he found what he had been looking for. There sat a couple of pages which described, no, which in fact were the beginnings of letters, though each was very short, the handwriting clear. It was Franza's handwriting, the pitched schoolgirl's handwriting from her high school days in Villach, which had developed no further and was still that of a fifteen-year-old, as if the end of the war had also sealed the handwriting in its final form—formal, very clear, but with nothing within it that would say who this person was.

Dear Martin, I must write to you. Dear Martin, I don't know where to begin or what I should say. My dearest Martin, it's so terrible, and yet I fear there is only you, which is why I'm writing you. Dear Martin, I'm so full of doubt, I must write to you. . . . That was all. Different dates, all of them from the last two years, the pages yellowed in part, in part dirty, then a folded page: Dear Martin, yesterday in the café as I sat there with those little packages, suddenly I could say nothing.

But when had he and she been in a café, and which one? He couldn't recall any time when she sat surrounded by small packages and couldn't say anything. He stretched out his legs and stared at the beginnings of these letters. What had caused his sister to write him letters that barely got beyond the initial greeting, and why were they lying here in this drawer? He took the rest of them out of the drawer and saw that some were written on better paper, proper stationery. My Sweetheart (that one wasn't to him), now I know everything (what?), I believe I know it all. My feelings are certainly no longer your business. (Did his sister have feelings? What kind? In any case, what a cold sentence, My feelings are no longer your business. How painful. No date. Most likely a letter from the past year or even more recent.) The next page: My dear Leo, we must separate. But I can't even bring myself to mention it. You know why I can't talk about it. Also no date. His sister only dated the ones to him, and the beginnings of the other letters had no dates. On the last page, which began exactly like the one about the need to separate and whose sentences were only written out in a different position on the page, there stood a line of stenography, which couldn't have been from Franza, for she didn't know stenography. That meant it had to be from Jordan, for his shorthand was recognizable from the folders. Martin took out his fountain pen and tried to copy down the symbols in his notebook as best he could and stuck them in his pocket. He debated whether he should take the pages with him, then he decided on another solution, namely to leave them lying on top of the desk so that the Professor would see that he had had them in his hand. Despite this, he still felt the disadvantages of an incomplete education. No knowledge of shorthand, and here everything was in shorthand, and it was time for him to go.

He shut the bottom drawer and let Frau Rosi give him a suitcase and a large cumbersome bag. She didn't know where the good lady had put her special suitcase, for she must have taken it with her to Baden, something that clearly bothered Frau Rosi, though it was a situation that clearly wasn't her fault. Here no one was responsible for anything, not even Franza's disappearance. The smirk with which Martin looked back at the office was brought on by his imagining that this person so worried about the suitcase would later on that evening relate how he had been here and had taken some of Franza's clothes with him, as well as what had happened at the desk, which he'd left behind for anyone to see. Dear Martin, I must write to you. He would find out just what it was she had wanted to say.

And so with this ridiculous sense of triumph he left a noble Vienna house and two streets later caught a taxi, leaving a noble Vienna district as well, but without having told the Fossil his opinion of him. Since he knew less and less about him or what indeed had happened, this would have to consist of the opinion he had always had of him, namely how he had always gotten on his nerves with those pedantic sentences with which the Fossil had always dismissed him. That haughty tone had never bothered Franza, even though there was no need to use it at home, it being somewhat moralistic, and always there, and his sister seeming to fall for it.

Yet as he traveled toward the city and still had not given the driver a destination, having told him to just drive toward the city, since he had not yet solved the Nemec Problem, and because he couldn't solve all problems at once, and Nemec was pressing to come visit him over the weekend in Carinthia, and because he was thinking about the moralistic tone, the disgust, the beginnings of the letters, and Elfi Nemec's peculiarities in bed, it suddenly struck him that he had to return home immediately, and so he said to the driver: The South Train Station. Franza must be at home. Whenever something happened between them, there would always be this: Each and every time they would know where the other was at any critical moment, and he knew, against all reason (and reason itself he had learned to respect, for it had always stood by him), that he only had to catch the train in order to solve his little mystery.

For it was like the time when, as a teenager, Franza was hanging around with the English soldiers, learning some

English, and then suddenly turned and ran away and kept running, all the way to the Gail River, into which the gang from Tschinowitz had thrown him and in which a ten-year-old could have drowned as his senseless schoolmates looked on from the shore. That's when she showed up, and although he had not seen her running, it was as if now, years later, he could see her, a barefoot wild thing pulling her little brother out of the water. Clearly, he had been crazy to come to Vienna. She must have gone home, for she was either dead or at home. There was no need to alert the police. Nor Jordan. Conclusion: She could only be dead or. . . . If that was the southern train he could see, right on time, dusky, covered with soot, and if it indeed would soon be leaving, then finally this oppressive station would be behind him.

"He will not break a bruised reed or quench a smoldering wick."

A night journey. Return to Galicien. Matthew 12:20. How irresistible Galicien is, the love for it. Now he was totally exhausted and slept on and off. Yet such love is irresistible. At least he could bring her a few dresses. Beyond that he didn't think of anything, for nothing else occurred to him, since he was unable to formulate even a sentence. Yet he thought, The Jordans of this world, and how did that sentence go that Franza had always said to him? The Jordans could not be vanquished, but love is—no, it went quite differently than that, for it had been her special saying: Among a hundred brothers. He would have to ask her what that meant: Among a hundred brothers. And what did he himself mean by this other phrase, "The Jordans of this world"? To him this one person represented many, only because he made him so angry and from the beginning seemed so suspicious, there being no other reason. What in fact did that slave to honor and glory know? Within Martin's inexhaustible storehouse of anger there existed over a hundred words with which he trampled Jordan, or the Jordans, in the dust. Who in fact was he? The more his rage became bound up with his exhaustion, the more exhausted he became. Images of his sister rose up inside of him. Only now, at night, as he approached her, he could not imagine her running down a hill, and no longer could he see her barefoot, her legs scratched, wearing a cloak made out of curtains, the curtains from the kitchen. She had always worn those rags, a Ranner, a vulgo Tobai,* the last of a long line, a mythic figure who had pulled him out of the Gail, who had gone into the cold water.

It was for this figure that he searched his childhood, no longer having much recollection of it, except for certain words, a couple of images, "The war is over," planes just above the tree-tops, white bread, a captain, jars of marmalade in which he stuck his fingers and then licked them, soldiers and then more soldiers, always friendly, and who also transported their mother to the village of Maria Gail. Did he remember the funeral, or had Franza in fact not taken him? The wailing of the relatives, one Nona, one Neni,* both of them ancient and as helpless as the children, a father on a list of missing persons, on many lists, no funeral, then no longer any Nona, and no Neni, only Franza, who presented him to the soldiers who then gave them white bread and chocolate, and also a captain who one day took him back to school, and Franza, who went to school as well. Then darkness. Gaping holes. Nemec would never believe that it all had to do with his sister.

The trail from Warmbad to the Gail River, which is labeled as trail #21 by the tourist bureau and acclaimed as a superb wildlife area as it travels past Zillerbad and along the Ziller Creek, also runs part of the way through a romantic wooded area. The entire hike to the Gail takes 1 1/2 hours and provides beautiful views to the north (see trail #10). The point where three countries meet. Three languages. From here we can retrace our steps backward (see trail # . . .).

Martin had the taxi take him only as far as the railway crossing at Warmbad. He needed to walk, yes, along the Ziller Creek, though at night he couldn't see anything and there was no thought of turning back. He unwound from his long journey, the many hours in the train, and breathed deeply. Soon he could hear the Gail at the bend in the river, the unmistakable sound of where the Ziller Creek flowed into the teeming water. Now Martin could ready himself for the musty house that still belonged to him, for Franza had gotten the money and he the house, and a bit of money as well, which he had used to finish his studies, though the house was still there. He knew every bump along the path and gave sway to each of them in much the same way that the path followed the banks, always keeping the right distance from the river's gravel bed, as if he had a sixth sense for the contours of this landscape.

At least the Fossil had never set foot in this part of the world and could not lay claim to the signs and names by which everything here was coded, nor had he ever known the Franza who walked about carrying a jack-o'-lantern, who in the afternoon had climbed the ladder to the hayloft with Martin to tunnel through stacks of hay, who had taught him how to carve pumpkins and roast corn and to live stretched out in the hay as if that was all he would ever need to live. She always took him along with her, traipsing around, looking for food, washing him and dressing him and undressing him, as they made promises to one another whose content he no longer knew, only that they spoke of how they would live together when he "grew up," though she thought she already was "grown up" at fourteen or fifteen, she was sure of it, that Gitsche.

But how could he have forgotten that! For that's what he had called her, "Gitsche," the Windish' word for girl, "Gitsche," who was the essence of all the Gitsches with slanted, expressionless eyes.

Yet later something came between them, for though one day both were living in Vienna and he had met her again in Café Herrenhof during his first semester, he had to abandon the word "Gitsche," choosing stubbornly instead to latch on to Franza, even though her fellow students called her Franziska. Soon everything fell apart between them and they had nothing more to say to one another. This young lady had changed her hairstyle and dropped the Galicien accent, exchanging it for a different accent in Vienna, walking through Herrengasse and through the Kohlmarkt as if she had never walked over the Matchstick Bridge at home. Because of more pressing matters, he didn't ask her any of the questions he should have asked, and later only thought of one or two from time to time. Only much later did he want to know more from her, for she had known their parents longer and must have missed them more than he did. Father, for example, and not only because he was on the missing persons list, but rather because of the two black warts on his face, which he had wanted to ask about the first time he had seen her with Jordan. While saying good-bye, after the initial tensions between a husband and a brother were over, he noticed that the Professor indeed had two dark warts on his face, something that had slightly shocked him. It occurred to him that Franza was looking for someone to watch over her, though he couldn't imagine that to be true, for she had always watched over him. Nor could he imagine that she was looking for someone or something that wasn't him, and that she had married her father, or at least that's how he thought of it on first impression, reducing things to the lowest denominator, though later he revised it to "father figure."

Ten years later, as Martin was thinking about warts as a reason for marriage, he reached the house and opened the door, but without having to look for the key under the empty flower box on the window ledge—the door was open, it had to be. A light burned in the hall and the door to the kitchen was open a crack. He soon could see the bench in front of the ceramic tiled oven, but first he saw her feet stretched out over the end of the bench, wearing bright socks, her shoes having toppled to the floor, looking pathetic. He remained standing at the door as she sat up, turned toward him, and grabbed hold of the oven's tiles, remaining there, slipping and yet grabbing on, half sitting, yet hanging. He quickly went to her, kissed her on the cheek, and before he could kiss her on the other, she turned her head away.

No. Don't look at me.

He tried to take her in his arms.

I knew that you would come. Finally you came. I knew it, that's why I'm still up, I knew it.

Martin still had not said a word, for he had seen her face, which she now pressed against his coat. He hoped that she had not noticed anything in his face and also that he had not said anything. What matters is that you came, that . . .—but she stuttered so that he could not make out what she was saying, only that she kept trying to say something but couldn't speak. He kissed her and held her tight, kissing her soiled and sweaty hair. Don't say anything, what's important is that you're here.

I . . .—but she could say no more. She cried, but it was something more than simply shedding tears, for she trembled and her body did something he couldn't ease with his arms, a convulsion whose spasms got stronger and stronger. She trembled and tried to push him away and then grabbed hold of him again as he kept saying, Franza, Franza. There was nothing to do but keep saying her name and hold on to her, though he didn't know how much longer it would last or how much longer it could go on. He continued holding her, suddenly easing up and then holding on tight, not thinking of her at all, but rather that this was an impossible situation, and here in this house, miles away from a doctor or telephone. As she collapsed, as if she had neither muscles nor bones, and he lay her head in his hand, checking to see if she was dead (no, she was not, only mortally ill), he came to his senses, realizing that he only needed to, that is, only must get through the night with her and then in the morning, and then immediately he would . . . , if only the morning would come!

He lifted her up and took her into the bedroom, where there was nothing but their grandparents' twin beds, and laid her on the bed that he had made up for himself. As he did so the mattress began to rustle the moment he touched it, giving off a terrible sound in the dead silence of his own breathlessness. It was the straw in the mattress, but Franza lay there completely still and didn't seem to hear a thing.

He took hold of her wrist and searched for a pulse, or what he would have been happy to call a pulse, but found nothing, or at least it was too weak, and trying to count the beats was useless since he had no idea what pulse rate a person should have. He then undressed her, but it was much more difficult than he imagined, for Nemec and Karin and Fanny wore different kinds of bras and garters, as he violently unhooked and ripped off everything. If only she weren't so heavy, though of course he had never had to unhook something on anyone who was unconscious.

Then he looked down at her and didn't know what else to do. He was hungry. He couldn't just stand there and stare down at her. He went into the kitchen and cut himself a couple of slices of salami that he had left there. The bottle of wine was also half full, but he had forgotten to cork it and the wine was flat and sour. He balanced a plate, a glass, and the bottle in his hands, carried them back into the bedroom, sat on the other bed, and began to eat hungrily, gulping it all down and looking at her while considering what to do.

It had all ceased to make sense, everything he had thought of on the return journey, and what he had remembered. This was no longer the Franza of earlier days, and no longer the strange lady, the always elegant strange lady of Vienna, nor was there anything left even of Galicien, except the fact that it lay at a distance from the railway, the highway, and from every other connection, and that you still needed eight hours to get to Vienna in order to get someone to a proper hospital. Back to Vienna twice in the same week! That was really the last straw, though no better idea occurred to him nor did he want to think about it anymore.

He began to drink as he considered the entire myth of childhood and its puzzle, if indeed there was one to consider or recall again. He thought over it all, chewing bread and salami and drinking wine, the dull weight of the situation bearing down on him, which perhaps at one time he had remembered as being bad, but not as bad as this, and not here in this run-down cabin, this last little remnant of a once-imposing estate, which had in fact not been that imposing, but only was considered so in the region between Dobrowa and Tschinowitz, where one could belong either to the large estates or the small ones. This place had once been considered large in Galicien, a realm and a name, though that was no longer true. Instead, it had electric lights and running water and only two sheets that were no longer clean, between which Franza lay, but no sense of comfort, no doorbell one could push, only a useless, no longer familiar sense of welcome, a hot plate with two burners, a couple of hand towels, rags, and an iron washbasin.

He should perhaps have made tea for Franza, yes, tea, in case she could drink or needed to or wanted to. This place was not even good enough to put a sick dog to bed in order for it to die, while for Fräulein Nemec he naturally had reserved a double room with a shower in Warmbad, which was good enough for a three-week affair and for Elfi Nemec, who, though she currently was an unemployed model without any prospects in business or industry, was not in the least calculating, thus making her pursuit of Martin seem all the more genuine. Still, he did owe her a decent hotel, and she expected that, even if her passing interest in a notoriously underpaid scientist made her quite selfless enough to pursue more favorable acquaintances less zealously.

Nonetheless, he had never given the impression of living in poverty, and not only because of her, but rather because, like thousands of others in Vienna, he had sought to maintain the appearance, and convey to her the feeling, that she was not involved simply with a young man who had prospects of a future career at the university, but rather with someone who through his acquaintances and circle of friends belonged to that stratum which, even after a total upheaval in the social strata, still represented a thin, exclusive upper crust simply by the vocabulary they used, the jokes that only they understood, the manners they maintained, as well as the unmannerliness they afforded themselves—and indeed how much they do afford it! Thus Nemec, with her handsome figure and the proudly tender tilt of her head, always caused one to think of her as posing in front of a portal with a swarm of pigeons taking off behind her, or standing upon a fallen balustrade with her beautiful hair flowing in all its calculated wildness, or pulling on her gloves as a blind man with a hat entered the picture while walking along the sidewalk—all of it reminding one that Fräulein Nemec never wasted her beauty on simply anyone.

For an eternity could pass in this city before anyone found out about the run-down sublet in which, between the many ill and the macabre, inbred families, someone lived who during the day passed through the doors of the Demel Café on the Kohlmarkt with complete self-confidence or held tickets to a premiere that evening, or who in some tasteless postwar apartment complex worked and vegetated and yet thought himself a part of that upper crust, despite living in one of those apartments built right after the war whose architects were racketeers, speculators, and gangsters who had long since disappeared with the down payments, no longer held accountable for the badly fitting doors, cracking walls, and the suffocating oppressiveness of the rooms, an oppressiveness from which as little emerged as from the untenable great labyrinth of rooms found in the older districts and villas that remained locked up and moldering away.

For the secrecy of a Viennese apartment is almost impenetrable, even by one's own best friends, while those who dare to invite people in are usually the nouveau riche or old money and have nothing to hide, as well as a bathroom one can allow guests to use, servants or cooks who open doors, drinks already prepared, and refrigerators in the kitchen instead of roaches. Others, however, call each other up and agree to meet in the same restaurants and cafés frequented by those without such fear, choosing to meet there in order not to betray each other's secrets. Always there were accidental encounters that opened Martin's eyes and shed light on the relations of a successful university professor or a journalist or a successful woman, be it a death, rarely an emergency, and even more rarely a shared trust, for in such matters the maintenance of secrecy was a matter of respect and honor. You simply took down someone's telephone number, since the address was treated like the cartouche of an entirely new proletariat, for you never made use of it, or at least did so only when you wanted to write someone a letter while on a trip, or if someone couldn't be reached while you were in the city, since you never actually showed up on his doorstep but instead sent a telegram.

As for the women allowed into these apartments and rooms and hideouts—no matter who they were, they always kept their mouths shut and said nothing, for that was also an agreed-upon arrangement, as a Viennese woman would always admit whom she was seeing or sleeping with (whether it be an affair or a liaison, the two not being synonymous), yet she would always keep quiet about the location and her lover's financial status. Elfi Nemec, for instance, grew up near the inner city, but it was the wrong side of the ring road that circled the inner city. Hence, she asked no questions, nor did he, and so she knew no more about him than did all the others—namely that he had some connection to Carinthia, that somewhere down there in the south he had a house way out in the hinterlands, or what could be called a house, and a family, or what could be called a family, but nonetheless something, for he went there from time to time, perhaps to ski in winter, maybe to swim during the summer break. Indeed, though he wanted to bring Nemec to the inn at Warmbad, he would never have brought her here to the house.

As Martin looked around the room, he thought about what the house was worth, which no doubt some of the farmers in the area had already calculated in their heads, while some dope from the city had also figured out whether or not he could buy it, or even a German, for recently the Germans had extended their joy in conquering the world to buying up property in this remote area. Yet when he first thought about selling, it was because of Franza, since he couldn't help thinking as she lay there that he had to do something for her. As he thought deeply, estimating and calculating a price that he knew hardly anyone would pay, he forgot the terms of his parents' estate, which stated that he promised never to sell. Yet even as he remembered that, he tried to think of a way out. What did he owe his sister, what in fact did she really mean to him? He simply had to help pull her through, head back to Warmbad and the desk clerk at the inn, and slip him a tip in order to get him to let him use the telephone. In the middle of the night the Professor might have the decency to listen to him as he gingerly broke the news that he had accidentally come upon Franza, and because he didn't feel it was his business to interfere, Herr Jordan should come fetch his wife or have the Red Cross pick her up, since he alone was responsible for her, and furthermore was a trusted doctor and her caretaker, and he certainly couldn't allow himself to divorce a near-corpse.

Meanwhile, he, the brother, couldn't do much more for her, for he had his tickets for the plane and ship in his pocket, his bags were packed, and he had before him a singular opportunity that he didn't want to give up. He knew nothing about pulse rates or about someone being seemingly dead or even about illness, which it certainly was, and he could not take over such a responsibility for more than a day (the responsibility of the psychiatrist, wasn't that one of the Fossil's own phrases?), for the Fossil was so good at taking "responsibility." To Martin, quartz and epidote formed a finely textured mass, the components undulant and smoothly grained, and about slate or hints of subaquatic volcanism he could talk with pleasure, or when it came to the odd sample rich in chlorite and epidote, with isolated traces of feldspar—but he understood nothing about his sister's closed eyes and whether they concealed something or what that something might be.

Sample #331, that he would have gladly explained to the Professor, but here his sister was cut through by pain and by something he was unable to explore, given his specialty, for he had no desire to describe or identify his sister's dissected soul, which was from the Modern Era and not from the Mesozoic. Only rocks provided solid ground, and had structures, textures, and locations. Franza only had words, and then silence. Also, he had no intention of returning to Vienna, and no intention of. . . .

Martin stopped drinking. The wine was really sour. He stood up and went into the kitchen, took down the bottle of schnapps from the shelf, and quickly took a couple of drinks from it, because tomorrow was what was important, tomorrow was what he wanted to come. He could also call Alda, since

Alda's goodness, willingness to help, and thoroughness filled him with warm confidence (which the schnapps also supplied). She was a doctor, had completed her residency, and would know which doctor and where he could bring Franza, for one could only wish for a good old friend like Alda in a city where you could rely on no one.

So he toasted his own good fortune as he took another drink. Alda would straighten out everything. But as he set the bottle on the table he suddenly felt caught in the act. Franza stood in the doorway, her stockings hanging down, her dress on sideways and open at the back, looking as if she'd been resurrected from the dead. She looked at him urgently, still not saying a word, as if he needed to understand something. Then he said quickly as he turned on the hot plate, I'll make you some tea. He busied himself with the water, then pried her away from the door frame, took hold of her arm, and brought her back to the bedroom. I'm feeling better, she said, I need to explain it all to you, I'm feeling much better. She wouldn't let herself be swung back onto the bed, but instead remained sitting on the bed and resisted his excessive, cumbersome worry as he said that he simply had to lay her down. Just lie down, I'll bring you the tea. But I don't want to lie down. Martin let her remain sitting, for he still felt guilty. Can't she accept that one can drink schnapps even though someone else lies there seemingly dead, looking blank as a stone? He said, There's so much I have to think about. We'll think about it together once the tea is done.

There's nothing more to consider. I've already done it.

Franza spoke coherently, but very slowly, as if she had to force each word from the base of her tongue out toward her teeth. Soon it began to go better and she could begin to articulate as her face regained its composure, something having come back into it which one might with some assurance call life, though Martin simply thought her pulse must have returned or her circulation.

Look, Franza, you need to get out of here. I'll call Alda first thing tomorrow.

No. Not tomorrow and not at all. You won't call anyone. I don't want a scandal. You need to stay right by my side. Go make the tea. Then come to bed.

When he returned with the tea, which he had not bothered to strain, she began to talk while still sitting up. Meanwhile, he undressed in front of her as he used to long ago, though this time she didn't help him into his pajamas or rub his feet, even though they had always been warm. Martin was happy that she was alive and talking and wasn't crying, upset, and angry anymore. Yet she wasn't quite right, was she? He couldn't believe this was the first he thought of this, and he began to think about the immediate family and all of their distant relatives. In the immediate family there had been no mental illness, which was hard to believe in a country in which such ailments were endemic. But that's how it was, yet despite such reassurance, what Franza said was crazy, namely what she had done or thought she had done and conjured up.

By now he was completely sober, yet everything seemed even more crazy. She had found her purse and taken out her passport and held it out to him so that he could study it quietly as she took a sip of tea, after which she swallowed a tablet with her tea, coughed, and absentmindedly pulled her stockings up a bit. Meanwhile, the dress—which was what he would have called a designer dress, as he thought of Nemec, since recently at night in Vienna the talk had often been about dresses and recent collections, and "designer dress" had stuck with him as a code word—in any case, Franza's designer dress looked worse than the rags she had worn as a young girl. Dirty, wrinkled, stained, it looked as if several mouthfuls had already fallen onto it and she had simply wiped them away, though she continued even now spilling some tea onto the designer dress. He had seen it coming as she held the cup at an angle and then made fidgety movements over the stain. However, they weren't about the dark wet stain, but rather she seemed to be dramatically searching for something, as if she were constantly searching for something as she swiped back and forth with her hand through the air, then grabbed hold of her head again with only the hand holding her passport still free, the passport itself being brand new and containing a single visa.

Martin looked at the passport, first in a dutiful, then a disturbed manner, and read the words "Good for all countries with the exception of," though a visa with the Arabian stamp was there. She hurried to explain how she had gotten the new passport, asking whether or not he had noticed (her voice growing ever more rushed) that her own name was printed in it. He had not noticed and obediently looked at it and saw that there was no longer any mention of Franziska Jordan, neé. She had taken care of all that after her disappearance from Baden, which in fact she had visited not for the sulfur baths but for an operation. She hesitated. An admirable achievement, noted Martin to himself, for she knew exactly when he wanted to leave, and she was hoping to go with him. She still had enough money to do it, though it was all that was left of the great Ranner fortune, the Ranner essence no longer in her. He let her talk on and on, gave her back the passport, took the afghan from the living room, rolled up an old flannel blanket that lay beneath it and set it at the head of the bed, and stretched himself out on the rustling of the slack straw mattress, and thought of cursing, since he was no nurse and wanted to sleep.

You have to take me with you. You must.

He let the light burn, for she asked him, suddenly changed once again and with tears streaming, to let the light burn. And as they were going to sleep, as he still tried to help her along by asking "What? What exactly do you mean? What are you thinking?" in order to get this entire madness out of her, since one couldn't argue at five in the morning, especially given such mad statements, no matter how much they contained their own kind of logic, he finally said again, this time more sharply: You must see the best doctor we can get in the best clinic available. This is madness. You can't stay here, and I can't take you with me.

You will take me with you. And I'm not going back to Vienna.

By midday Martin hardly knew if she had cemented the commands "you must, you will" into his thoughts while he slept or if she had simply begun in the morning to try to convince him that there was no such thing as the best doctor or the best clinic for her in Vienna. As long as she carried the Fossil's name, she had no chance of being sick like the others were, not amid his power base, which inspired more fear in her than dying on a straw mattress in Galicien or while on a journey, one on which Martin wouldn't even take a healthy person, for since she could only walk and talk and breathe for a few hours at a time, he wondered how he would even get her to Genoa, half doubting that he could.

In this way a day passed and then another, the moment of decision approached ever closer, but he called no one. He dressed her as if she were a child, held onto her tightly when the madness came on, and bathed her, later walking with her a few steps away from the house to the foot of the hill, and once all the way to the Maria Gail church when she insisted on visiting the graves. They walked around the graveyard in the springtime sun, and Franza plucked a few weeds, though he hoped she wasn't thinking of weeding the neglected graves entirely. She made a token attempt at doing so, then she said, "This isn't the nicest spring, it's the second nicest." He looked at her with suspicion, but then she stopped talking about the nicest spring and the second nicest, and they began to study the names on the gravestones and conjectured which ones they might be related to. Certainly she was related to Gasparin, for shouldn't our name really be that, asked Franza, and aren't we also related to Katzianka, Napokojs, Wutti, and Kristian "V Jezusu Kristusu Je Življenje In Vstajenje"?' And then she was astonished at how few first names had always been in use around Galicien, the same ones recurring over and over, Martin, Jakob, Kaspar, Johann, Albin, and not many more, Elise, Agnes, Terezija, Márica, Magdalena, Angela, and then again Elise and Josef and Magdalena. They kept repeating. Not only had Ranner and Gasparin repeated themselves, but also other names by which they were known, such as vulgo Tobai, meaning that they were baptized twice over, like the House of Austria with its sixfold set of names constantly repeated until its collapse, and even afterward suffering the urge to maintain a memory, the names standing for something that no longer was.

Martin noted that Franza was also suffering a collapse and that through her sickness she was also suffering the sickness of the past and manifested many of the same symptoms. She looked backward, spinning amid the past, clad in those ancient names, and only when he spoke to her did she seem to awaken, but as if she had almost forgotten that she herself was there, submerging herself again and draping herself with the last name that had in fact been her first, herself surprised that it no longer covered her entirely, but rather only the bare essentials.

He, however, would no longer have anything to do with this demise and death, of that he was certain, for he would somehow extract himself, having no need to dwell on the memory of the past here in front of the graves, since they meant little to him. As far as he was concerned, the cemetery could be closed, plowed under, for he certainly had no plans of being buried here. If it were up to him they could begin the collectivization of the fields and make an end of the worship of names and spells and this endless agony over the meaning of names, behind which lay property, and the monstrosity of the ownership of property and the desire for it. Certainly Franza, like him, no longer was a person concerned with owning things, but she was also a fossil, for she still insisted on keeping hold of Galicien, despite so much having been taken from her, an inclination that was also revealed by the story of her forged passport. He, however, didn't want to succumb to the old wounds and entanglements, but rather to branch out and rise above them. That's why the worst name he could give to anyone whose way of thinking and feeling made him feel uneasy was "fossil." And that went for all such impositions that had ever existed, all such oppression, be it that of the oppressor, such as Jordan, or the oppressed, such as Franza.

He then apologized silently to his sister for calling her a "fossil" and promised himself to acknowledge who she was, even her faults, because she was being destroyed, yet he hoped she would discover just what had caused her destruction. Even her trembling and confusion did not completely erase her talents, which made possible her move from Galicien to Vienna, where nobody would understand her strengths, and from which she was now in retreat, though at least remaining true to herself. For she had not forgotten where she came from. She didn't walk around here innocently as he did. He could have been anywhere else looking at a graveyard and names, and he wanted to get her past their mother's grave quickly, but she didn't budge. He didn't want her to notice too easily that in these last few days he had wanted to remove and take away everything from her, be it the view of a mountain, of an old familiar place, a path marker, a photograph. He hoped that nothing unexpected would happen, for he hated it when something unexpected happened, and it was already enough that he couldn't understand and was unsettled when she said something like: This is not the nicest spring. These allusions! Their manifestation right in front of him. So what if it was the second-nicest spring? It would be nice enough for him if only this entire spring were not ruined.

On the way home he said, It's not much farther, pull yourself together, it's not much farther. But I know how far it is, and I can't go any farther. So he dragged her home. Why wasn't this the nicest spring or at least one as nice as all the others?

He went through the same routine, though this time he drank less schnapps and was able to look calmly on as she slept, the novelty having worn off. With her pale and seemingly dead, unable to do anything more, he let her lie there as he read through the books he had brought along in order to prepare himself for the journey. Now and then he laid down a book near her, such as his beloved Breasted,* as if he were setting a piece of cheese out for a mouse in order to get it into the trap, but she never touched a single book. Yet there was no word of any change in her plans, while only her lack of interest allowed him to hope that in the end she wouldn't come along. Alda could still be reached and tomorrow was another day, and the spring was still the second nicest, though for him it was spoiled by this game of cat and mouse, which she didn't want to play.

Franza continued to say nothing about Vienna. When she broke out of her deathlike trance, she began to speak at length, going on and on, but about nothing, or at best about things from long ago. Do you still know? Do you remember? No, you wouldn't know about that. No, back then you were still too small. Is that so? No, there's no way you could know about that. Such madness would turn him into an idiot.

Back then. Always back then, about which he knew nothing. It was hard to make out what Franza remembered of the occupation and Englishmen and "parsitans" (as the ten-year-old called them, his hands slapped by her because he built bazookas out of tin cans and wanted to look for Allied hand grenades with other children instead of listening to Franza's fanciful monologues). In Galicien, after the Germans retreated, one lived on rumors that, completely exhausted, they had filled other towns and streets and would never retreat from them as they had from Galicien, this being the last throes of a monstrous power that had long since disappeared from Franza's consciousness.

Indeed, she was convinced that the Germans would never be heard from again. They would retreat ever farther to the north and down the other side of the globe, passing from day into night and disappearing, or at least retreating to places with names like Kiel and Magdeburg, the last two sad soldiers whom she had given something to eat having been from those places, which for her didn't exist on the globe. She wished that they could return to their towns and to their families, though she didn't think they should fill up Galicien, which for reasons of space didn't have enough room for so much chaos. On the one hand there were the partisans under Tito who were on the march, while the Croatian rebels' had not yet ceased fighting and Vlassov's hopeless band' of anti-Soviet and pro-German troops had begun to plunder the upper valley. This stirred up the rumors, as the farmers of Galicien, who were panicked not so much by war as by the word "plunder," decided to flee to the hills with their livestock and supplies of flour and corn and sides of smoked bacon that they had kept concealed from the Nazis, now hiding them in the caves and burying what they could, deciding to wait it out in the upland caves, yes, until. . . .

"Occupation." That was a word that Franza pinned her hopes on and which she carried around inside of her. She always imagined countless soldiers with loaded rifles occupying every square foot, a swarm of locusts investigating and patrolling every inch of Galicien. And "rape," that was another word' that caused Franza to imagine things capable of taking away the spring, and since there was no one she could speak to, rape and armies turned into longed-for heroes and troops who were on the march, which was for the good, since nothing ever happened in Galicien, absolutely nothing, only the village dying out and the place belonging to her alone as she waited for a miracle and for something miraculous to occur.

Now and then planes still flew low in dense formations over the houses, and since they took precise aim on anything that moved, she once had to throw Martin to the ground and cover him, for she was convinced that as long as she wished for it strongly, she couldn't be wounded and not even shrapnel could touch her. And then one time a bomber patrol returning south from Vienna released a couple of leftover bombs, collapsing the little train station as a waiting train full of people from town was thrown from the rails, tearing the people within to shreds. Then it was quiet again. During that spring death was a given, as well as life, for at the same time it was so easy to live—you simply walked around with a head held high, and if there were shots you walked calmly on. Shots fired from the muzzles of guns and the quiet that followed, those meant nothing to someone like Franza.

But for the first time Martin became a burden to her, for he didn't understand and didn't share her sense of wonder, which was what she called her sense of restlessness. She grew up during those days, shooting up tall. She was always on the go, running around and throwing herself down amid the meadows to gaze up at the sky full of droning as she saw the squadrons appear. Yet how did one properly greet these heavenly hosts? Who was up there and who was it that made the spring and dying and not dying seem so easy? Maybe she would in fact die and would not live to see what she was waiting for. For bombs could still fall from the sky, and on Galicien as well. But with every squadron the weather improved, nor had there ever been so many flowers in May. Between the initial alarm and the main alarm the grain still grew high in the fields, and that alone was what Franza noticed and no longer the alarms. Nona and Neni had both become so hard of hearing that they hardly understood when they were told that they no longer needed to live in a cave, and Franza would have to yell into their ears each time she returned from the village. She screamed that the war was almost over. It's beautiful outside. I went swimming in the creek. They'll soon be here. Those are only the bombers. And Neni asked as he chewed tobacco whether she had heard anything from Vienna or about the Kaiser. Franza yelled that that was another war and laughed loudly.

One day she walked the hour's journey to the highway in order to keep a lookout, for neither during the night nor in the morning had there been any planes. She dragged along a reluctant and feverish Martin, who held a large handkerchief with dark green, blue, and red checks up to his face, blowing his springtime congestion into it. He was hungry and, to Franza's exasperation, seemed to use his fever as an excuse to whine, while she was waiting for peace to come, for the swarm of locusts, for the invasion and the troops. And besides, it was noon and the nicest of all springs.

Franza had fallen into such a state that there was hardly any more room in her body for such excitement. They're coming, finally they're coming. It means peace, Martin, do you understand? But what came was something other than she had imagined, something that didn't worry itself about two children and was not just troops, as four tanks appeared quite slowly in orderly formation. She almost fainted, for it was overwhelming. How was it possible that a day and a moment could culminate in the mind of a fifteen-year-old, a date that would enter into the history books, but with no mention of Galicien's liberation and two children watching from a country road?

The tanks had reached the children and the soldiers laughed, some of them waving. English soldiers, said Franza, who didn't even know what English soldiers looked like, though there was so much that she knew intuitively during this time and which she recognized the instant that it happened. She ran along beside the tanks, which didn't turn toward Galicien, but rather, without slowing down, traveled on in the direction of Villach and simply passed them by. And as the tanks pulled away from her and she couldn't scream because of her joy and didn't ask the soldiers anything, who themselves were unable to say anything but just laughed and waved, and because it suddenly was impossible for her to smile back since she had to cry, though she wanted to let them know how happy she was, she ripped Martin's snot-filled handkerchief out of his hand and waved the crumpled rag. Peace is here. She gazed on at the tanks and then back the other way, but nothing more came, no one occupied the villages and streets, and it was hard to believe that peace had come to a country road, leaving behind a cloud of dust.

That evening the war once again came to an end in front of the armory in the village. Although Franza had wandered around the village the entire day, she hadn't noticed the arrival of the jeeps. The soldiers had already gotten out, and now real, live Englishmen stood in Galicien with maps opened wide in their hands, and they did nothing but speak English with one another.

All of Galicien rested on Franza's shoulders, and because of that she walked toward them, trying to muster her courage. English had been her elective subject, though it had always been dictated to her. Despite translating some from one language to another, she knew no sentences that could be used in such a situation. In addition, since during German class different parts in Schiller plays had been read aloud, there was more Schiller in her head than English dictation such as "I am, you are," none of which was useful, though she had to try. She put together some sentences and hoped that she'd get them out, even if she didn't get as far as saying the last words of Schiller's *William Tell:* And therefore I declare all of my servants free,˙ for man is born free, is free.˙

Instead, as she stood in front of a soldier, she said: Sire. Either he didn't hear what she had said or didn't know what it meant, and so she said again to another one who looked at her in a friendly manner: Sire. And then she noticed that one of them didn't talk like the rest. He was very tall, thin, and big boned. His mouth moved as if he had a speech impediment and stopped after every third word as if he needed to take a breath and relax his jaws and stretch his palate. That was when Franza, for the first time in her life, demonstrated her instinctive discernment, a quality that later would help her make her way outside of Galicien, as she looked up at this uniformed soldier and, as she kept her eyes glued to his face without looking away, said to him with confidence and for the third time: Sire! And this Sire happened to be the captain, though that she would learn later, since she couldn't make out any signs of rank on these khaki-clad beings, having up until then only taken men with gold or silver on their jackets to be officers. And yet she said to this manifestation of peace and to this man, Sire, and he looked at her and listened to her with a condescension befitting someone who represented peace, though he did it without insult. Then she took a breath and began her recitation.

"Sire, this village is yours." Was that it? She spoke so clearly, as if she were standing in the back row and had to be heard at the podium. "We have no arms." Wrong. Weapons were called something else, as she looked at him intently and said, "We have no Germans and no SS, the people has left" (was that right, or was it lived?) "the village because of fear." And Sire and peace, this king, this first man in her life, showed consideration and understanding as well, as she ceased to recite.

Later she would walk through the village accompanied by the captain and other soldiers, her own sense of wonder still there. "This is my brother, Martin," she said, and the captain asked her where her father and mother were, that is, if she understood correctly as she tried to watch the words coming out of his mouth. She decided to answer the simpler question first by saying, El Alamein, and in case he thought that she didn't know that El Alamein had happened early on in the war, she added that her father was probably dead. "We miss him," she said, and thought to herself, He is thought to be missing. More difficult to explain was the mother's situation, what with the Villach hospital and the operation, or whether he could help Franza travel to Villach and look for her. The six-foot-three, thin manifestation of peace said he would take her to Villach in the jeep, not right away, but tomorrow or the day after, for he had more to do than look for mothers in hospitals, though Franza was glad they had understood one another, despite the English being so difficult.

For weeks afterward she continued to call him Sire, even though he had suggested a couple of times that she call him Percy, but that simply wasn't possible for her, for she never could have called him that. At night, when the grandparents and Martin were asleep and finally no one else was in the kitchen, she undressed herself in front of the mirror that hung above the sink and observed her body intently and with distress. She rubbed the skin on her arms and legs with the washrag, and felt so thin, nothing but skin and bones. Although for once she had enough to eat, it would take longer and was for now hopeless, for she had no hips, only two bumps that stuck out, and breasts that were too small. And he was so bony it was hard to imagine how it would be, for he was certainly a bag of loose bones held together by a uniform, and she couldn't picture him in a suit.

By the time the people had finally come down from the caves with their livestock and supplies, the situation with Franza and the captain and the jeep was old news to everyone, for he had taken her to Villach, and there were the Englishmen who had brought her mother back, and the captain who had gone with her to the funeral. To Franza there was nothing in the least suspect about this, for her Sire came quite often and picked her up and Martin too, or stayed for an hour at the house, but he never held her hand and treated her in a condescending manner. Instead she was treated not like a child, though not very differently than a child, him saying once to her, "You are a strange little girl," as she held onto his sleeve in order to keep her eyes open while walking through the hospital wards and the stench and the groans (wading through blood, this court full of blood, she thought). Nonetheless, she did keep her eyes open because he walked with her through all the corridors where soldiers lay and partisans and the wounded or simply sick women and men, the two of them passing the tired and irritable doctors until they came to the woman doctor from Vienna who was not irritable and who also remembered a Frau Ranner and what had happened and had talked to Franza with such understanding, explaining that this too could be endured, and then chatted in a friendly manner with the captain in her good English.

Franza thought to herself that the two grown-ups could handle anything, for Dr. Susanne Santner of Vienna was also tall and above all tenderly plump, completely enwrapped by lovely flesh. And throughout that nicest of all springs this woman played the most important role in Franza's thoughts, for soon the captain and Dr. Santner saw each other again, and even before the two of them, who often took her places, brought her along to dinner, Franza had already guessed that such a long bony man needed such a warm and tall woman and not a thin spindle. If she felt tears come it was because she was so happy, for she loved the love that they felt, which she took to be an enormously tender love, though she especially loved the Sire's love of the Viennese woman and looked at her Sire ever more searchingly to see if he was happy and how happy he was, though it was impossible to tell, for he didn't change, didn't glow, and only Franza glowed.

On her lay the afterglow, though the captain remained the same, arriving as lanky as ever and stammering, which she learned from Dr. Santner came from being at Oxford, making it understandable why he was different than the other soldiers who spoke so fast and laughed a great deal and were friendly, but who also seemed like children who, after an exhausting day, relaxed and played games that seemed childish to Franza, although she played along with them, listened to the radio, and performed a couple of dance steps nonetheless. Franza always spotted him first, and it was never hard to do so, and not only because amid the twenty khaki uniforms that stood in the village square he was taller and a captain, though like everyone else he drove a jeep. Peace lasted the entire spring, there was no school, and there was a man who never laughed at her and always took care of her, but who didn't want her, or to rape her, for there was no thought of that.

When she suddenly learned that he was returning to London and had said nothing about it, she should have been shocked on Dr. Santner's behalf and felt bad for her, but instead she found herself shocked about his going to London, even though he said that he would be back. She knew even then that he would never return, for the troops at the front were all being replaced, and she knew that, so why had he spoken about returning? Would he at least take her hand now? But no, as he moved to get into the jeep as if it were simply a normal departure on any given day, she suddenly threw herself at him, feeling her bones knock against his, wanting to wrap her arms around his neck, but only reaching with her fingertips as far as his throat, as she said, Thank you, thank you, in both languages. As he bent down a little and kissed her, they suddenly kissed each other in a great rush and several times, as if the jeep would simply drive off on its own without him if they didn't hurry. With that, Franza's first love came to an end, and she remained behind, with no afterglow, only dazed, the glow flickering out within her, as she stood amid the dust cloud that floated behind the manifestation of peace as it drove away.

These kisses, perhaps ten in all, that had tried to represent "thank you" or "you're welcome" or that there was something terrible about the moment, also were special in another way. For although they were Franza's first kisses and none would follow for years to come, she knew that they weren't real kisses, but rather what she called English kisses. He had kissed her mouth violently and with closed lips, though she would have gladly opened her mouth, because she didn't want these types of kisses, but rather others. Yet amid such hurry she couldn't solve this problem and didn't really know what she wanted. Later Franza often looked searchingly at the abandoned Dr. Santner, feeling sorry for her and hoping that she had not been kissed in such an English fashion. But she said nothing to the doctor and didn't ask if letters had arrived from the captain, because for Franza it was somehow better to think that nothing more would come, that there was no point of dispatch or return address for Sire.

She thought of the story of that spring during one of the explorations that Jordan had conducted with her, though she left out the part about peace and other things, as well as the beauty of the spring in Galicien, because naturally Jordan was not interested in that, but only in the circumstances surrounding the first kisses and Franziska, which had to be investigated. Yet in the middle of her ardently faithful description a phrase returned that she said out loud, one that as yet had only been in her thoughts.

Those were English kisses. Jordan, who never allowed a sentence to pass by without interpretation, interrupted her, saying, That is extremely interesting, what you said, English kisses. That's a slip, for you must have meant angelic kisses, but she replied sharply, No, not at all, to which he said, Please don't keep interrupting me, as he studied the little problem and analyzed her kisses on both the linguistic level and the experiential, as both peace and Sire fell by the wayside, being of no use. Franza allowed herself to be analyzed as she strained to keep listening and not interrupt him again, until she saw her English kisses weighed, cut apart, and pulverized, divided up and dead, herself now purified and sterilized, having found her place and calling in life. After that there was really nothing more that could happen.

Later, at a conference in London (sponsored by Her Majesty the Queen, who naturally was not there but whose name appeared on all the information sheets and daily programs above a long list of committee members in fine print, women and men, all of them titled, who also had nothing to do with psychiatry), she was allowed into a club one time, along with other women, at an evening in honor of the guests and the international man of science to whom she was married. In the maze of doctors and wives and committee members, she recognized him again immediately, though after fifteen years he looked not a year older. She was thrown off for only a moment by the fact that he wore a suit as he passed by, obviously having had a tailor able to give his long frame a certain elegance that it had not had in Galicien, though it was still able to bend in certain places where other bodies were not able to bend.

She tried to come near him and noted that he still spoke breathlessly and was only somewhat uglier than what she had remembered. And that must be Lord Percival Glyde,˙ if Jordan's English colleague wasn't mistaken, though she'd have to check the list later, although it wasn't that important. They continued to stand at a slight distance from one another and were swept toward or away from each other by the crowd. From where she stood she didn't listen in to the conversation but rather to him alone. He sounded very polite and at ease and continued to talk in a superficial manner. As he sat down at a table with someone, she turned away from a group of people, headed toward the table, and sat down next to him. He asked what country she came from and whether it was her first time in London, and she replied that London pleased her a great deal, but she had seen so little. After the fourth question and answer she debated whether it might possibly shake the foundations of the club if she asked a question, which was not a completely senseless one, as she asked, Do you know Austria? And indeed he was not shaken, nor did the walls of the club collapse, for it was a completely normal question, one that remained within the boundaries of the club's etiquette. He said, Yes, but unfortunately not well enough, having gone to the opera once, Karajan the conductor. She then asked, And the countryside, you don't know it? He said, Yes, of course, a bit, but the club began to tremble somewhat, no doubt out of abhorrence at his directness, as he continued on, saying, Just after the war, at the end of the war with the army, though before another direct question came he was saved by a lady who was thrilled to see him again. Meanwhile, Franza went mute. She had the waiter bring the same drink as he had drunk, a whiskey, and said in his tone, But with water. And please, no ice.

It was time to go, though as they left he had to ask someone else a question and answer one as well, and so she took Jordan's arm and said she was incredibly tired and that must be too much for him, these eternal parties, after which they chatted in a London entirely clear of fog about the people and the lectures, as Jordan talked on and tore apart the London conference and the slim pickings, as she walked along, holding his arm, angelic, and debated if she should call him up and see him, for now she had a body. She still owed him that. No, not him, but Sire. Then she laughed, since neither Percival Glyde nor a captain in the army would understand her, while Jordan was lucky to have said something funny in the same moment, and thus took her laughter to be related to that.

But if he had known, he would—well, what?—find one of his little theories reduced to a shredded heap. For it was a long way from the onset of peace to the middle of an extended peace, and amid the latter there was nothing one could do. In peacetime you no longer represented a prize, nor could you simply curtsy in front of him as a representative of peace, for he no longer was important to anyone, he as such, and the peace having become a mirage. And no one stood anymore at the edge of a road, somewhere in Europe, feeling as if she would collapse while trembling, or simply stand there forever in a cloud of dust, as the four tanks rolled on—which could no longer be seen.

Someone like Franza was such a fossil that she had to live constantly amid a sense of magic and marvel. Martin knew no magic, for he was content to be like the painter who said that before he painted a picture of a landscape (as an irreducible magical image from which others would then construct their own impressions), he first had to know its geology. That was well put. And before Martin could know something of his sister and complete a portrait of her, he needed to find out just what kind of ground she stood upon.

No, more than that, for he was already somewhat familiar with the terrain, but he needed to know what had been covered or had shifted, what had migrated, what had formed folds, and what hanging walls had remained stable. For geology had wonderful words. Hanging walls. And what kind of geological inclusions still existed inside her person? Why had something gone wrong and what could have disturbed her so? Such questions of a general nature he had only asked earlier while in the field, and only when he no longer focused intently on his work and deadlines, but instead relaxed in an alpine meadow, ate his lunch, smelled early snow coming on, or tried to guess when the rain would come that would prevent him from working further. There, at the back of the beyond, as he scornfully referred to the area since he was sick of it, he had thought about the social makeup of rocks and various rock formations disturbed by apparent faulting. And even today he still thought of some sentences that he had written down as initial conclusions in his study.

"It must be concluded that both rock formations must have suffered (suffered!) a final metamorphism, and likewise a mechanical realignment as a result of a subsequent overthrust." But could the same be said of human beings? "A morphologically striking quartzite formation turns out to be imbricated along the Rannach Line." The *Ranner* Line. But the Ranner line would soon run out. The last of the line sat there in Galicien and could no longer even share the names they once had for one another. At one time it was because during that nicest of springs the difference between their ages had been too great, and later, when the age difference became less important, a void had opened up between them involving their separate interests, milieus, social circles, and concentrations of bacteria, while even now, when all the differences between them could be explained, there was an illness whose characteristics were not yet completely known, a secret as well as an illness.

What had they indeed done to her? And what residues were still within her?

There were only a few places in which to discover Franza's strata. In general he had been shocked by what he had seen of her in Vienna, something that made him think of someone bent down, polishing shoes. Most likely Frau Rosi had polished the Fossil's shoes, but what Franza stooped to there in Hietzing had been more irritating, for not even Nemec had ever debased herself to him, or the photographer who had "discovered" her, the way that Franza went around in such a sanctified manner and got involved in discussions that had nothing to do with her. Since he had only this point of reference, he kept thinking of the ghostly evenings in Vienna during which she ran around like a spinning top as the Fossil patted her shoulders heartily, jokingly, erupting with a laugh that informed the others how well things were going for the two of them and that Franza belonged to him. And even when he was alone with her, when they met for an hour in a café, it wasn't she who came, but rather a facade, for whether he liked it or not, he had to bear listening to what her esteemed Fossil was up to—"my beloved Leo"—a ridiculous phrase that even now made him want to slap his forehead in frustration.

Indeed, Jordan was called Leopold, and the letter he had seen had been intended for him. But what would Franza have written to her Leo when she was still together with him and clinging to him? Minister B. was also now his patient, which meant that he would soon get the Medal of Distinguished Service, First Class, though naturally such an award wouldn't matter to him, for now he would certainly have to go to one of those unspeakably idiotic evenings at the Palffy Palace. It was all so awful, but still she clung to the medal.

And then they were supposed to fly to a conference in London, and in the fall to Buenos Aires as well, although Buenos Aires probably did not happen, for he heard nothing more about it, but instead Martin heard about this enormous responsibility. You know he has such an enormous responsibility, Martin, her face taking on a wrinkle of worry here and there, for there was this annoying bad blood between Jordan and Frankl on the one side, and Jordan and Hoff on the other, and he could see because of the worry over such bad blood that she stirred the sugar in her coffee for minutes at a time. As far as he was concerned, the Fossil was free to cause bad blood in the pursuit of his own ambition or to shove others aside because of his desire for power, but why should Franza suffer as a result? She had never argued with anyone or stood in anyone's way, except of course when it came to him, since she had often argued with him, but that was something different, and why should his Franza allow her coffee to get cold because of others?

That's the way it had always gone when they had met, and he would have loved to say something to her, his proud, silent one, his deathly pale sister. Especially about how early on he had sometimes gone to Frankl and Hoff's lectures, thinking the Fossil would be hurt or annoyed. Instead he only wasted his own time, while this irrational defiance of his brother-in-law, to whom he had no other way of demonstrating his disapproval as a twenty-year-old, later seemed ridiculous, especially after he had been sent to the mountains, where amid raspberry bushes and snakes he gained his first distance on Vienna and his sister and the Fossil. He had his rocks and the ages of the Earth, and Franza had a life at the side of someone whom she had demonstrated was someone who made her let her coffee get cold, and she couldn't expect, given his own perspective, that he would see things from her point of view as well. Instead, it was better to have the folds of the Alps and the field, the serpentine and slate, the hornblende and granite. He would rather bite into granite.

Oh Franza, how can someone with an old Windish head and a face the spitting image of Nona fall into such a trap!

They stayed inside the house for most of the time she remained in bed, though she was not as silent as in the first days. It also relieved him when she groaned and let go and cried, Don't go, stay, hold me, don't go. Above the bed in the otherwise bare little room there hung two oversized photos replete with wide wooden frames as if they were paintings from the palace at Schönbrunn. The photo of Nona hung above his bed, a wedding photo such as one never saw anymore, herself at eighteen but looking older than Franza at thirty-three as she lay on the straw mattress. Still, Nona was undefeated, gazing across at the picture of Neni, yet also beyond him, who, with his mustache, confidently looked ahead at the death of the Kaiser and that of his own children and the pneumonia that would arrive sixty years later, though he too was undefeated and under attack only by the picture opposite, whose face was not ready to sign any armistice in a silent marriage war that they would end together, and out of which each would emerge the victor. They were both the unvanquished, the two of them up there, and Franza said, without sarcasm, that she felt the same.

Were you in a war then? asked Martin, amused. No, said Franza, not me, as Martin thought, She really has no sense of humor. But weren't you married? He couldn't let it pass. But Franza said, No, not me. Not me at all. He discovered that he had not only gotten Franza to walk and to stand and to talk, or at least talk her way around it, but also that she sometimes was able to ward off the spells when he spoke to her. She used him like an oxygen tank, listening eagerly, herself also talking a bit, but only within certain bounds as he tried to assist her breathing and not tire her out, though she wanted keenly to know what he had done "at the back of the beyond" and in the years since.

(Don't pretend now that you ever were interested! Don't pretend . . .)

Yet still he talked to her, for he knew that he had to pump something into her that would help her to function, not a coin per se, but something about his work, a thought, something that she could latch onto. She always seemed to be interested in something, whether it was Nemec, Karin, Fanny, or his outings to the Wachau region west of Vienna. He presented his affairs to her like the gift of a toy, and with each toy she busied herself for half an hour and then wanted a new one, and he gave her as many as he could. In other circumstances he would have felt shabby in talking about Nemec or Fanny like that, but this type of indiscretion was something different. She needed that in order to get a chunk of time between herself and the time about which she didn't speak, and so she was even eager to hear about geology. She still did not speak about the trip, the same way she didn't talk about "Jordanian" time, for it was as if she wanted to protect them both, the past and the future.

On the last day Martin once again looked for a way out, for he wanted less and less for her to come along the nearer the departure date approached. If she couldn't or wouldn't go to Vienna, then certainly there were other countries. There must be clinics in Switzerland, and "Swiss doctors and Swiss clinics" soon became for him an extended leitmotif of cleanliness, purity, and responsibility, but if Switzerland was still too near Jordan's power base, then there was also the Mayo Clinic. This idea totally fascinated him. He had just recently heard someone talk about it, though unfortunately he had not listened closely. They said it was exceptional, the best in the world, and one only had to wheel her through the entrance and onto a conveyor belt and she would come out healthy on the other end—such was the kind of progressive treatment offered there. It also occurred to him that a word like "Mayo" not only had a fabulous ring to it, but would also come with a fabulous price tag, not to mention the travel costs, though there must be a way to afford it, though for a life nothing could be too expensive, could it? If he thought about it, there must be a hundred thousand people who should be at the Mayo Clinic, but perhaps 2 percent had the chance to be admitted. He would at least have to call Alda about it, for once you thought of it, one didn't give up on a name like

"Mayo" and such an opportunity without pressing further. In addition, in a Mayo Clinic a Mrs. Jordan would not draw attention, and no one would bother himself with this apparently lifeless European woman. She could even be known as Mrs. Smith. They didn't attach any importance to names. Or she could try traveling on her forged passport since it was no longer difficult to enter the States.

That evening Martin felt very happy again, although he had second thoughts about the Mayo Clinic. Franza had packed her bags and made it obvious that she understood this was the last night in Galicien and that she was quite capable of remembering her resolution. He was happy that the dangerous Galicien episode was over and he had something to do. He loved to pack with a sense of deliberation and careful consideration, whereas Franza, when he looked around and saw what she was doing, simply stuffed her suitcase full as if it were a duffel bag. In the meantime, she thought about what she needed to buy in Genoa, for though she had plenty of clothes, and indeed the right kind, since Martin had grabbed summer clothes in Vienna, she still talked about needing underwear and a bathing suit and sandals, as he began to feel gloomy about Genoa.

He organized the supply of medicines and checked over it. In order to keep Franza busy he thought of having her do it, since she needed to understand such things. Yet it turned out that she knew nothing about it, since she had never heard anything about stomachs or intestines or yellow fever or malaria in her world, but only about the white man's psyche, which was clearly under siege, as he could well imagine just by looking at her, and so he pretended to turn over the job of the final check of that bag, praising her when she recognized a gauze bandage as a gauze bandage. Then she said she would like to go for one more walk in order to get some fresh air, and it wouldn't do any harm to get out a little, just to take a few steps. After studying her, he asked, Do you think you can manage it on your own? and she replied, Yes, of course.

He then repacked his case of books, being dissatisfied with its present arrangement, for nothing was on top that should be on top and lying in the open, ready to be studied. He sat down on the bench in front of the house after everything was finished and smoked, feeling everything was in order and ready, just like his bags. Somewhat bored, he then stood and walked to the Matchstick Bridge, thinking he'd certainly meet up with her soon, for she had never taken any other path. Then he realized that it was the first time she had gone off on her own since they had been in Galicien.

He began to call her name, but there the water was too loud. He heard his own calls, but nobody else could hear them. He ran to the end of the bridge and took the path along the Gail just as he had done on the first night. He kept calling her name, then would stop, call, run further, toward Tschinowitz, until he stumbled upon a motorcycle with its headlight on, although it was still twilight and not yet dark. A man stood by the vehicle and looked down at the river, the motorcycle resting firmly on its stand. There's a woman below walking into the water, said the man with a satisfied gasp, as if he had finally come upon something exciting, such as a house on fire or an accident. Martin ran down with the man to the stony banks of the river, but the man was faster and let himself slide into the river as Martin slipped and tried to catch himself, his foot landing against a pile of garbage that began to topple, himself reaching the bottom as the man pulled Franza onto shore, though she in fact had not gone under, but only waded in.

There was no other way to think about it, and from where he stood, nothing to do, for it was not a "leap into the river." Here there was no "Bridge of No Return" and there was nothing that lent itself as the setting for a dramatic leap, and

Franza was not at all lifeless or a waterlogged corpse, and in fact didn't even seem to be cold. Only the man was freezing and began to tremble, and as the three of them climbed back up the path, Franza kept saying, Forgive me, please forgive me, while Martin said nothing. Then they were back standing next to the motorcycle with the dripping man, both of them apologizing to him, together and alone, though none of it made him any more dry, as he got the idea for the first time that they owed him something as he looked down at his wet and ruined suit and said something about getting cold and catching cold and schnapps and how was he going to drive to Müllnern like this.

After some awkward negotiations, the man drove back to Galicien with Franza on the back of the motorcycle, and Martin walked back to the house. Thus the last night was like a morning songbird eaten by the cat. They sat there together with the man, who was from Müllnern, and emptied Martin's last bottle of schnapps. He had probably never felt better, especially after he had undressed and put on Martin's almost new winter suit, which Martin had given him, and which fit almost perfectly, though he would later have to hem the pants. Of course he would also keep his mouth shut, though Martin was afraid he would not be able to drive the vehicle to Müllnern. Clearly they underestimated a man from Müllnern, for a bottle of schnapps had no effect whatsoever, and he could still drive fast and straight as an arrow. He doubted whether he should let him drive, but after midnight Martin let him go, obviously an experienced, knowledgeable, schnapps-besotted rescuer who lightly swayed, but who, like a rider in the Wild West, clamped the motorcycle between his thighs and, as ever, headed his horse in the right direction.

They both went to bed right away without even saying goodnight. Even if Franza didn't avert her eyes, Martin did, for he couldn't bring himself to ask: Why? Why had she done that, done that to him, why to him, and why did he have to spend his last evening with a motorcyclist from Müllnern? That was hard to take, yet he couldn't find the words to ask. He turned out the light and Franza let him turn it out without complaint. She no longer insisted that it burn the whole night through, and she was asleep before he was. He listened to her breathing, mechanically asking why inside his head, though since that led to nothing, he noisily turned toward the wall and turned off his thoughts just as he had the light.

The next day, quite early, a delivery truck from Tschinowitz took them to Villach. On the journey Franza mumbled something about having the sniffles, which wasn't really necessary since she was already on her second handkerchief that day. He had the truck stop at a drugstore on the main square so he could buy some decongestants and aspirin and something else ending in "ycin" that the druggist had recommended, and he threw the medicine into Franza's lap with an ironic smirk.

Neither had looked back at the Gail or Galicien, but instead sat in tense silence across from each other. At the train station they bought newspapers and stood reading the headlines as if it had just dawned on them to find out about what was happening with the labor unions in Vienna and the American president and the choral society from Federaun and the trolley workers strike and the dairy farmers association and the new summer bus schedule and the film industry and the Theater-in-der-Josefstadt and yet another launch at Cape Kennedy and a plane crash in Beirut. Martin would have preferred to have read about the plane crash in his paper rather than in the one Franza was reading, just as, oh God, he could see another ship was reported to have sunk in the North Sea again, but as the train arrived he noticed as she folded her paper the words "Business Section" on the upper left of the page she had been so deeply engrossed in the entire time.

So Franza read the business section, something he would never have expected, and he couldn't help laughing out loud, unable to keep down his amusement at the thought of her reading the business section. Franza looked at him uncertainly, yet with relief, although she had no idea why he was laughing, but at least it meant things were good between them again. She clambered onto the train and took the suitcase that he handed to her as he continued laughing. She squeezed herself even more tightly between the suitcases that he tossed on so that there was just enough room for him as he closed the door behind him as if making certain that the river and the evening and Galicien didn't come along with them.

Just before the border, as all the bags hung in the netting above them, Martin asked her whether she could still recall the sentence from the book, no, the poem. She briefly looked up at him, as if she had to think hard or couldn't so quickly come up with what he meant, and then opened the business section and looked for the article about crude oil (since crude oil set him at ease? because he knew something about crude oil?—it was hard to say). She then said in a neutral voice, one far removed from the young Franza who liked to recite with great enthusiasm: Among a hundred. She hesitated and pressed smooth the business section and said, Among a hundred brothers. Yes, I know that, said Martin impatiently.

Among a hundred brothers, there is one. And he ate her heart.

And what else?

And she ate his.

That's all I wanted to know, said Martin, for I couldn't remember it exactly. He took her newspaper and gave her his. Now you can read mine and I'll read yours. And he felt the urge to laugh again as when he had boarded the train, but she continued to read and looked as if she didn't want to be disturbed.

He began reading again. Customs and the border patrol would be coming up any minute, and Martin, who to say the least had never felt very comfortable in the presence of gendarmes, border police, officials, and policemen who caused him to feel more cowardice than courage, sighed and took her passport, putting it together with his as if she were his wife and they were the Ranner passports, hoping that nothing would go wrong, that reading newspapers would be enough to convince them, and that his sister, or rather his wife, would not be taken away from him by some border official. Franza began to stir as the first official arrived. She reached over for Martin's cigarettes and lit one up, although she hardly ever smoked. She crossed her legs and stretched out and quickly gave the official a direct and friendly look, then quickly looked out the window with interest, while Martin, who had no talent for acting, but instead hated such things, allowed the ceremony conducted by the border officials to descend upon them, all the while feeling unconcealed bitterness as he presented a face by now full of suspicion and discomfort. As the train finally pulled out of Tarvis he would have loved to slap Franza's face or throw her from the train and see her crushed beneath the wheels, but not here in this compartment, not as she sat across from him with tender eyes, speaking little sentences, such as, Is something the matter, dear? and, Would you mind opening the window just a crack? Meanwhile, she appeared almost distracted and behaved as if they had spent an entire life traveling together across borders with a piece of paper that had something false written on it.

chapter two
jordanian time

As they left Genoa, Martin decided to remember this departure always. Then came this awful departure in Genoa, he could imagine himself saying, though he was wrong: Later these hours would hold no special place in his memory.

Why didn't you leave? he asked Franza. I don't understand it. You only needed to pack a suitcase in those first weeks, you could have called me, you could have simply left. I don't understand you. Every single moment cannot have been so awful that, as you say, you're unable to think of any part of the past without screaming or beginning to tremble.

But it's because it wasn't that bad then. I didn't know yet what he had planned for me. It's simply hard to explain. Goodness, I can't breathe, she said, laughing.

Her breath wheezing, she stared at her hands on which blisters had formed. Look, I'm shedding my skin, she said, everything will be all right, for I'm getting a new skin. I'm certain that it's not contagious. You're shuddering because of me.

What are you talking about, said Martin and checked the door's bolt again. He was so exhausted and also had trouble breathing in the stale air of the cabin as he poured two full glasses of mineral water. What do you think of the ship? he asked.

Every moment that I spent with him now seems to me a disgrace, every single one, she said, though that can't be true. What a disgrace.

There's no disgrace in that, with having lived with a pig, Martin said curtly.

You can say that because you've no idea what it means. Only now do I wonder about the other women and why all of them disappeared without a sound, why one no longer left the house, why another turned on the gas, while I myself am the third who amended herself with this name, becoming the third Frau Jordan. It's as if over the entire time that lies sunken in darkness a spotlight now shines. Everything there lies naked, grisly, unfathomable, full of evidence that can't be overlooked, and yet how willingly I believed them to be dumb, ignorant, at fault — worthless creatures who through their departure into silence condemned themselves to their own failure in the face of a higher morality, a higher authority, a standard that I wanted for myself alone. I felt I was above them, flattered, as if perhaps I could knight myself, having earned such an accolade through effort and cooperation and the renunciation of my own way of thinking, which should have just begun to take shape. Yet I hung myself with my immature thinking, with my careless rapture for his charged wire of thought, for had I touched a high-voltage wire, causing electrocution, severe damage, and burns, it would have been faster and gentler, and certainly no worse.

What other girls long for I had to work hard at, namely, to look into the last room, the marriage with Bluebeard,˙ ever curious about the last room, to be slain by secret aims and methods and to kill myself by pondering the one figure who, for me, wasn't transparent.

Why was I hated so much? No, not me, the other within me. There are many possible explanations, and you'll have them as soon as I tell you three stories, but as yet I don't have them myself. I have no way to account for the choke marks on my throat, for my peeling skin, for I am peeling everywhere, the result of a diabolical experiment. Oh, why didn't he simply kill me. It's so unjust.

I don't know why during those days I met so many people who knew something, each one knowing something different, things that contradicted one another, each sentence a minefield on which I stepped. Alda said that she felt so sorry that things were going so badly for Leo, though I didn't know myself that things were going so badly for him. At home he whistled and played his tapes as if he were happy as a thief about something. What could it have been? That I was feeling bad she simply didn't know, so I kept quiet and tried to figure out what was going on.

He had spoken with her, she said at the end. She only wanted to say that, generally, a divorce is always something very sad. Certainly very sad for both sides. I stared at her and then left. I stood on the street and then felt the pain, this odd pain. I thought that I wasn't yet over the flu. I had to lie down immediately and take a couple of pills, that was it, but in the evening he came home and said, So, the lady lies in bed and reads. I stood up and dragged myself around the apartment. I read the galley proofs and sealed the envelope, the page proofs having arrived, which I looked at after dinner. And then I saw that in the acknowledgments expressing gratitude for the help of Riedel and Prohaska and Emmi my name was missing.

It wasn't really the fact that my name was missing that bothered me, but rather that it tipped me off to something else: He wanted to erase me. My name should simply disappear in order that I could disappear for real later on. And then it hit me all the harder: If any name was expendable and no longer meant anything as a signature through which everything could be verified later on and by which each could be held accountable, the same was true of everything I had visibly done, which in fact I had done exclusively for him. That had cost me a number of years, and because of my own zeal and sense of conviction had given meaning to my life.

I took the first packet of page proofs and brought them to him and said, You have to proofread all of these yourself without me making any remarks, especially the introduction. After an hour he brought the pages back to me in the living room and said, It's fine. I immediately opened to the pages of the introduction and saw they hadn't been changed a bit. Then I looked at him.

Yes, I simply looked at him, and then it occurred to me what his strategy was, for he was above all else a renowned strategist. He smiled and said, Now we can treat ourselves to a small whiskey, it should all be finished soon. He poured me a glass and brought it to me. I didn't take my eyes off him, and yet I knew that I would never be able to ask him a question, to say something to him. Cheers, he said, you've worked hard. I lifted my glass and then I knew that he knew exactly what I was thinking and enjoyed it. I suddenly said that I had been at Alda's. Well then, what's our lively one up to? I said, She's not so lively anymore, she's worried. When it's someone else's business that's when she comes to life, don't you think? Yes, I thought, as I choked on the whiskey. Then I stood up suddenly and noticed my teeth were chattering somewhat, I couldn't speak anymore, and I wanted to get out of the room before he noticed it.

He laughed, pouted, and held me back. Your flu always comes in handy whenever you want to ruin an evening for me. Do you have a fever? I shook my head. You're letting yourself go, he said slowly, don't you think? The way you look you shouldn't constantly run your fingers through your hair. You should stand straighter, or do you think that walking stooped over is attractive? What's this? What's this? Little Franziska in tears? It's so predictable. A delightful evening. So delightful.

After an hour I could hear him screaming. I held my head and he screamed, things having gotten out of hand again, myself glued to the chair, motionless, and the sentences slashing into me. I no longer knew what he actually wanted, what he was talking about, but whenever I was able to shut myself off there came a blow, a sentence especially honed that penetrated my head.

Then I said something during the night: I think differently, I don't think like you, although I knew there was no context for it, but that was what ran through me, this helpless sentence with which I suddenly wanted to stand up for myself. Excellent, he said, let's have it at last, because for once we want to hear what you think.

That's not what I mean, I said, but in general I think completely differently than you do. Yes, completely. Like the way that people walk or breathe or carry themselves.

Ah, the enemy in my own house. Why don't you finally say what you really think of me. Perhaps that shining knight with his multiple sclerosis comes to mind, though I can't measure up to him, not having it myself. You'd be pleased to see the same thing happen to me. Someone with MS can do whatever he wants. It's impressive, and the man himself plays it up and operates his little blackmail so well.

Franza jumped up: Don't say that. That . . . , that's unfair. That's monstrous. You shouldn't say that, certainly not you.

Yet why shouldn't he say it, he, Jordan, who of course saw through everything.

Yes, she said, exhausted. You see through everything. She wanted to add: Except yourself. Then her cowardice defeated her once again as she whimpered, I don't want you to talk, you don't mean what you're saying, I know you better than that, you don't mean what you're saying. She turned toward him and laid her arm across his neck. He freed himself and yelled, I know what you're thinking, and Herr Prohaska will be fired after his next insubordinate act. It occurred to Franza that he needed Prohaska, and again she trembled for Prohaska. She didn't know what she could do, how she could warn him, prevent a confrontation, for it would look as if she were opposing her husband and she thought she couldn't do that, given everything she had said to Prohaska. She began to murmur to herself, I'll go crazy yet. I will without a doubt go crazy yet.

During the night Franza got up and went into the bathroom. She suddenly knelt down upon the bathmat and prayed, her hands clutching at the edge of the cold tub. All she could think to do was whisper, Nothing will happen, everything will be all right, he won't torment me anymore, I won't be so tormented anymore, though she became confused, for it seemed to her crazy that she was kneeling in the bathroom, trying to prevent something from happening. I will do anything, anything, for it all to come out all right. I will love him all the more so that things go better. She crawled back into bed and listened to his breathing and remained awake until the first light, when at last she fell asleep.

But the craziest thing is that, I mean, you wouldn't believe it— when Prohaska showed up Leo was a different person. Full of charm, he courted him, gave him Greek cigarettes, the two of them laughing. That was a real surprise, one of many. I couldn't stand it, for it seemed to me so devoid of any logic, especially this warmth after this outburst of anger. If any of his friends, even one of them, had any idea what he thought about them (since he saw through everything, which led to his unshakable certainty), no one would have even shaken his hand. No, it would be unthinkable. When Prohaska said that day (and this was the last straw, but only for me) that he would like to go to the movies with me, I went pale. But then *he* said, Oh no, my dear, it would give me such pleasure, poor Franziska gets out of the house so little, I believe it's been over a year since I've gone to the movies with her, that would do you good, little Franziska, my poor neglected girl. She doesn't have it easy with me. Yet I found an excuse, for I wasn't interested in going to the movies with Prohaska. There was correspondence to be answered, the taxes overdue. When we had a moment together alone in the hallway, I said, I'm not going, understood? He acted as if he didn't hear what I said. I had to go. Children, at least grant yourselves a couple of free hours, dear Prohaska, it would give me such pleasure.

At the cinema, between the newsreel and the main feature, Prohaska said to me, He is such an extraordinary man. I worry that he will hold something against me, I'm really quite ashamed. He laughed in such an odd manner, this forced laughter, and at first it irritated me, my suspicion undercutting my feeling of pity, even to the extent that he might have noticed. But I was wrong; he, of course, didn't notice a thing. You know what I think, he said, laughing some more, the automation of this laughter sounding so horrible to me as he suddenly hit me with the remark: You are also extraordinary. You have killed a tiger, and even if you've done it unwittingly that says all the more for you.

What did you say? I gave the impression that I hadn't understood. It occurred to me that earlier Prohaska had been on a hunting expedition and just what this figure of speech stood for. Franza laughed almost hysterically, inquiring with a couple of monosyllables addressed to Prohaska's gaze. If she understood correctly, he was worried if she was clear about how important a man Jordan was. Oh yes, of that I'm certain, that you can be sure of, she said. No need to worry about that. Well then, everything is okay then, said Prohaska, speaking quite loudly now.

After the film was over Franza gave absentminded answers and said good-bye quickly. Prohaska's strange talk had completely unsettled her. He should have said nothing at all. A man whom she respected had tempted her in the assumption that she would save herself in the end. I think I will go crazy yet.

The strategy was put together by the field marshal in charge of my immortal soul, which itself had begun to seep away. For it's true that I have an immortal soul, Martin. As for the psyche, no one knows what that is, not even today, for it's only set down to biological/sociological conditions—yet I pit such foreign words against one another, and nothing is lost, there being something there that science can't capture, which hopefully you know. That something is the past, and by that I am defined, in conjunction with the latest point of view. Nearly the latest. In accordance with the Jordanian. How do I think, how do I remember? No longer as I did in the past. It's a force that moves through my head, that unrolls itself chronologically, presenting an accumulation of scenes, always the same ones, then I connect them. All I need is a ship's cabin, a glass of water, and I think of a glass that was thrown past my head. But then there is more, the next one comes, there are shards of glass, then I arrive at my border, a wall, and I stand there and my lament carries through a large space, one like a desert, without onlookers, without confidantes, facing no one. You utter a word, and I move with it and am swept away on a flood of words that washes outward and upward from my head and then back again, breaking over my head. That's how I remember. In a different way.

Earlier I would have said: And then we flew to London for a conference and lived in such and such hotel and met these people and saw Trafalgar Square and visited the British Museum, and the summer after that we were in the countryside outside of Salzburg and at night went into Salzburg for the festival. A wet summer. Today I remember that he said as we walked along the Salzach, I'll cut your ear off and throw it in the river. And then the remarks during a thunderstorm, when I was afraid: Turn and look at it, a better show than *Everyman*,˙ open your eyes. And I obediently opened my eyes and was even more afraid. I told him that my father had always brought my mother home quickly during a thunderstorm, then closed all the shutters and stayed with her. This story only hardened Jordan's opinion that it would have been better not to have become mixed up in this family, and if Franza now said, Please hold me tight, as the lightning struck the nearby lake, followed by the loud bang common to Salzburg storms, that would be a reason not to hold her tight, at least for pedagogical reasons, as well as others, since it was silly that such a "grown woman" should behave so.

Before Franziska was even thirty she was declared a mature woman, though I reject whatever one takes that to mean. The flight from reality, female behavior, typical woman.

You yourself say "typical Franza," don't deny it, that's what you think, even if you don't say it. But I was always something typical—a model which he tinkered with, which he had at his disposal, for I had to feel what he ordered me to feel, and if he declared that a woman couldn't sleep with a man without his leaving his mark, it only being natural, then of course there was no example I could have dared to counter with, Martin.

But what is evil, what is it?˙ They say today that it's nothing secret, it's conceivable. Yes, the mechanisms of aggression, self-interest, these shed some light on it, and yet they don't, although I don't want to look for anything at work behind the world or within it. Nonetheless, it has always frightened me whenever someone has lost control, such as a train conductor at the gate because someone doesn't have a ticket. This hatred, this awful hatred that stirs the blood. What causes a conductor to feel such hatred because of a ticket? What does a Jordan have to hate and be disgusted with inside a person?

I think that's it! One paralyzes someone, cripples him, strips him of his unique characteristics, his thoughts, then his feelings, then deprives him of the instinct for self-preservation, then kicks him when he's down. No beast does that. The wolf doesn't kill a humiliated opponent, for he simply can't kill him. Did you know that? He's simply incapable of biting the throat when it's held up to him. How wise, how lovely. Yet mankind, possessing the strongest weapons, the strongest beast of prey, has no such qualms.

I can reconcile myself to the wolves, but not humans. Today they all shake their heads, just as in Vienna we all shook our heads over every single story that surfaced about the sufferings of the prisoners during the war. (I'm sounding like Leo's book, which is not what I want. I want to get away from that.) They analyze and ponder it all and seek demons and brutality as if one knew what that is. How sublime their explanations, how provocative their insights, as if one really seemed to understand it all, and then, how sublimely they understand it and do what they need to do, no effort or expense spared.

Just last night I dreamed that I was alone in a gas chamber, all the doors shut tight, no windows, and Jordan held the knob and was letting the gas in and—how can I dream something like this, how is it possible to want, at the same time, to ask for forgiveness, though he'd be incapable of killing me, there being nothing more despicable. And yet I still dream of it and express it, something that is a thousand times more complex. Post-traumatic stress. I am a prime example of post-traumatic stress, for there's no record of memory that I can play that doesn't release its contents with a scratchy needle, no summer day upon which a noxious shower of rain does not fall, no night during which I am not obsessed, and because he made his notes, no forgetfulness that is not buried in Freudian slips and meaningless babble. I wasn't sick at all, I didn't come to him as a patient, I trusted him. What is a marriage other than trust, to place oneself in another's hands, all that you are, however little that may be.

F.'s preference for French kissing, stop, lust not sensuality, stop, I think I'm choking with laughter, F. overheard while talking on the phone. F. most likely lesbian. I'm choking, no, with laughter, no, it's really nothing, a scratchy needle on the record of memory. On the next day a report on personal feelings, the dossier of love. These are all contradictions. As a result the world is blown sky high, finally the fire is lit by the fuse, the dynamite having begun to stack up from the first week onward. Year after year. F. summoned to speak. F. pleads for forgiveness. E. would never have done that. So far they are different, stop.

Why should I admit to that? What should I admit to?

If I admit that I've made a mistake, you'd say I was behaving holier than thou. If I admit this, like in the dream, then it's much worse, for then I die twice over, once as well for him, my idol. What were you trying to tell me back then? It was only an opinion. How could I take the opinion of a twenty-year-old seriously? And no, of course I no longer know what it was. I don't know it at all anymore. It's so painful, for he is not what he appears to be. No, it was not just my own deceit. The strategy, the calculation. Promise me that you'll never be calculating. I've been used, I've been part of an experiment, an object for the private thirst for knowledge of a scientist. The physique was assessed, gauged for its type, the physique and character, myself only surprised that he didn't submit my handwriting to analysis. I have to laugh. They do that in companies these days, it's standard practice. Including dreams as well, I related everything in a dutiful manner, but soon after I learned what dreams can involve, for I always dream of him. It started in Baden, when I was first able to explain it to myself. Out of fear. Earlier I was afraid, but now I feel fear. I hold myself tight. Fear is not something we learn, it is something else entirely. It's in the body, nothing otherworldly, and it's not an idea, it is terror. It is terror. The sickness of our time. Oh, don't make me laugh.

Inside him all went silent when he was with me, the goodness draining out of him. He no longer heard the voices that he heard when he was out of the house, the laws under which he worked collapsed. At home there was nothing but lawlessness, the fanaticism with which he perhaps wounded himself, the blows, the urge to destroy, the need to destroy someone else. He didn't like women, and yet he always had to have a woman in order to provide him with the object of his hatred.

One day a woman from the neighborhood came to us with a ten-year-old who for months had continued to bark like a dog, sounding just like one. Then we had the nymphomaniac who had no sensitivity to touch whatsoever. I felt that she had slept with as many men as the barks released by the child, that being her own way of barking. Sometimes I had the feeling that the entire city was full of these "fates," which they always referred to, no matter what may have happened to them, and who either allowed themselves to be treated or stubbornly persisted, the evil ones, the dark ones. But our house was naturally on the sunny side of the street, for we had a spotless villa which I had no reason to associate with such sorrow. He was the guardian of health and I his subordinate, he being as well my mentor and my judge, my benefactor, whose coldness I needed to learn as a prerequisite.

And I never asked myself how we lived or if it was the right way to live, or whether alcohol was something that only made alcoholics tremble, or what someone like the young Herr G. could be dreaming of or wish for. G.'s case involved his dreaming that his wife climbed into the toilet and flushed herself down, thus committing suicide and freeing him of her presence.

And then they were all pressed into a "norm," those suffering from eczema who ripped and scratched the skin off their bodies until blood flowed, hatred for their children the cause, each evening a heap of aggression arriving on our doorstep, one broken shard after another presented to me to learn from, though I learned nothing. Instead, I took it all in, considered it, made an effort to speak informatively about it all, and when that didn't work, slight tremblings would interrupt the study session, like a dog barking. I tried to do it, I tried to understand it all, though such attempts were always bound up with pain as I looked at Jordan and tried to comprehend what he felt, as I thought to myself, he feels nothing, not the way I do. He feels something, but it must be something different. Now I realize that these syndromes were like a drug to him.

Why did it never occur to me that he dissected everyone until nothing more was left, nothing remaining except a finding that belonged to him. It never occurred to me because I mistook his intensity as being part of his profession, never asking if it was unnatural that he cut himself off from his brother, from his child, from his wife. I know you can't understand it—he couldn't allow any person to deviate from the norm he established for them.

When did it begin? At first you think, not at the beginning, but in the end you see: at the beginning. Something warns you, and yet you don't listen to it, pushing away this feeling which later you realize was your initial feeling, really the first you felt. You are warned. Through the way a head is held, through the movement of a hand, through a voice in which there's a hint of something, and before you know it, perhaps a month later, you notice something different in an arrogant gesture, or something touching, sensing a history behind it that has never been revealed to you, something uncertain, not seen every day. At that moment you love the voice as you listen to it with a sense of melancholy, and when it becomes aggressive you hear something bold, and you're pleased by it, the swindle having been brought off, there being no need to deceive yourself, for the deception produces new deceptions.

Nothing warns you again, the signal is given only once, the first time you are in a room with others and it occurs to you, watch out, watch out. The next time you have a title to latch onto, a lecture, followed by boisterous applause, a couple hundred idiots overcome with wonder calling out the name, or a needling critic, yourself swayed by an address, a name printed on the page of a journal, as you hear "make sure to watch out" once again, which your skin, your muscles, your hearing, and all your senses have called out to you.

You nobly shrug off a half-true story heard amid gossip, nor do you want to hear another one. It's cruel to come to you with such stories, for there are stories about everyone, even yourself, and you forget to distinguish the kernel of truth amid the dirt, having to work too hard to find it. Then you let yourself be helped from the car, you have coffee in a quiet little street, you lie in bed in the nineteenth district and gather together your documents. Your residency card is found and must be submitted, the residency card issued by your town which you want to leave behind as you practice writing a name in order to be able to write it with ease. Then you leave the justice of the peace. A couple of hours later the door of an apartment closes behind you as someone lifts you up, after which the lock is turned, yourself laughing with someone as if a wonderful spell has been cast upon the world with the closing of this door, the exchange of names, you not thinking for a moment that you could have been tricked or that this trick could have been played on others before you. It's awful, it is a disgrace, a history of disgrace you begin to bear, though you are still laughing as you hang your clothes in the closet where earlier others hung.

Is that what you think, is that what you really think, that it isn't a disgrace at all? I see, that's what you think. What then is a disgrace? Something you can't escape. Yes, that's true, but that's only part of it. It's easy to escape from one another when everything is going well, or nearly well, but it's not at all possible with this slime that you wipe off your face, so many unanswered questions that I continually pose.

Throughout the day I stew amid these questions, asking continually: Why did you do that?—and when you've done it: Was that intentional? Why do you want to destroy me? What have I done to you? Sometimes I wish that it were only thoughtlessness, but one can't do that simply out of thoughtlessness, no, that can't be. He knew very well that someday I would have to figure it out, for he could not have anticipated my death, since I was so healthy and so much younger than him, and thus he could not have counted on that, but rather just the opposite, which meant that in ten or twenty years' time, while putting his work in order with his assistant, I would find these records. And so what he also wanted was that ten or twenty years of living together would come to ruin in just such a moment. That's what he wanted, you understand.

You say fascism, but that sounds strange, for I've never heard that word used to describe a personal relationship. No, forgive me, I have to laugh, no, I'm not crying at all. But that's an interesting idea, for it had to begin somewhere. Why does one only refer to fascism when it has to do with opinions or blatant acts? Yes, he is evil, even if you can't use the word "evil" today, but rather only "sick." Yet what kind of sickness is it when others suffer from it and not the sick one himself? He must be crazy. And yet there's no one who seems more rational. I can't explain it to anyone, there's nowhere to go to prove that he really is crazy. He tormented me constantly, but not haphazardly, or at least rarely, but nonetheless intentionally, everything being calculated, tactics, always tactics. How can anyone be so calculating?

What useless questions, if that's the way it is, yet until now I hadn't noticed that sadists are found not only in the psychiatric hospitals and in the courts, but also here among us with snow-white lab coats and titled professorships, armed with the intelligentsia's tools of torture.

No, no.

Franza then said: Why does someone want to kill his wife? Why does someone who hates women live with one? Why liquidate her, making sure not to lose face in public, for the public is his only judge and has no idea, separations being only the unfortunate affairs of love, and the law itself, which is even more ridiculous than public opinion, doesn't pay attention to the abuse of others, their belongings amounting to nothing more than trifles, the public thinking it's all a joke, or at worst very sad.

When did I find it? I didn't find it at all. It began otherwise. I came back to the apartment after shopping and stood there with the door open because I couldn't close it while carrying all the bags and packages. Because doors and windows were open somewhere in the apartment there was a gust of wind, and a window rattled so hard against its frame that the pane popped out. I quickly threw the door shut and left everything lying in the hallway and looked at the mess around me.

On a sheet of paper there was something written in steno, and I knew that it had of course blown in from his room, and so I gathered up all the sheets and laid them on his desk. As I glanced at the top sheet, the one that happened to be there, I considered whether I should try to put the papers in order or let him do it. Then I read it. No, it didn't occur to me at first what it was, for as I read it, it seemed to be about a stranger. Here and there I could see that F. was written down, though that didn't disturb me, but rather the content, which swept over me like a chill wind, there being no better way to say it. I still didn't take it as referring to myself, and I took in hardly more than half a sentence: F.'s self-confidence, something that still needs to be shaken. Her self-awareness, her lust, her vitality.

Yes, I can recite each sentence. I will see each sentence before me until the end of my days. It's good that I know all about them.

It's a terrifying dream (hand me the water, please), it's something that I see played out inside my head, but I see now how it could be staged. But if the Mediterranean doesn't get any calmer, Martin, I won't be able to stand it. I want to get out of here, I want to get out. It's like in the dream, though there it was worse. Yet it happened in the same head that now rests on the same cushion, and how can I be expected to stand it. A few minutes ago the gas chamber and now the ship's cabin. My head, my head, Martin. No, you shouldn't hold me tight, I want to hold onto myself, or onto you.

I was in a large room. There were thick hoses that were ribbed hanging from the walls, screwed in tight, and I look around and see there are no windows and no exit, yet enough dim light to see Jordan. I can't speak any longer, though I move my lips and ask what we're doing here. He looks at me and in his eyes I can see it, though he doesn't say anything either, yet it's in his eyes, what he wants to do with me. He goes over to a wall and turns on a hose, and then turns on the next one, and the gas streams in through the first one, and Jordan turns on yet another one and the gas streams in, and that's when I woke up, the world no different.

Earlier I never paid attention to dreams, nor did they amount to much, usually hazy and full of wandering and sometimes colorful, but now, how menacing, because it doesn't seem strange, it's part of me and I have come to inhabit my own dreams. The puzzle of my days is more important than the puzzle of my dreams, for you should understand that there's no dream puzzle, but rather the puzzle itself, the puzzle of days, the undetectable chaos of reality that tries to articulate itself in a dream, which sometimes in a composition brilliantly reveals to you who you are.

Otherwise there's no way for you to understand it, and then your dreams are useless, amateur productions, and then nothing goes right, a bad dramatist chopping up the scenes, confusing the motives, and who has the hero die too soon, exchanging characters from earlier scenes with those from later ones, until suddenly the dream pulls itself together and is suddenly a hit, a Shakespeare having loaned a hand, a Goya having painted the scenery, lifting itself suddenly out of the valley of your own banality and presenting you with your own great drama, your father and a henchman named Jordan together in one person as equally important as any great figure. The anthem begins, the first subterranean communication that the ancients are at hand, your mother, whom you never think about, leaning against every wall. Your free-floating fear, for which you have no basis, presents a story that assaults your sight and hearing, and you know for the first time why you feel such angst. I saw a graveyard at sunset, and the dream told me: That is the Graveyard of the Daughters. And I looked down at my own grave, for I was one of the daughters, and my father was not there. But because of him I was dead and buried there. Maybe in your waking life you know something about a graveyard of children and who is guilty of your death. You'll never know for sure, but you think about it, as hard as you can, though it will never come to you.

If you ever experienced this in the same manner within yourself, perhaps during the trip through the tunnel, or during the night, then you know it is true. That's it. You can swear by it. Your tyrannical brain, its secret workings between the cortex and middle brain, its acts set down in the passages of the middle brain and their manifestations in the cortex. Why did you call him the Fossil? Oh no, you're wrong, for he's more contemporary than I am, for I, I, I am from a lower race,* and I have known since it began that it's one that has wiped itself out. That's what I am, and he is the type that rules today, that succeeds today, that attacks and lives to do so, for I've never seen a person with so much aggression. It's what sets him off, like a gem, what makes him a shining specimen—the predator of the year, the wolf pack of the year, there being no contest, for what I have realized is that I am from a lower race.

Or perhaps it's a class, for I have been exploited, used, manhandled, enslaved, my golden Galicien skin stripped away, myself gutted and stuffed. In Australia the aborigines were not exterminated, and yet they are dying out, though clinical research is unable to come up with organic reasons as to why, it being a deadly doubt that infests the Papuans, a kind of suicide, since they believe the whites have stolen all of their goods by magical means. Weren't the Incas wiped out by ruthless bandits, and the Murutes of North Borneo are dying from contact with civilization, while earlier the races who had been introduced to alcohol destroyed themselves through the same kind of desperation. And as for me, someone tried to break me, my instincts, my little piece of heaven, setting off the war within me, while in the south there grew honor, pride, and something else, it was a trio, can you help me with the third? I must have had it, what was it? There was a third thing, something to do with loss, something that was lost. Don't you have the courage to tell me? Did it have something to do with courage? Am I getting warmer? I must be close. You don't know it either. But you will. Yet you don't know it, because you've never been without it.

He stole all of my goodness. My laughter, my tenderness, my capacity for joy, my compassion, my ability to help, my animal nature, my shining rays, for he stomped out everything that rose up until it could no longer rise again. Why someone does that I don't understand, but it's incomprehensible why the whites took all the goods from the blacks. Not just the diamonds and the nuts, the oil and dates, but also the peace in which such goodness grows, and the health without which one cannot live. Or is it that the riches of the earth go hand in hand with those other riches, which sometimes I believe. Nor can I live any longer, because he has my things. Yes, that's right, our silver bread basket, for instance, our bowls, and I can't stand it as I think to myself, his hand can't take the bread out of the basket. Better that his hand turn leprous, better that the bread simply goes moldy as I continually think about it, since in my mind this bread basket takes on the dimensions of a huge barn full of harvested crops, it getting worse each day, this suffering that makes the magic possible, for I am a Papuan. You can only rob those who live by magic, yet for me everything has meaning. Already it's better, for I can keep some distance on the dream and study it calmly. It's not as strong as before.

Often I ask myself, I ask myself, having asked myself. What are you saying, that I don't listen to you? Yes, it's true, I hardly ever listen anymore. Everything is in such tumult that I can't hear what is said to me. But still I know what you said an hour ago in the train just before Milan. I thought to myself, you'd prefer to deal with a science, one where everything makes sense. You even said that although geologists have barely left the Middle Ages behind and know nothing about the Earth, there are still three theories that hold true. Nice, nice. Who always says "nice"? In Vienna everything is nice, isn't that so?

But when your experts on the Earth know nothing about the Earth and all of you can only say a few things about the crust, how can one know anything about people? And why has it fallen to me to know more in order to guess about one single ungraspable person?

Now the one thing I know is that he—does it bother you?—that Jordan has spread fear. What's that? You say that when someone spreads fear he himself can never be free from fear? Ah, everything is so sensible. One dips someone into the solutions offered by psychologists, and then everything is explained. But what did he fear? He did not fear me, nor others. I certainly feared him, and I must have been purple with fear, my color returning for hours at a time, followed by the change of color when near him.

Was it always that way? Probably. At first just a bit, then stronger, and at the end very strong. And I heard about how people were getting sick, and I didn't realize that I would become sick, nor what from.

Yes, I believe there is such a thing as Bluebeard, and Landru* must have been an amateur, a charming little criminal.

I was caught in this labyrinth, in the entire house, I mean. In our apartment I spun around like the mobiles in other rooms, inside this syndrome, and you have no idea how many syndromes there are. If you had dates or something else indicating when it began (was 1526 the battle of the Mohács?),* they would still apply, for our battles were always against such syndromes. But for me it meant something else. I was suddenly no longer a co-worker, no longer married. I was separated from society with my husband, living in a jungle in the middle of civilization, and I saw that he was well armed and that I had no weapons at all.

But what am I saying? I'm missing the central point. No, no, I wasn't in any jungle, I was in the middle of civilization, along with its definition in the dictionary, and its verbal ability to handle any situation. One day, as the apartment was being aired out, for Rosi was always airing out the place at certain hours when I was not home, though this one time I was home, out of his room blew the pages from his desk into the front hall. Rosi picked up these pages and carried them to the desk, while I caught one that had blown as far as the front door. I then carried it back, reading it over as I returned it. I couldn't read stenography very well, but enough so that what was on it immediately caught my attention. Then I went back into the bedroom and remained sitting on the bed with my coat on until I began to sweat. Do you know what I'm about to say?

Martin didn't know what she was about to say or what he should say, so he said at random, Do you mean his affair with Pfaundler? But everyone knows about that. Yet Franza, who didn't know what everyone knew, didn't interrupt him, because she was astounded by this news.

No, no, you have to remember about him (she was now somewhat upset about the suggestion about Pfaundler) that everything for him was a pretense. I don't know if back then he already wanted me to find the stuff, though certainly he did later. But maybe that was also because I had already begun to find it. Because from then on I would often come across a page, sometimes with only notes written on it. It took me a long time to understand it, at least a year, then I understood for certain that they were about me. He was working on me, he was working on me as his case study. He hounded me. And every page on which I appeared hounded me all the more.

One day it had gone so far that I no longer even knew when it had begun. Suddenly during dinner, while eating Wiener schnitzel and some fruit, namely an apple, it was, you see, just like the apple in the fable, for when I had a piece in my mouth I began to cough it up, though I knew that I had not swallowed the wrong way, certainly not, but suddenly I coughed it up as if it were poison, and I continued coughing and coughing until I couldn't breathe. I spit out the piece and he stood up somewhat impatiently and slapped me on the back. I don't know why his patients always say he has such gentle hands, for it was with a hard hand that he slapped me on my back like a carpet beater. Then I couldn't breathe at all and fell back against the chair as I thought, I'm dying, and slowly slid off the chair and lay upon the carpet. Then he began to give me some pills. Of course sometimes I didn't know what he gave me.

The next time I got into the car with him I began to cough again as soon as we drove off to the opera, though there was no slice of apple in my mouth. We were always going to the opera. I don't really know why, but we had a box, though neither of us got much out of victims, I mean opera, yet we went to the opera the way others go to church. At the coat check it began again. I didn't want to check my coat and said, Let me have my coat, and I looked at him as if he wanted to rip the clothes off my body. He said, Get a hold of yourself, do you know where you are? I told him he should bring me straight home or at least let me have my coat. He was in a complete rage because he had to bring me home. He gave me a shot, but then he began to scream at me continually, saying that he wouldn't stand for this tyranny, this behavior and affectation.

And I fought against such behavior. I took the pills secretly myself when the spells came on, or just before. Yet the spells became more and more frequent, nor did I know when they would occur, you see. But to whom am I speaking? To you, of course, but to which persona? Certainly to you, but with whom am I talking as one persona to another persona? I'm talking about a kind of behavior, about not wanting to take off my coat, not wanting to get into the car, not being able to get into an elevator, not being able to board a plane, for I'm talking about ridiculous behavior, the most ridiculous in the world. Namely this—I'm talking about fear.

Close all the books, the abracadabra of the philosophers, the satyrs of fear who manipulate metaphysics but who do not know what fear is. Fear is no mystery, no end in itself, no existential condition, nothing noble, not a concept, and, God willing, nothing that can be systematized. Fear is indisputable. It is an assault, it is terror, a massive attack on one's life. It's the guillotine to which you travel in a cart to your executioner while stared at by an uncomprehending crowd, a public audience, and my audience was my murderer. But this one didn't just gawk.

Fear, angst, where are the needles, the cardiograms that can read it, which notations and which prescriptions can encapsulate fear? I can only say what is, the same way that historians can only say what is, and you simply have to swallow what is and was. Otherwise no one questions it, even when no one has the means to digest this history. One must only have the means to deal with one thing, namely fear, which must not remain free-floating. Nothing free-floating, to the devil with these syndromes. I sat opposite my opponent, and I had nowhere to go, not to the police, not to the courts, not even to Alda. What could I have said? My husband, please excuse how ridiculous this sounds, for it substantiates nothing, is murdering me. I am going to be murdered, help me. That's what I would have had to say, but just imagine in this society someone coming along and saying: I am going to be murdered. Could you please say by whom and why, could you give us some facts, some evidence? I had no evidence. I had run from any kind of consolation from others because I didn't have the kind of fear that could be talked about, but rather the other kind, that which one decreases with psychopharmacy and the shots and lying down quietly, and which can increase simply through the fear of such fear.

I felt like an animal that runs back and forth in its cage, and even if I'd been able to crash through the bars with my head, I would have still been in a cage, in the cage of his notes which followed me, which had abandoned me.

But I am speaking to you. You are not just sound and smoke, my brother, you are my guide, and in the end, when I have found my direction, you will be there, understanding nothing and supporting me, and you will talk over all of this idiotic stuff, saying, Are you feeling pain again, lie down, or, Just wait, give yourself a little break.

After a year the episode with the slice of apple was forgotten, nor did I choke during a performance of *Turnadot* or *Lohengrin*. You should never question me, he said. So I did not question him. We played a princely game. Silence, pretense, silence, then more pretense.

One night I began to cramp up, trembling with cramps, and I took my cushion and went into the living room to lie down on the sofa. He screamed at me again, but I no longer listened and let him scream, holding onto my cushion and trembling. I knew that he would soon stop, for he had to be in the clinic the next morning, so he had to stop, and then he stopped and let me go.

The next day I said to Rosi that she should move my things into the guest room because I was sick. That was my first daring act, for I said I was "sick" even though I was not certain. She brought me breakfast as soon as he left the house, and I didn't touch it, though I'm usually so hungry for breakfast. She warmed up the tea after a couple of hours and boiled another egg. The orange juice sat there, not a thing was touched. Then I began to think after she mercifully left me with the second breakfast. After half an hour, when I didn't hear a sound in the house and was certain that she was busy with lunch, I went into the bathroom used by guests and patients and dumped out the entire breakfast, one glass after another, then poured all of the coffee into the toilet and pulled the chain. From the bathtub faucet I drank a glass of water from the glass used for brushing teeth. At lunch there was vegetable soup, schnitzel, and fruit salad, but I dumped it all into the toilet, myself only feeling thirsty. I only trusted the water supplied by the city.

On the second night Riedel stopped by because he wanted to speak to me about a chapter for which I had the documentation, though naturally not in my room. I said that it was good that he stopped by anyway. At first we talked about the chapter, but then I began to sense that the chapter intensified my fear, so we talked about all kinds of things, though I don't know for how long. After a while Jordan came in through the door, saying sarcastically, I hope I'm not disturbing you, but it seems to me you're feeling much better. I said, Yes, I'm feeling better. Riedel wasn't a friend, but at least he wasn't an enemy, and he could be trusted to get some soup to me via Rosi. I had even grabbed hold of his hand once or twice when these bolts of lightning suddenly passed through my head, these bolts of second thoughts. I didn't want to second-guess him, but instead simply talk about something, anything, about the quotes and the case concerning B.

Then I read a quote.

Suddenly I said to Riedel, This part has to be left out, there's no way we can make use of it. Then he gripped my hand and said, You have a fever. No, I said, no, you realize we can't include this "Forgive me for crying." Why did the investigating judge say something so awful as "There's no reason to be afraid"? Forgive me for crying. Those others also cried at Nuremberg.˙ And they also said: Forgive me.

Oh my dear one, forgive me, forgive me, Martin, for crying. I only wanted to say that it's too much. It's all too much. And this disgusting banality. The boss's wife lies in bed and has something against asking for forgiveness and crying. Have no fear, witness. But only the witnesses feel fear, a maddening fear, for what they could bring to light is even larger than the sun that is measured and gauged and set down in a study. But the sun is not a witness. A probe will land lightly upon it and be easily singed, even on the sun. It will soon be dissected, causing a few flares to shoot out, stirring up the weather a little, though the weather will only manifest itself beneath the atmosphere. Everything I say has to do with the atmosphere. My dear brother, who reckons the value of the pound and the piastre, and the time, and with your Breasted in hand, and with your reservations about me and our trip without any clear good or purpose, and who has abandoned Fräulein Nemec because of me, and who busies himself with an unfolding itinerary and little jokes with an Arabian boy, whom you don't care for too much and who certainly doesn't care for you—my dear brother, forgive me that I take you at your word and say to you: I will not be found again, I'm traveling into the Egyptian darkness.

chapter three
the egyptian darkness

I

They have gone into the desert. Light pours down upon them, the sky's discharge accompanied by heat, as well as a dry and pleasant odor. The immense sanatorium, the immense inescapable purgatory, though open on all sides—inescapable, subdivided into the Arabian, the Libyan, fine grained, full of stones polished smooth by sand, otherworldly stones. Everything about it is Saharan. The Sahara. Like an institution, it had engulfed them.

"Likewise the foreigner. . . ." "Because what he (the foreigner) finally wants to do, he will never. . . ." Martin cleaned his sunglasses, smearing them with sand. "He will never be able to forget. He recalls. . . ." Martin tried it again. What does he recall, or what calls the foreigner back? "He will desire it (the desert) until the day he dies."

Everything empty and yet more immediate than anything that claims to exist. Not simply nothingness. No, the desert has nothing to do with the nothingness speculated on by the holders of endowed professorships. It escapes definition. "It is something absolute, denying all half-measures." Martin read, because he relied on his books. Because it made him angry that he couldn't see through his glasses, and that he was being told something that he couldn't feel. He slammed the book shut, much to

Franza's relief. For him nothing here was absolute, nor a half-measure either. It only made him question why a city suddenly stopped, why Cairo, which contained over three million people, spread out as far as the sand, while other cities shifted into garden plots and suburbs. Here a city ceased from one meter to the next, the highway out of town ending at a dirt road, while for Franza's sake he had hoped that the last house would be a rest stop so that she would be able to get out.

A nine-hour journey. The prospect suddenly made his bones feel weak. The desert bus, which took its time while driving through the city, increased its speed after the first hundred meters on the dirt road as if it were beginning to feel in its element and wanted to show what a desert bus really was. Nonstop to Suez.

Sire, I will come. I am in the great padded room of the sky, light and sand all about me. Franza leaned against the side of the bus. She avoided Martin's questioning gaze and stared continually out the window, where for him there was nothing to see. Could that be a sign, Martin asked himself, wondering if she had enough control over herself to conceal her fear. But he knew nothing of "Sire" and "I will come," and when she stroked his hand or laid her hand on his arm, he thought she wanted to be soothed, and so from time to time he took her hand and pressed it in order to soothe her.

The bus rattled on toward Suez and stopped in a side street before the main street, a couple of pumps on the brakes barely stopping it. Suez was a surprise, for no immediate drama presented itself to the eyes, nor any trace of a past war.* Martin and Franza remained in their seats, trying to decide if the mass exodus of Arabs meant that Suez was their final destination, leaving them to travel on alone. Then they got out as well, deciding that this was a rest stop. They wandered a ways down the main street and came to a shack with chairs where some men were drinking tea. Franza kept looking down the side street at the bus to make sure it wouldn't leave without them. Then she relaxed and drank some tea, though not like the way she drank coffee at Café Herrenhof or the Opera Café, surrounded by packages, with letters at home that began, "Dear Martin, I must write you, I really don't know where I should begin, it is so awful, and I only have you. . . ."

No longer afflicted by syndromes affecting her every extremity, she didn't let her tea get cold by stirring it constantly while suffering bad spells. Her inflamed eyes simply did not reveal if they shone from such illness or because it was hot. She said, Suez. Is it really Suez?—as if she wanted confirmation from Martin that it was Suez. He couldn't do anything but concede that this hole in the wall was called by that well-known notorious name. He swatted away flies and said, Alas, another unavoidable error! If you can just hold out and hold yourself together for just nine hours, then we'll reach the sea, and then you can relax.

Franza kept quiet and again looked past him. He didn't completely believe it himself. This was not like traveling to Portofino or Cannes to lie on the beach, dismissing in her thoughts two places that she had only heard about in passing. Did Martin have no idea where they were or where she was, and did Suez mean nothing to him?

She had spread *The Egyptian Gazette* over her head. Martin tugged on the white cotton hat that struck him as ridiculous. No, he did not know where she was headed. He should stick with his tickets and maps and schedules, keeping faith in a bungalow by the sea, as well as phone and bus connections. Since she had staggered off the bus a struggle had begun inside her between two opponents who set upon each other with vehement determination, neither having more to say than: I. I and the desert. Or I and the other. The absolute and no half-measures, I and I began to go at one another.

Martin, who was hungry, was surprised that she offered to do something, to willingly leave him for the first time in order to go to the bread shop she had discovered, managing the exchange of piastres on her own and returning with two pieces of flat bread. He wanted to say something encouraging to her, but in this heat, which had steadily risen as if someone had turned a faucet handle too quickly from warm to boiling, he could neither wet his lips nor offer a thank you. He would have liked to break out in laughter, if only he could have laughed. Because here a general course of study was beginning about which he had no idea, rather than a trip for the purposes of a study. Would Franza collapse, toppling from the chair after a couple of minutes? What does one do in Suez with a white woman who collapses or sobs or begins to convulse? Because she looked so impenetrable and complained about nothing, he thought it possible that she might topple from the chair, clutching a piece of flat bread in her hand, and die. But she sat there and ate the entire flat bread and drank another glass of tea. It just didn't seem possible after these scenes that went on for days in the ventilated cabin of the ship amid the comfortable climate of the Mediterranean, during which every roll of the ship and view of a couple of powerful waves seen through the porthole made it impossible to pass a single hour. She sat there in front of the shack, holding up entirely, not even interested in the city's people, curious about nothing, not even the pajamas people wore in the street or the clouds of children who moved with the clouds of flies along the street. It was as if she had always sat here.

He leafed through his guidebook with sticky fingers. The Suez Canal. Travels for a third of its length through natural lakes.

The Great Bitter Lake and the Lesser Bitter Lake. "Bitter," also a name. He hoped that Franza's thoughts were not back in Vienna again, for she was capable of suffering a setback as a result of any name or coincidence. The same was true on the ship, where everything was too white for her, where she never realized she was on a sound ship, but instead remained in Vienna, rolling about. With her endless lament she beat on the cabin door as if she had to get out of Vienna, out of her apartment, or out of an operating room, as again she imagined a surgeon, a sterilized surgeon dressed in a snow-white uniform, throwing herself onto her knees before him, begging him to give her the fetus so that she could bring it to Hietzing in a canning jar.

Martin didn't want to think about the canning jar that she had bought at a housewares store in Baden. He no longer even knew what a canning jar was. Years ago in Galicien, meat and vegetables had always stood in canning jars in the cellar. But this canning jar, which she wanted to fill with alcohol and take to Hietzing in order to present the Fossil with a scrap of flesh he could look at until his dying day, even if it wasn't a child, this idea about the canning jar was something she thought up herself. What a person will think of! She lay with the jar on the floor of the operating room and on the floor of the ship's cabin. Martin was frightened by every passenger who walked by, as well as the suspicious steward of this haunted ship, for her only child was. . . .

My only child, my child, give me my only child. So that it doesn't end up in the incinerator. Martin didn't want to believe it, but she had insisted about the incinerator. There they had burned the scrap of flesh with many other scraps of flesh and dumped it into the sewage system, those white devils.

Who today still falls to their knees, who would even think of it? On your knees you risk being immediately transported to an asylum. No one in the world from which they came fell to his knees. But he believed Franza now. She had done something so monstrous as fall on her knees, saying, You have to let me have something of the child, for then I'll be able to eat it,* a piece, and I'll be able to think that it might be his heart. They can't take it all from me, for I would rather eat it if it's not meant to live.

The sterilized surgeon stood next to the speechless anesthesiologist (whom Martin imagined as speechless after spending hours trying to find a vein). The germ-free surgeon had to leave the operating room again and call the Fossil, one professional to another, not mentioning this monstrous scene while consulting with him since it was something that could not be spoken about over the telephone. Instead he would only raise doubts he might have about her nervous condition, for the talented surgeon had seen just about everything, but never once a woman who wanted to eat her child. Yet all doubts were laid to rest. Jordan, the psychotherapist in charge, knew best whether there was any cause for concern, and Jordan the authority assured him authoritatively: There's no need to worry.

Franza stood up and said amid Martin's tormented daydream, Don't think about it anymore. I can promise you that I've forgotten all about it. How did she know that he was thinking about it? He hardly ever knew what she was thinking about.

She looked across to the side street. The men in the djellabahs and pajamas had gathered again without the driver having blown the horn or called to them. She ran a couple of steps and turned around, motioning to him to hurry.

I have already eaten it. I swallowed a piece between Cairo and Suez. Up until now I was only missing the sand necessary to swallow it.

She pulled him along with her.

I will never again throw myself down on my knees. Not before any person, not before anyone white.

The whites. Finally they were nowhere to be seen. Here she no longer had to turn around and hear them behind her and be afraid of being strangled, pressed against a wall in fear, pushed from a car into the snow. She ceased to be afraid of being yelled at by someone, ambushed, and strangled. She no longer had to hold still for any experiment. Another experiment was beginning, and that she would perform on herself.

With the exception of Franza, there were only men in the bus. Light brown, brown, darker, two or three of them black. Franza turned her head from side to side. The window was not enough to satisfy her. She had forgotten the incident when Martin brooded and tried once again to understand what had happened on the ship. She looked outside at the branches of the canal and the sluice that must have something to do with the canal or was the canal, a thread of water that collided with the desert. Then only the desert was there again. "It consumes the entire man" — ah, how many times we had that in a lecture or in seminars. And whatever part of the man has not yet been consumed— "never losing its hold on you"—will be consumed nonetheless. What the desert encased (encased! what a pompous word) was erased (at least it rhymed, although it seemed forced). Meanwhile, Martin felt discouraged. Someone had actually written that!

'Ain Sukhna. Once reached, the first settlement on the coast, one of those recommended resorts. The promise of a seaside spa, the lie revealed by a couple of pitiful houses. Martin felt very clever, for he had not given the resort a moment's consideration.

At the military camp near Hurghada, nine hours of travel long since having passed, there was still nothing to see. Yet behind the rolling dunes there must have been huts, since two men, probably engineers, had pointed in this direction, if Martin understood correctly. They got off before the others and waved goodbye. Then everyone got off the bus. Martin and Franza were the last to do so, neither of them questioning or trying to decide anything. All of the others must have expected that a house stood here at such and such a distance and in which coffee and water pipes were served. In the friendly middle-of-nowhere room furnished with tables and flowery chairs, they lolled about on the stools, exhausted, while half of the men stood in line along the length of the hall that led to the toilet. Some smoked water pipes and stood up when the others returned.

Six hours earlier, along the dirt road, in front of a striped barrier at a checkpoint where nobody was checked as the guard spoke for a short time with the driver, the scene had looked different. All of them had walked a ways into the desert and stayed there a while, their faces turned toward the desert. Franza had remained behind on the bus with the guard, having said to Martin, Why don't you go? At first she didn't know which way to look and accepted a bottle of Coca-Cola from the guard and drank a little. Then the image began to seem grotesque to her. Thirty or forty urinating men who could be swallowed up instantly by the desert. She imagined their feet sinking, their djellabahs fluttering in the breeze.

Franza went to the other side of the bus and, before the first men returned, took off her underwear, twisting out of it beneath her dress, and stuffed the sweaty nylon and lace into her suitcase. As they traveled on again, she said to Martin, I couldn't stand it anymore. Do you think anyone can see that I don't have anything on underneath? But since they had left Europe behind them, there being no reason for her to remain a white woman with habits, taboos, and residues of the past, Martin stifled a critical look and said that it didn't matter at all and it would be much better if she dressed more sensibly. He pressed the newspaper back onto her head since the window seat, which she didn't want to exchange with his, was getting hotter and hotter with the sun. You need a hat, nothing more. We'll buy one as soon as we get there. A hat, though only bread had been available that morning. In Hurghada there must at least be a hat!

Between the driver and the suitcases piled high since they'd left Suez there stood a couple of bottles of yogurt, some vegetables, and a crate of fish, everybody looking at them since the ice block that had been placed on them had melted into a clear watery substance. Martin watched Franza staring at this crate, the first interest she showed for anything in this country. Never the slightest worry about food, about fish, even about the canteen of water that the conductor passed around from time to time with a metal cup from which everyone drank, each of them careful not to take one sip too many. The first two times Martin and Franza had politely declined; the next time Franza didn't look at Martin in order not to have a "no" thrown at her with his glance as she drank quickly. Martin said nothing, took the cup away from her, pretended to drink, and then returned it. He then shoved the book toward Franza.

It is not advisable except in the best hotels.
When possible, peel fresh fruit.
When not possible, wash it with soap.
Then let it sit for 10 minutes in potassium permanganate.
Drink tap water only in large cities.
Drink only boiled water and thin tea or mineral water.

As a preventive measure against malaria, take 2 tablets of Resochin Bayer each week.

Outbreaks of billorzsiosis, Egyptian tapeworms and intestinal parasites, and prickly heat occur regularly.

Change sweat-soaked underwear regularly, washing only once a day with soap.

Don't shower more than three times a day, using one part mercuric chloride per thousand.

Pressure bandages, snake-bite incisions, disinfectant, Behring pharmaceuticals, 10 ml.

They both had to laugh as the letters and words swam before them under the glaring light.

Yes, dear old Behring and all its good advice, said Franza. And hopefully you don't shower too often either.

Who here feared the bacteria catalogued by the whites? Who washed out a cup? Who boiled water? Who disinfected the lettuce leaves? Who closely examined the fish? Hunger, thirst, discovered once again. The danger, discovered once again. The ears, the eyes, were sharpened, directed toward the outer world, a sense of purpose having been regained. A roof over one's head, overnight accommodations, shade, just a bit of shade. The gas needing to hold out, no flat tires, no fouled spark plugs, the axle needing to hold. The way must not be lost, the signs marking the road need to remain visible. The dirt road is narrow, hardly visible, since there's only room for the wheels on it.

The wind comes up for the first time and digs into the sand, the wind-born earth dispersing powerfully into the air, displaying its true nature. The eyes and the desert meet, the desert settling upon the retina, sweeping away everything, breaking upon it in waves, once again settling in the eyes, remaining there for hours, days. The eyes grow ever more empty, noticing more and more, growing large in the only landscape made for the eyes.

How subtly the desert seduces one in marching out its delicate designs. What are you looking for in this desert? says the voice of the desert in which nothing can be heard. Why am I so desolate? Why is the Red Sea so full of sharks, full of the most terrifying creatures? And the voice doesn't answer since it's still in the desert. Someone had reserved this desert for himself, and it wasn't a hotel chain or an oil company.

That evening in Hurghada, Martin stood with the hotel manager in one of the unoccupied little bungalows. Franza, who had already figured out that there wasn't much more to Hurghada, looked casually at the two of them. There was nothing to discuss. No water had come from the pipes when she went to wash her hands. The shower was dry as well, the sink dirty, crusted with dirt, sand and sea insects crawling around inside it. The water doesn't come up this far, the pressure is too weak, explained the manager. They went down with him to the beach and moved into one of the older huts thrown up as an attempt at maintaining a settlement in the face of a hundred kilometers of no-man's-land and the onslaught of the sand. Franza was satisfied, for the shower trickled and she could put up with the rest, even with the fact that from now on sand would always be in her shoes, sticking to her skin, and seeping through her dress.

Martin and Franza entered the main house and walked to the dining room, which looked like dining rooms found anywhere in the world. Table settings, a bar, people talking with one another. It was already too dark to see the beach, the sinking sun mirrored in the Red Sea. She stared through the window at the

Mecca of this incredible sunset. Of the foreigners in this room, they were the only ones who had come here to relax. At the bar a television crew was holding a discussion, each of them taking turns at trying to telephone Cairo about a permit, supposedly to set up their connections, though on this night Cairo was not reachable from Hurghada. It wasn't clear to Martin, who went to the bar and ordered a beer, what the crew wanted. Something about heading further south in order to film something, but was it the Red Sea from offshore, or the desert together with the Red Sea, or, since glass-bottom boats were available, did they want to film sea fauna and coral reefs beneath the Red Sea itself? Then the talk was all about a glass-bottom boat and how that wouldn't work for what the team wanted to film, and how Cairo still hadn't called back.

Besides the Arabs who were spread out in disconnected fashion throughout the room, there were three crab-red, exhausted natural historians from Paris who were also interested in the Red Sea, but only for scientific reasons. The three gentlemen were the laughingstocks of the dining room, because their shoes, suits, and suitcases lying all about had already fallen apart, only the diving suits and cameras remaining intact. They were having a beer, though of course they had not ordered until the sun had set, their hats still on their heads as they lifted their beer glasses.

Martin's gift for quickly ascertaining his surroundings and for sketching the outlines of a personality from scraps of conversation (the Frenchmen kept talking about the natives—hopefully none of the Egyptians understood French) worked whenever he got away from Franza for a bit in order to come back to her with a couple of bits of information. He waited on her like a traveling storyteller, for she merely sat there and waited for the meal. Since waiting for the fish that the waiter had presented to them only made him more hungry (a fish that no doubt they would see again each noon and evening), he stood up and said that he wanted to go swimming before the meal, for it had been the thought of a swim that had helped maintain his spirits during the journey. Franza nodded, for she wanted to be alone and to practice remaining alone, and she was still occupied with the trip, which he wanted to forget.

Unexpectedly, Martin came back soon. He sat down and didn't have the guts to look at her. There's nowhere to get into the water. I'll have to check it out for sure in the morning. There seem to be jellyfish. No, not just jellyfish, not just a couple of them, he corrected himself as he saw her laugh. There must be an entire minefield out there. The next morning the minefield lay there, consisting of little lilac-colored jellyfish swaying in the water because of the minor high tide. After lunch they all lay in the sand, so thick that one couldn't even step between them.

Martin stood on the beach and ranted. How can someone just build a hotel here and invite people to a relaxing spa? What a country, what a sea, he said. She laughed at him. Further on or down below there must be a swimming beach. But Martin said bitterly, It says right there in the damned book that the nineteenth-century Egyptian travelers always avoided the sea, and that only in recent times—and sure enough, we have to be the first. But the earlier travelers, they had the right idea.

As they walked a few kilometers south, their clothes draped over their arms, he tried to figure out what they could do. They would still have to wait four days for the flight back to Cairo, and he refused to take the bus. He thought of Cairo because of Franza. He really wanted to go to Luxor, although there were rumors that there was no longer any room there because of a state visit.* Yet Franza thought that Hurghada was fine. She lay beside him in the sand and rubbed oil and spray on herself and him. Nowhere was the beach any better. She walked back with Martin only for a while, and then she walked along above the beach until she reached a sand dune on top of which lay a set of huge flat bones, a battle scene that the sun had picked clean. There she got dressed again, for the village was visible, stuck in the desert.

The tanker was still at sea. It was the subject of conversation at all the tables. The manager went around asking that the showers not be turned on and that people not wash. The water reserve, the only one within a thousand kilometers, was not in danger, but for the first time Martin and Franza understood what was going on with the water. For the couple of square meters on which the hotel attempted to grow plants in front, and for all of the fellahs and bedouins who had the right to stay here, there had to be enough water from Hurghada, because on an arid coast this priceless water belonged to everyone and none could be refused. An unspoken law held sway before which a sophisticated and calculating hotel manager and two foreigners had to bow as well. Water was more precious than caviar and gold, than diamonds and land, more expensive than a month's salary or insurance, or the right to vote or an entire bill of rights. It came under the domain of the oldest law and could not be violated.

You see, said Franza, there's something here that even I can't be denied. I am discovering my rights.

For the first time he thought that it had been right to take her along, for he might be surprised at how well she could adapt here and learn so quickly. She no longer walked stooped over, and she sat all scrunched up at the table less and less. Water was a key part of a battle for existence within each last traversable square meter between a murderous sea and a couple of sentry posts in the desert. It brought something to life in her, as well as the pride with which she said: I will discover my rights here.

Martin, who because of his sunburn could no longer stand and had a fever, making him a weak guardian, said to her, I think you will get well here. She nodded, then began to cry, but in order that he did not see it she pressed the damp washcloth from which the water had evaporated to his face. Franza continued to display a stubborn reluctance about returning to Cairo, though she didn't make her feelings clear. Either she didn't like the city or she wanted to press on further from here, perhaps further south into the desert, her wild instinct having begun to surface as his courage wavered.

There was no doubt that her skin had begun to heal as a result of experiencing real necessity. Something (what?) was helping her to gain control over herself, for she no longer trembled for hours on end and was becoming brown and fit. He burned like a piece of grilled meat and, despite his flawless circulation coupled with the heart of a geologist strengthened by work in the mountains and coal mines and used to all kinds of exertion, he could only lie there and suck on his washcloth.

Yet he soon recovered and rode with her into the desert, asking her: Why don't you want to go back to Cairo? She gave no answer to that. They did fine with the horses, but Franza still had camels on her mind, though she was afraid of the dromedaries. Climbing on and landing, as they called it, made her afraid of the camel. She always felt like she would fall off the front when the animal stood up or knelt down. I no longer have enough time to learn how to ride a camel. I could go very far on a camel, she said with a resigned voice, but she still grabbed his hand each time she saw a tent and two or three camels set off against the desert with their slow, kingly heads. Only the promise of going further into the desert dragged her away from them. But under no circumstance did she want to go to Cairo. It's because of that woman in Cairo, thought Martin. It couldn't be anything else.

In Luxor only one hotel was taken over for the state visit. The two of them got a room together in a beautiful old hotel, though it didn't have the air conditioning that Martin had longed for since Qena after one of the French scientists there had told him about the air conditioning in Luxor, which was now reserved for the foreign dignitaries. In Luxor trucks full of soldiers were emptying out. Most of the soldiers looked as if they had just been stuck into a uniform for the first time that morning. They walked through town with baggy pants and open jackets, the town itself decorated with strings of lights. The soldiers walked hand in hand like newlyweds, most of them arm in arm. Even by the time the president arrived only every tenth soldier carried a rifle. Martin couldn't understand how the others could be expected to guard anyone.

All of the people had come out of the houses, the women as well, hidden behind veils extending to the ground and squatting as a group on the pavement, laughing and cooing. If one looked at them sideways, one could make out the faces and the hidden babies, faces of young women who were the wives of those men who looked hard, impenetrable, and had grown old too soon.

A tall Nubian was strewing rose petals on the street, and in front of the hotel bedouins were playing on tiny instruments. One of them stepped out of the group that had gathered around the musicians and began to dance by himself in what little space the onlookers provided him. During the dance he unwound the white sheet that wrapped around his head and finally let it drag behind him on the pavement. One man after another asked to be allowed to dance. As they heard the strange cries that broke out amid the village festival, Franza and Martin came out in front of the hotel. Martin walked away with her as soon as the limousines had passed.

It was embarrassing for him as a foreigner to look on unmoved, for he much preferred to read the newspapers that kept mentioning Aswan and always Aswan and the huge dam, now and then interrupted by a couple of condemnations of the

World Bank and praise for the Soviet engineers. Obviously they were caught up in a historic event, not just a couple of hotels that had been taken over. Martin cut out articles from the newspapers in order to take his mind off the bloated American women, all of them over sixty and decked out with canes and giant hats, who had taken the joy out of the hotel's main hall. In earlier times this hall would have reminded one of a renowned traveler being served in style while traveling on a steamer up the Nile to the granite quarries and on to Elephantine. Although nothing was out of place in the uniforms of the waiters, nonetheless the guests no longer existed for the waiters, for they were no longer guests suited to the tulle baldachins draped over a cool bed for the Nile winter. It was May, the Shepherds Hotel long ago having burned down in Cairo, no longer any room for the whites, and Luxor was a village that was being displayed by one president to another who, short and clad in white in the glowing heat and wearing a white hat made for a child, wanted now to see the temple at Karnak as Martin and Franza rested and waited for the one-day event to pass.

The state visit to the temple and to the hydroelectric dam moved along that same evening toward Aswan. Franza countered it with the question of when they would be able to head into the red Arabian desert again, which they had hardly seen. Martin couldn't manage to get her to see that she was disrupting his plans, and that there was still a lot here he wanted to see. She had not arrived at Luxor but instead at a point in her illness, not having traveled through the desert but through her illness. In the evening she collapsed. I have seen how I will die, she said. I saw it amid the mud.

Earlier that afternoon they had traveled south on a sailboat and landed on a peninsula. She had buried her feet in the mud and asked him to pack her in mud. You will see, she said with feverish excitement, I will be healed by the mud of the Nile. He covered her more and more, taking great pleasure in doing so. She began to look like a mummy, distinguishable only as a raised profile on the beach. Before he covered her face tenderly with a thin layer, she added, This will do just the trick. Then she lay there completely still and felt the mud slowly begin to dry.

Martin stood up because the presidential ship was sailing by. Like the women and children who waded into the water, he also held up his hand like a visor over his eyes. He reminded Franza that they should go, since the sun was unpredictable. Before one's skin became red or brown it could be suddenly burned. As she tried to get up, Franza noticed that she couldn't move, and then that she couldn't speak to him. As soon as she tried to utter the first unheard word, sand crumbled into her mouth and eyes, and the mud held her tight to the ground like a hundredweight. She was walled in. He looked down at her impatiently, not knowing that she was unable to call to him or explain. She tried to scream. He still didn't notice a thing. Her bathing cap was like a lead weight. She was buried alive.

At the hotel her pills fell on the floor. She searched around, asking, How many have I already taken, Martin? You must know. I think I have to take one more, then it will pass. How many pills?

Martin picked up the scattered pills. He had not kept track; he didn't really know what was going on. As she began to come around she said in a serious voice, It's often been much worse than this. But Martin had never seen her in a worse state. She played with the tulle canopy and talked continuously. Was that a glimpse of history? she asked ironically. Tomorrow is the fifteenth of May. Something of that day will be recorded in the history books, and I will have seen that day. What have I seen? A limousine, a ship, and rose petals. Then they will open the sluices, the water will come out. History will dub it the Day of

Water. And I was buried alive. My story and the story of all those who make up the larger history, how do these find a place within the whole of history? Are they always left by the side of the road? How do they find a place?

Franza wriggled in the mud. The sand ran into her mouth, choking her. With one more outburst she would really choke. If she screamed the sand would collapse and fill her windpipe. Martin tried to lift her up, but he couldn't move her. He knocked away the hardened layers of mud. Why didn't you say something, why didn't you say something! She staggered into the water while crying, spitting out the sand, submerging herself in the Nile. I wanted to scream, I kept wanting to scream. But I simply wasn't able to scream.

"When the choking began, I immediately left the room. I don't know if he noticed it then. I locked myself in the bathroom. But I didn't know whether or not he knew for sure. Now I'm certain he was waiting for me. Yet did he know how much I already knew?"

Now it began again, and without meaning to do anything, Martin had been at fault. Franza continued to tremble with her thoughts, her hands and feet twisting. She tumbled even further and repeated something about the notes in Jordan's files, the case of F., myself turned into a case! Then she rambled on breathlessly, My body, it's completely violated, violated everywhere. I can't go on this way. I can't. How often do I have to dunk myself in the Nile in order to wash away all traces of him?

Martin had already begun to think he had to get her mind off of it, but he couldn't manage to speak with her, neither seriously nor jokingly. It wasn't so easy. He bent over her, kissed her on the neck, and pulled the sheet up higher on her chest. He had to convince her to sleep with someone, and it had to be soon. He could indeed do it himself and would have done it when there was no other way, but he didn't want to take such a risk for them both, least of all for Franza. There was also the question of whether that was the kind of help she needed. But he had to get rid of the Fossil. Those couple of days in the desert had fooled him, for the devastation was only getting worse. She was mortally ill.

He traveled alone for the first time through the Valley of the Kings. For an entire day he dipped in and out of the tunnels and cliff graves. On the return journey that evening he met the two young Arabs. He ate with Franza that night, and then went back into the village to meet up with them. They walked down the banks of the Nile, took a boat, and then he returned late at night. Franza woke up and said, I know where you were. And you slept with someone. Martin didn't reply and only said, You have to come down to the Nile with me some night.

An enigma. During a night on the Nile, which I shall never experience, during a night on the Nile when there are no village lamps lit but rather the stars. On the Nile, on the upper Nile, far away from the shadowy years during which no star hung in my mouth.* Martin, who was "blown away" (as he called it) as he climbed around the temples, or stood there gazing at the stars, or walked with her through the forests of columns and through this powerful necropolis, saw that Franza only felt chilly. She didn't see the "glorious colors" of the city of Thebes that Martin imagined with the help of the colors that still remained amid the ruins, the starry heavens painted on the ceilings of the tombs. He could see the golden streets leading to the colossal statues, yet she saw only desert. She sat down or stood, feeling crushed beneath these columns, while he found them to be, without question, a wonder of the world. For they spoke so eloquently of death to him and served so well as a great homage to time and the continuation of time, not eternity, but rather as a search for perpetuation within time through gold and stones and mummification and symbols. She learned to read the symbols easily. There had never been a history easier for her to learn. Everything was here. No message within it, but a history.

Franza said: They have violated the graves. At first Martin thought she was thinking of the grave robbers he mentioned in his lectures. Therefore the graves of the dead had to be dug even deeper in order to make it harder to find them. But she remained stubbornly insistent. No, not the plunderers. The whites. They violated the . . . , they didn't allow the dead to rest in peace. The archaeologists. They dragged off the dead. She stared into the grave of Tutankhamen and said, That's such an outrage, it's all such an outrage. Don't you understand? That's what they did. I can't stand it. I feel the shame of it within myself, because no one else senses it.

With such differing perceptions they walked through the city of the dead. For the first time Martin could understand Franza again as she looked at the scratched-out symbols of Deir al-Bahari within the temple of Queen Hatshepsut. Every symbol and face on the walls was eradicated as they walked through the destruction, though not as the result of plunderers and archaeologists, but rather destroyed in her own time or after her own during the reign of Thutmose.*

Look, she said, but the pharaoh forgot that though he had eradicated her, she was still there. It can still be read, because nothing is there where in fact something should be.

Martin was uncertain what she meant, but it was in fact the

strangest thing he had ever seen. This urge to destroy, carried out with chisels, this desire to erase a great figure. He asked himself why it had occurred, for there was nothing written about it. And if ambition was the motive for Thutmose, then he could have silenced many other dynasties as well. But the temple of Hatshepsut stood there, an enlightened stone inside this dead city, something Greek a thousand years before there was a Greece. Hence, no need to learn about the Greeks, for Martin hoped that he'd never have to visit Athens in order to see a couple of harmless Greek lumps of stone, since after this it simply held no appeal. But Franza couldn't understand that. She only said, He was not able to destroy her. For her this was not a stone and not history, but it was rather as if no time had passed and it was something that consumed her entirely.

In the large tent in which carpets were spread out, a scene out of *A Thousand and One Nights* covered with a layer of wretched poverty, the children were awake the entire night. They smiled at Martin and poked Franza very gently with their fingers, grabbing hold of her reddish-brown arm again and again, since it still looked white compared to theirs. The children, the quietest Franza had ever seen, weren't children at all. They made flirtatious glances and gestures. Because she didn't know what to do, she said to Martin, The children here are not normal, have you noticed that? They're just different children, said Martin, hoping that she would get away from the children so that they would leave her alone.

But they're not children at all, Franza repeated again and again. She began to cry and repeated the sentence a few times more. Martin patted her hand as if to say, Don't cry, damn it, stop crying. It's a wedding.

The fat Egyptian woman in the transparent dress (fat enough such that a couple of sequins weren't enough to hold everything in, unlike the small, tender, black-clad women of the village) art-lessly moved her belly. There were only children and men in the tent. Young and old men, all of them withered and with dark eyes. They had ridden in on donkeys from the fields, a farm implement held to the chest like a weapon, looking dangerous only when they were on the donkey, threatening, and then up close no longer threatening as they shifted position to make room for Franza, talking in a staccato voice with Ahmed and Sallah as a bottle of Coca-Cola was pressed into Franza's hand.

But the children. The children continued to paw her and throw her those looks that said love me, love me. None of them was older than thirteen, and yet already the little ones had the eyes of seducers, though nothing of it was to be found in the grown-ups who smoked without pause. Franza looked search-ingly at Ahmed and Sallah. They were still beautiful because they were still young, though they no longer had that look.

What are you looking for in this desert, in this dead city? The west bank, the east bank, no matter which bank, only desert is there. In the street of a thousand sphinxes, of a thousand ram skulls, you headed home flanked by your fear, flanked by not just one sphinx, but a thousand, made of stone, with hands that can grab. In this particular landscape, which says nothing, which expresses nothing, how much there is that one can say nothing about! What do you want here? A pure expanse before your eyes into which you escape, chased every day into the desert and going into the desert again in order to drink in yet more desert with your eyes?

Where is the Gulf of Aqaba! Still on the run, crossing the Nile, at night on the Nile, in the shadow of a sail which alone is dark. What do you want in this desert? Why not get involved with a foreigner who has the aura of a simpleton tortured by words that smack of deeds that still make him tremble but are not punishable by any article of the law. Thus will I discover my rights. But the alibi of the whites is strong. Don't forget that. They tried everything to eliminate you, to blow you to bits on their minefield of intelligence, which they misuse in order to make you serve their plans and schemes.

The whites are coming. The whites are landing.* And if they are driven back, then they will come again. No revolution or resolution can prevent it, nor any controls over the currency. They will come again in spirit if there's no other way for them to come. And they will resurrect themselves in a brown or black brain, which will become white once again. They will take over the world through such indirect means.

Pain, a rare word, a rare thing. In the natural history of man, it's something that is allotted to the body, migrating from the body and becoming explosive inside the brain. I am in the desert in order to shed my pain, and I cannot shed the pain that runs through my head, through my lungs, that rages through the vessels of the heart to my twisting extremities, this maddening pain that every couple of hours seeks another area to explore, locking my jaws, making my teeth chatter, numbing my hands until they seem cut off from me, the bowl slipping from my hands. If I cannot shed it, the pain that is packed into my knees, that which causes the pupils of my eyes to reel after each momentary death, if I cannot shed it. . . .

Martin looked at her focused, unblinking eyes and slowly closed them, breathing on her lightly again. What was she looking for in this desert?

He couldn't bring her to the Gulf of Aqaba, but he swore that he would bring her back to life here or kill her in order to put an end to it. But at night he got up while she was asleep, for she often slept very well now, and went to meet the two Arabs.

In the wedding tent Franza sat all tensed up until after midnight. The belly dancer continued to move her belly and the music kept repeating itself, a strange litany. Franza could barely hold herself up anymore, but she did so for Martin's sake, and because Ahmed and Sallah saw the lengthy affair as only a shortened version of a three-day wedding. She didn't want to wait around for the arrival of the bride and groom any longer.

In the courtyard the camel had lain down when they had arrived and entered. She had spoken to it in the way that she had spoken to the cows and horses in Galicien years ago. When she let her head fall back heavily on the hard chair, Martin stood up, along with the two Arabs, all of them crossing the courtyard. The camel was no longer there. A few meters away in the sand, Franza stopped. She had stepped onto red sand, but the sand was not just red; she was standing in blood. Then she looked over toward the lantern on the stable wall. There the camel lay, some men standing around it, its throat cut.

Franza did not move in the bloody sand. Martin said, Come. She replied, I can't go any further. The men had huge knives and were cutting up the camel. She had understood what was happening before Ahmed and Sallah explained it to her. But I will not walk through this blood, through this sand covered with this blood. . . . She was pulled by the arms by a white and a brown hand, forced to wade through the bloody sand. The camel, they had killed the camel. I know what I look like. I look like the camel that is staring at me. It was a gift to the bride, said Ahmed. There was no other way out from the tent or the courtyard.

In the wedding tent the children climbed over the chairs and through the rows to Franza. She saw the cretin only when

Martin pointed him out to her. She saw him and yet didn't see him, for she had never seen such a horrible-looking figure, not even in a picture of hell. With his head bald, he sat squatting on the earth, his twisted arms covered with biblical abscesses, his legs twisted as well, himself no bigger than a child. The children stepped on his feet, two little girls held a bottle of Coca-Cola that Ahmed and Sallah had paid for to his mouth. He is a holy man, they said. Look, Martin commanded, but she stared fixedly past the cretin, though she had seen his grin as she stared beyond him. She didn't want to glance at the ground where the children stepped on him, himself grinning without feeling their footsteps upon him. Then some other men brought the cretin a bottle, and Franza thought, If I am going to get up, then I will have to look at him.

At one point a crippled foot reached as far as her sandal and she said, Martin! Then the cretin touched her. She let the Coca-Cola bottle drop in the sand under the wooden chair. She stared at the belly dancer. It must be three in the morning, Martin, it's late. But I can't step over him, I can't do that. He is already inside of me. He travels within me, and that's why I can't look at him. The cretin had a huge skull that seemed to be attached directly to his hips.

Hashish, hashinin, assassin,* a derivation of murderer, assassin, cannabis indica, hash, and by how many other names was hemp known? Sallah and Ahmed had only been able to get a small chunk, but a very good, hard, earth-brown chunk nonetheless. They tested it and allowed Martin and the crazy Irishman to touch it. Desmond had put on a djellabah and Franza, irritated, said, You look like you're dressed up in a costume, disguised, nor would she allow Martin to put on a disguise. A Soviet engineer who worked on the hydroelectric dam at first wanted to stay but then decided to leave.

They sat at the table and began to carefully empty tobacco out of the cigarettes as the two young Arabs cut up the chunk of hashish and took over the mixing of the tobacco. Then the cigarettes were slowly filled again, not too loosely, not too tightly. It all took place with extreme care, like a ritual, a ceremony.

They all began to smoke at the same time. After the first three drags Franza laid the cigarette in the ashtray and said, I don't want to. Martin gave her the cigarette again and said, Do it. Do it for your own sake. What did he want from her? She no longer understood what he was ordering her to do. He had decided something for her. He wanted to place a wedge between her and the illness, or between her and Vienna. She began again to smoke, obedient, sensing nothing. Silence was the custom, nothing needed to be said. As Martin gave her the third cigarette, she noticed how the faces of the others turned inward, and she saw for the first time the soft smiles on the brown and dark brown faces. The Irishman had stood up and stretched out on the carpet, having already smoked his third cigarette.

It happened, something happened, at first unnoticeably, then more quickly. The smoke began to move through the body in swaths. Franza felt it in her thighs as it began to press upon her skin and hold her down. Feeling panicked, she wanted to stand up. Where had the others gone, where are they, where is everyone? It was unbearable to sit there another minute—if indeed it was a minute, time having disappeared, no longer any time, the room spinning, the body in opposition to time and the room.

Since there was no one to help her, she crawled down from the stool, letting herself go, and crawled along the ground with open eyes, thinking it was dangerous for the lids to touch the bottom rim of the eye. She reached the terrace that was covered with carpets and lay on her back, her eyes directed at the light in the room. At the end she had inhaled very deeply, holding the smoke in her lungs until she vomited, but the nausea she felt was not like that before she vomited: It permeated her entire body.

Franza closed her eyes and let herself be shoved down. Down where? Out of horror she wanted to push back, for she no longer had one body, but two. She now had a double. She placed a hand over her breast, but there she felt another large hand attached to another large body. I have become two people, one who is huge and one who is my size. Her two bodies, lying on their backs, were suspended. The four feet were lifted up, the two heads remaining on the carpet. I must become one, and all she could think was that she had to become one again.

Straining, she forced open her eyes. Everything was there, just as she had left it: the room, the lamp. She saw Ahmed's djellabah, his arm dangling down, then she pressed her eyes closed again. Her body was held in a vise grip, her hips and back pressed against each other, squeezed tight. There was no possibility of shifting positions.

Beneath her closed eyelids ran a string of symbols bedecked with black and white ornaments. The hieroglyphs danced beneath her eyelids. Her eyes opened again, opening quick as lightning despite the pressure. This indecipherable writing had to stop. She assured herself that everything was still there. The room. A warm, stale odor from the Nile. The hieroglyphs had stopped. Then it began again. She pressed her hands hard against both her bodies, her hands feeling everything inside, all the arteries and veins, all the muscles, all the bones, feeling as if an X ray were piercing through her, no one able to illuminate a body and dissect it in the way that this feeling probed through her.

She threw herself on her side and rolled onto her back again. The minaret from the mosque. The assurance that it was there, that it was able to be seen, the vise grip loosening its hold. She flew toward the minaret, came back to the carpet, flew toward it again, then began to smile. A flurry of thoughts midflight, thinking something, incredibly fast, too fast for a brain to handle, thoughts causing new thoughts to break away and whirl. The whites are coming. Don't think, just don't think any longer and such thoughts will be vaporized. Once more the eyes have to, once more the eyes have to open. I will fly again, I will come, Sire, I will come.

Franza didn't know when she had come around again and what her other condition had been just before the return flight, before she landed in sleep with one body, having become one, or when she had gone to sleep.

She awoke, awakened by Martin, lying on the carpet. Yes, she had gone out on the terrace last night. The morning was bright, already too hot. They went back to the hotel with clear heads, never once needing to grab hold of their heads. They tried to speak about the night, but Martin didn't understand Franza, or at least the part about her body having a double, nor did she understand what he had heard. What was there to hear? Martin made a couple of attempts to explain the musical sounds that he had heard and then gave up. The hemp had taken them to different places.

Far off, again on the Red Sea, further south, black Egypt replaced red Arabia as they drove in a car toward the Shell oil fields. No gas can, no water. Martin and the two men wanted to take a dip, to find a place to go swimming, but they came straight back, since the water was teeming with snakes. Franza walked into the water in a shallow spot. After she tested it a bit, since it was water that couldn't be trusted, she lay down flat in the water, then on the beach. She sunbathed and fell asleep. The men drove off to fill the car with gas.

On the loneliest beach in the world she stood up and began to walk along this hellish pool jammed with jellyfish, spiders, and crabs, while on the beach the stinging, pinching, and creeping creatures that had become stranded there flew off in all directions between her feet. She began to run and stepped always on the stretches of sand that were free. In the bright sun there was nothing to see, then a shadow wandered along the dirt road. She heard the sound of a car, thinking that must be the car. But the noise and the shadow disappeared and she kept running.

Then she stood there, looking for a place to stand between what crawled, pinched, or wanted to pinch. The sun stood exactly above her. Then she saw the image, there in the red Arabian desert. No longer the recurring image of the woman in Cairo, no longer the puddle of blood around the camel, and no longer the cretin. She looked on disconcerted. I see. And now once again. I see what no one has seen before, an image.

She took a couple of steps, too slowly, and the image retreated. Her skin began to burn. I have to run in order for it to become more clear. It's him. I have to go to him, but it wasn't Martin who was receding. It is him, it's him in the white coat, he's stepping out of the image, he's come from Vienna wearing the mantle of comfort in order to take me home. No, it's a terrifying coat that he's throwing off, but it's not him. My father. I have seen my father. He's throwing off his coat, his many coats. She laid her hands on her head so that it wouldn't burst into flames. But it's not him, he is not my father. Who is he then?

She began to run faster. Black and standing high, it began to cross the beach and hover above the sand and touched down. But black and dark and now crawling over the sand, rolling across, it came. God is revealing Himself to me and I am standing before Him. She ran faster and cried, cried, and because no word escaped her, only the phlegm from smoking the night before rising in her throat, she spit in the sand and ran further. I have seen God. Near enough to touch, between . . . where am I? Safaga, and between Safaga, just before Safaga, the surrounding mountains beautiful and over 6,000 feet high, in a tent near the sentry post. Where is the guard, the phosphate mining company, what used to be the English harbor? There has to be a way for me to reach it. The phosphate mines cannot stop the appearance of God.

She fell to her knees and there He lay, a black stump washed up on shore, a sea cucumber, a shriveled-up monstrosity, not even a foot long, and barely alive. That's what she had been running toward. She was still crying and grabbed hold of the creature and shoved it back in the water, letting it drift in the sea. I have seen an image. She remained lying there, suffering convulsions as she had in the hallway in Vienna, on a parquet floor, a linoleum floor, a hospital bed, and now again on the sand, on the sand bloodied by a camel, as she laughed and laughed and laughed—her laughter providing the opening for the decomposition that began: Who am I? Where did I come from? What's wrong with me? What am I looking for in this desert? Something happened and yet did not happen, since nothing can happen, only something stepped on her and alongside her walked something else, part death, part consciousness, part animal, part human, part of the five senses, one a sister, the other a woman, the flesh directed by the sun toward ruin, en route toward something that is unrecognizable.

She screamed. Martin lifted her up and they carried her to the car on the dirt road.

The Arabian desert is surrounded by shattered visions of God.'

❖

Following this section, Bachmann intended to complete another section in which Franza and Martin visit Aswan and Wadi Halfa, the ancient town submerged beneath the lake created by the Aswan High Dam, before their return through Cairo. However, this middle section was never drafted. —TRANS.

II

The hall of mummies is in the west wing. The sixteen layers of linen, growing ever thinner over the bodies of kings and queens, are fragile; that is, where they still exist. The skulls of the dead are visible, the foreheads sunken, the rest of the wrappings gray and muddy. For forty-five piastres one gains entrance to such horror; for five piastres one can see the entire museum. But the violators of graves, the hordes of soldiers, and bedouins in search of treasure don't crowd in here, but rather the public, armed with cameras, their faces distorted by intense curiosity, gathering thick as flies around the coffins, Breughel-like figures from Holland, from Germany, from Denmark, or some country with sensitive skin, their forearms sunburned and noses glowing.

Whether to use color film or not, that is the question. Martin walked quickly through the room, passing all of the glass cases and only concentrating on the names, because Franza had wanted to know who had dared dig up the mummies. She remained standing in the entrance, for right off she had seen Amenhotep III, the great legendary king and creator of the Colossus with the yellow star painted above his remote blue tomb. They had brought him here, and there she stood with a ticket, but she wouldn't use it, nor would she enter, despite a third invitation from the guard. She asked Martin, Are they really all in there? Martin had finally had enough (she could see it herself). He hastily rattled off who was on display here—all of the Ramses, Nefertiti as well, also Mentuhotep.

Franza stopped listening and looked at Amenhotep III with eyes almost closed and blinking, just as she had looked at the cretin while looking beyond him. She suddenly doubled up, her head thrusting downward, and vomited at the entrance of the room of mummies. A blob of tea and bread crumbs lay on the floor. Franza felt relieved, though she gagged a couple of more times. I have at least vomited at the feet of you violators of bodies.

The guard accepted a tip from Martin, but raised his arms in a helpless gesture, letting on that it was the heat. They simply can't stand the heat, these foreigners. Franza took the newspaper from Martin and wiped the floor. Two young Germans, who had continued photographing mummies and skeletons one after another, soon squatted down, propped up on their toes, circling Franza as they reloaded their cameras with film outside the room.

You can see the dead between nine and twelve, and from four to six. Here is an unused ticket. Here is someone who won't let you turn to dust, who will wrap you in linen again, who will replace your golden masks, lay you once again in the painted shrines, who is determined to bring back your sarcophagi, place you back in the cliffs, restore the darkness so that you may reign again and your symbols remain, the symbols of life, of water, the wingéd sun, the lotus blossom. You described your world very well. The living should describe the living. This is the restitution. This is the restoration. To seal the entrances to the tunnels so that no one finds them again. Thebes shall disappear, not a single cliff shall open again.

In the Cairo Tower (Cairo, the Victorious?).* Already in the elevator Franza asked, The Victorious, is that what you said to me? Martin thought, When and where does she notice anything, for she never listens, and then she comes out with a sentence that says she has been listening. Since she doesn't seem to listen with her ears, how does she hear? On which channel? And what a strange selection she always makes.

In the bar they met with "his" people, for Franza called everyone they had to see in Cairo Martin's people. They were an amateur archaeologist and someone on the staff of the American embassy. As they greeted one another, Franza and Martin were facing the huge dark windows that circled the tower, the lights of the city visible on all sides, as well as the other arm of the Nile embracing Gezira. Martin's people gestured proudly toward the city below as if they not only had chosen such a good meeting place but had created Cairo and the Nile for it as well.

The Nile seemed to be rising, itself a swift-moving snake. The Nile rose and sank quickly, the entire length of it. Franza leaned hard against the small table, her knees feeling weak, and then sat herself down on the stool that Martin shoved beneath her. As the waiter set down the cocktails and they all reached for the bowl of nuts, she tried hard to look at the floor in order to stop the spinning. She couldn't stand these windows that reached all the way to the floor. The windows were everywhere. She couldn't look up, no matter what they might say about her, as they talked about something there was to see from the other side. If only the dark shining Nile didn't flow through the window and across the floor so silently and shining. The voices also now gathered on the floor near her feet. Laughter, questions, talk, they wound themselves together in a whirlwind at her feet where she stared.

Then the Cairo Tower did something else. It began to sway, and Franza forced her eyes to look up halfway and said in the middle of the conversation, I have to go immediately, I have to get out of here.

She stood up and swung her hands to catch her balance. She

heard Martin excusing himself to the others, saying that Franza had a headache, after which she said to him quietly, It's the windows, only the windows.

The amateur archaeologist and the American stood up and paid. In the elevator Franza breathed a sigh of relief, even as it set in motion, herself chatting and smiling. The Americans led them all to the floor above. There were fewer windows there, only small ones that were placed chest-high in the walls.

The American said that the restaurant had a flawed construction. It was supposed to turn slowly around the tower during meals, but it never moved. But at the moment, as the waiter approached, there was a jolt, one not only felt by Franza but by all of them. Martin mustered all of the recklessness of which he was capable and said if they, the others, didn't mind then they should all leave right away, for his sister easily became dizzy. He made a couple of jokes about women and dizziness and feeling dizzy, but he got up nonetheless, and they left the tower to look for a restaurant in the city center.

It had gotten quite late. The owner of an Italian restaurant, himself an Italian-Egyptian, said on the such-and-such night to the so-and-so foreigners that he was one of the last of his kind in the country and that he would soon go to Australia. As he set the table, he did it as if he were doing it for the last time, because of Australia. As Franza willingly listened to him and got the impression that soon there would hardly be anywhere else to eat in the city, because everybody would soon move to Australia, the restaurant began to rock, even though she was on level ground, the glasses and place settings knocking against each other, herself unable to hold onto the table.

She took Martin's hand and pressed her fingernails into his wrist, afraid that she would rip open the veins, though she pressed her nails ever deeper, beginning to sob, hoping only that she did not draw blood and make him bleed. Martin, it won't stop, it's awful. She looked at him, although his head also rocked back and forth in the room and she could barely make out his features and kept seeing him at different angles. It's terrible, lay me down on the floor. Martin lifted her up as she said, On the floor, I want to lie on the floor. I think I'm dying, I think it's about to happen.

The next day the American came to the hotel with his mother to visit them in order to see how Franza was doing. Franza sat alone in the bar, which embarrassed her somewhat, because she was sitting there and not lying in bed, which is what one would have expected after such an incident.

Why had he dragged along his mother? And what a mother she was. Franza had never heard so many questions and pronouncements. She looked at the gaunt woman's sheer, pink dress and the pink rouge until she understood that she was there to help her, the woman having been informed of the dizzy spell the day before. Franza said, There was nothing wrong with me, it was the tower; I simply can't climb towers.

Franza kept both of the hotel entrances in sight, because Martin needed to take care of his own people since she was unable to do it. The woman was a witch, gouty and pink. She showered Franza with advice, invited her to visit her that evening, and then launched into Egyptian doctors, explaining that the embassy doctor was useless. Franza replied, But I don't need any doctor, as the pink witch talked about one illness after another, almost suggesting that Franza must have kidney stones or migraines. Franza wet her lips again with mineral water, and as the son drifted toward the bar at the mention of kidney stones and left her alone with this monster, the pink mother said that there was a doctor who worked miracles, a German, and that Franza had to go to this doctor, but in secret, for she also went in secret herself.

Franza thought that either this pink woman was insane or she was obsessed with illnesses. She had often seen that in Vienna, women about this age who ran to faith healers with pendulums and who swore by the examination of one's eyes for the proper diagnosis, as well as acupuncture and other hocus-pocus. The pink woman said with a giggle, Franza, my dear, there's no reason to be frightened. He's one of those Germans, you know the type, and he doesn't have a practice, the authorities don't allow that. It's quite exciting, said the woman. At first I was so agitated, but now a good many people go to see him, not only myself. I still get shivers in my spine, but it's as if the migraines and kidney stones have simply gone away.

The woman had taken her hand and bent toward her to whisper, He lives in Sharia al-Gabalya. Who? Him. But just tell him that I sent you.

The pink woman didn't let go of Franza's hand. Franza pulled her hand away and stood up. She introduced Martin, and the American returned, saying hello, and Franza thanked him for his visit. She then said, turning to Martin, Mrs. Holden was so kind to worry about me. It was very nice of you, Mrs. Holden, but we must go, for we're expected elsewhere. She looked at Martin quickly and took his arm.

You're hardly gone a minute and this is what happens. An awful woman, said Franza. What happened? asked Martin. Oh nothing, replied Franza, a bunch of chatter. She had kidney stones and the doctors here are apparently useless, the embassy doctor as well. That took a good hour, listening to all of her illnesses while trying to fight off a headache. Now I really do have a headache. I don't want to see any people, especially any of the expatriates. Don't you understand that?

On the island of Zamalek, near the Grotta Garden, in Sharia al-Gabalya, Franza found the houseboat. At first she couldn't make out the house number overgrown with vines as she looked down from the street at the wooden bridge. An unpainted leaky boat was tied up at the house next to the bridge. She walked hesitantly over the gangplank because a couple of its boards were missing. The branch of the Nile was narrow here. On both shores there were houseboats. There were lovely white boats with painted window frames in front of banks of bright flowers and abandoned ones facing dusty perennials as tall as a man, this particular houseboat being neither the worst nor the best.

She pushed the door open and entered a front hall in which a short, fat Egyptian lay on the carpet. Not Franza, but Frau Jordan, who was used to being admitted, asked in a distracted, assured voice for Doctor Körner. She hadn't been able to remember the entire day whether Mrs. Holden had spoken of Doctor Karner or Kerner, though it could have been a false name, while it wasn't until she was in front of the house that the name Körner suddenly occurred to her.

The sleepy servant stood up and motioned toward a chair. She waited for a long time, and the longer she waited, the less she understood why she had come, as though she had lost the reason why, as if she had lost it only at the discovery of the house number.

The servant returned and indicated that she should go up the stairs. Then the house began to move. Franza was dizzy. It's happening once more, it's happening again. She grabbed hold of the back of her neck. As she reached the last step, she clung to the bannister and saw that the steps led directly into a room, a man having stepped into it from a side door. He spoke to her in English and she immediately responded in German.

Who was it that sent you? Please sit down. I must inform you that I am not allowed to practice as a doctor.

Franza nodded. He was from Vienna, his accent was unmistakable. She had not known that. She had automatically assumed that he would be German.

I'm feeling dizzy, she said, happy that she could speak freely. I had thought—she tried to smile—it seemed to me that the house was moving.

Whenever a steamer passes it rocks. You get used to it. There's nothing better in Cairo than a houseboat.

Franza studied his voice. He didn't belong to *that* social circle. His voice contained nothing of Jordan's class, nothing of that haughty nasal tone. A thin, straining, middle-class German accent from Vienna. A face with glasses, brown hair starting to turn gray, a muscular body, stocky and certainly as tanned as the face, most likely tanned from afternoons at the Gezira Sporting Club. Otherwise no other distinguishing features.

Well, he certainly wasn't licensed, Franza thought to herself.

I heard about you . . . in the American colony.

Franza stopped talking and looked at the tattered furniture and then at the worn carpet. She had imagined the scene differently, a villa, himself looking like someone supported by the government or a secret organization. But things couldn't be that bad for him either. In fact they were probably pretty good. Tired, she tried to go on.

I have heard, or Mrs. Holden said, that you can work wonders, that you can even help the most hopeless cases.

He looked at her coolly and said that he was a doctor, an internist, to be precise. He could not work wonders, and that it would be better for her to begin by telling him what was wrong with her. Otherwise she should look for a quack.

I'm sick, said Franza, yet she felt that this sentence made her look foolish and quickly added, That's not why I came here. I know who you are.

She had said it, unable to take it back. For Franza it was like a silent explosion.

Some know that. It's known around here. You're not telling me anything new. Do you live in Cairo?

No, said Franza, I come from Vienna. My name is Jordan. I'm married to a doctor. She paused. To Leopold Jordan. She tried to look at him again as she cast a glance past him while holding her head at an angle. She noticed after a while that there was another reason why he didn't respond. The name Jordan, which for fifteen years had been a famous name in Vienna and in the international ranks, appeared to mean nothing at all to Körner.

He sat quietly behind the desk and played with a pen.

I don't understand. If your husband is a doctor . . . if you're sick. . . .

I don't understand it either, said Franza. She didn't know what else to say, but she couldn't just stand up and leave. The houseboat rocked again; she heard the waves slapping against the walls and held tight to the arms of the chair. The walls that were hung with calendars and bad reproductions of Austrian castles pulled her gaze upward. The monastery at Melk wobbled next to the door, then stopped moving and helped her to right herself. Nothing in this room gave the appearance that a doctor worked here except the white coat that hung on the back of his chair. Körner had not put it on.

My husband wrote a book. I worked on it with him.

She started to mumble. About the experiments performed on female prisoners. About post-traumatic disorders. She could hardly be heard as she pressed her hands together. I know all the documents. You were in Dachau and in . . . in . . . Hartheim. It just occurred to me today.

I have never performed an experiment on a female prisoner.

I know, said Franza, I know that. There were also other— she searched for another word, then used his own—other experiments made. Didn't I say that I know all the documents? The sulfonamide and phlegmone experiments, the spotted-fever vaccine experiments, the mustard gas and phosgene experiments.

They began to merge into each other, for she no longer had them paginated in front of her and couldn't just thumb through them. In memory, she tried hard to scour the shelves of the library in Vienna. That's also what made me sick, she thought, and then at last it occurred to her: the eradication of undesirables, the eradication, yes, the immediate eradication of the unwanted sick, the assisted deaths, the mercy killings. Two milliliters of morphine-scopolamine. In memory she had found Körner again in the chapter on the euthanasia program.

I still don't understand you, said Körner. What do you want from me? Then he made an attempt at irony that failed. To what do I owe the honor? He began to make short sharp marks on the pad with his pen.

Franza thought that it would make no sense if she said that she had a very good reason, an extremely good reason, to want to see someone like him who had done such a thing. He would think that she wanted to place him under inspection, and that wasn't it. She no longer knew how to put her reasons into a sentence that would make sense, for the reasons couldn't be expressed easily, and certainly not in conversation.

Something gave me the impression . . . I used to study medicine, then I stopped, to get married of course . . . the Hippocratic oath, she said, rambling on. All professions should . . . I mean, I don't know why the other professions shouldn't also . . . there's nothing they have to answer to.

And again she saw it printed before her, four times: 2 ml M.-Scn.

You didn't come here to give me advice. Do you want to spy on me or did you come from a scandal rag in order to take back a sensational interview from Cairo? I was never that high up.

But, said Franza, haven't you noticed that I haven't asked you a thing? I'm asking myself. I've asked myself for such a long time already. I'm asking myself. But she wanted to say: I'm sick, but not with something you can diagnose; it has nothing to do with circulation or the nervous system, with the heart or the lungs.

He stood up, and she knew that what he meant by doing so was that she would have to leave.

If you're not sick, he began, but then for the first time lost his air of certainty.

But I am sick, Franza said quietly and stood up. It's just that there's no way to help me.

She took a step back, but it was unnecessary, for she didn't feel threatened; there was nothing sinister in the air. In this room there was only a bad odor from the reeking Nile, but nothing that smelled of a crime. SS Captain Dr. Kurt Körner gave off no particular odor.

Forgive me, she said. The two of them stood there; he no longer pressed at her and she also didn't move.

She suddenly realized that she had said to him: Forgive me. On the last page she had left behind for Jordan there stood at the bottom: Forgive me. Not even her name followed.

In the Nuremberg trial report she had to stop reading when Witness B. took the stand, castrated, badly burned, his testicles having been operated on. But that was not what caused her to always stop at this point. She had already read too many court records and case histories, having read hardly anything else in recent years. Witness B. ceased to speak, but it didn't say that in the court record. Rather, it was as if he suddenly was swallowed up amid the paper on which it was printed. Prosecutor MacHaney,˙ after his question was not answered, then stated:

Witness, there's no reason to be afraid!

But after this line in the court record there was silence. And then Witness B., after the Earth had turned once again on its axis, said what summed up the entire page:

Forgive me for crying. . . .

Otherwise, in the entire court record there was no "forgive me." Meanwhile, from the doctors there were whole passages about orders and what was legally binding at the time, and "that I could not judge," and "that I don't know," and "I didn't know anything about that." The talk was always about "opinions." Silence never erupted, nothing ceased to be said.

Franza, in this still air, in this room, thought about forgiveness and records and eradication. What did all that have to do with a man in Cairo who stood there and had so little to talk about, as she did herself.

She nodded, relieved that he didn't say good-bye. She went down the steps and past the servant, who was again lying on the floor, and then across the fragile bridge.

Upon her arrival at the train station in Cairo, Franza had seen the woman. She had lain upon her knees, her hands pulled behind her back, bound with rope, cords of rope binding her hands behind her back, her feet naked, dirty, and bound together as well, which is what Franza had noticed first. The woman's head, a long, small head stretching upward, like that of Akhenaton's daughter, was bent back such that she had to look straight up and so high that there couldn't have been anything in her field of vision. Finally Franza had noticed the tall Arab who was twisting the woman's hair, not into a braid, but rather into a tight black cord, holding it twisted in his hand so that she couldn't move her head, as with his other hand he stuffed himself with yellow bean-sized kernels and smiled.

Franza had set down her suitcase and walked up to the group of men who were standing around the woman. She couldn't talk, her mouth having shut tight. Franza looked around for Martin, who was still busy on the platform next to the luggage. She stared at the men insistently, her jaws locked tight.

Martin, the woman! The man is crazy, he's crazy. She had

repeated the sentence so many times inside her that eventually she released it in such clear English that everyone must have understood it. The young man standing next to her had said with a comforting smile, He's not crazy, she is.

The woman, the woman at the train station. Franza, who had hailed a taxi on the street, asked to be taken to the train station. It was important to go back to the train station; she had to put an end to it. She told the driver to wait, got out, and climbed the stairs to the first platform. The woman who had been tied up and lay on her knees had been gone for weeks, the man from the country having waited for a train with her and then having brought her home somewhere in the upper Nile valley. At least he brought her home. However, he didn't bring me. . . . She began to sob. This woman will always be here, Franza said to herself as she nodded and walked away, for I have become this woman.

She got back into the taxi and returned to the hotel.

I am lying in her place. And my hair is twisted into a long, long cord that is held by him in Vienna. I am bound and tied. I will never escape.

Franza paid the money. She still had over three hundred dollars that Martin had held for her, and Martin must have had more than twice that much. That evening in the room she talked about how much they would need before they returned home. Will there be any left over? she asked. Could you give me a hundred of yours? I'd really like to go shopping.

Martin was astonished, for she had never yet wanted to go shopping. The desire to go shopping was surely a good sign. Martin didn't want to let on how positive a step her desire for money was, and so he just said, Then we'll go shopping together the day before we leave so that we can spend all the leftover money. One never knows what one will do before setting out on a journey. Does that sound all right to you?

During the night she got up and took three hundred dollars from his wallet. She folded the bills and stuck them in her passport, telling herself the reason was that he had given it to her anyway. Then she stopped searching for arguments and lay back down. And if I've stolen it, there's no need for him to be aware of it. No, he can't be aware of it. She lay there for a long time with her eyes open.

In front of the houseboat in Sharia al-Gabalya she was indecisive, but since she already knew it, the way into the house was like a familiar path. When she asked for the doctor, the servant said, as a noticeable sound could be heard from the creaking of the wood on the first floor above them, that he wasn't there. Most likely Körner had seen her coming.

She quickly went up the stairs and looked around. The room was empty, his white coat hanging on a hook on the door. She sat down on the chair that he had directed her toward the first time and tried to practice her breathing by breathing in deeply and then out. Körner yanked open the door and said in a repressed yell, Get out of here right now. What do you think you're doing?

Franza said, You misunderstand. She spoke very fast. I came back in order to ask you to do something. I've already told you that I'm sick. I have to ask you to do something and you have to listen to me.

He mechanically reached for his white coat and said quietly, but forcefully, You either leave right now or tell me what is wrong with you.

Franza thought, If only it were that easy. But she knew she had to talk, to be heard. She spoke again quickly, saying, I can't stand it anymore, I can't go on. It's my last hope. Don't you understand? Don't you at all?

Körner said, If you're pregnant and want an abortion, you could express yourself more clearly and calmly. But I don't perform abortions. You're in the wrong place.

Extreme agitation surged through Franza's head, through her hands, and finally her legs.

That's not the reason why I came, nothing like that at all. I've already told you that I know everything about you.

He didn't respond. Franza held the envelope with the three hundred dollars in her hand, cradling it between her fingers. She said, Forgive me, I think dollars are preferred to pounds here. I only wanted to say, I can pay in dollars. Three hundred should do it.

Körner sat down, letting fall more than just the weight of his body. My usual fees are paid in dollars. You can also pay in local currency. Don't make it so complex. But I can't imagine why you need three hundred dollars for an exam. What do you take me for?

I don't want to be examined by you. That's not what I'm after. I just want you to do it again. And I don't have any more money. Give me an injection.

Listen, he said as he stood up and walked toward her. What are you saying?

Nothing. I already said it. I don't want to live any longer, I can't go on.

How could she make clear to him that she wanted to be eradicated? Yes, eradicated, that was it.

I can try to get more money. You have to do it. For you it's just . . . she stopped.

I'm a doctor, said Körner. You're crazy. Who ever heard of such nerve?

Franza thought, I'm only asking for something that he used to do willingly and without being asked to do it, and yet now someone comes along and is not allowed to beg for it and pay for it. What kind of world is this?

If you are afraid of trouble, then give it to me and I can do it myself. But give it to me. No one knows, no one will know. . . . But give it to me. I don't know anyone but you whom I can go to. . . . She broke off once again. She didn't want him to turn against her. Perhaps it insulted his honor as a murderer or his honor as a doctor. These kind of people were all so sensitive. Suddenly she thought of Jordan, thinking the same of him as she did of Körner. Jordan had displayed the same indignation over such nerve and overpayment of the honorarium, spreading out his professional honor before the patient like a banner.

Listen, said Körner. I will forget all about this. You are, he cleared his throat, in a psychologically fragile state. I'm assuming all goodwill on your part. I can't write you a prescription, but I can give you the name of an Egyptian colleague. In the meantime, take one or two Librium each day. . . .

Franza shook her head.

I don't need any prescription from an Egyptian colleague, thank you. No Librium and no Meprobamate and no Dominal and no Megaphen. As you can see, I know my way around. I've had enough of them. They don't do any good. I want a toxic dose, fifty or sixty milligrams (it doesn't have to be gasoline, she thought to herself, obsessed with every detail). I don't want to do anything halfway. I don't have much more time.

She laid the envelope on the chair and ran down the steps.

The next day she returned again at the same time. The door was locked, so she sat down before it and let her legs hang above the water. Over the footbridge came the servant, turning around when he saw her and then returning again after a while. He gave her the envelope and said that the doctor had gone to Alexandria. Flown off. Gone away. For a week. She stood there stunned, the envelope in her hand. He had abandoned her. She walked past the servant. He didn't stop her as she crossed the bridge, entering the house through the kitchen door. She opened every door and went up to the first floor, walking through every room and back again, then out onto the terrace where she sat for a moment on a wicker chair, feeling weak.

Eventually she headed back the way she had come, wiping something from her face the entire time, feeling numb, then prickly, after which she began to cry, crying the whole way through Zamalek and in the hotel as well, where the bellboy looked at her as if he wanted to ask her something.

In the corridor she wiped away the tears. In front of the door to the room she took a handkerchief and comb out of her purse, blew her nose and combed her hair and put on her sunglasses so that Martin wouldn't see her swollen eyes. She took a couple of deep breaths, and when she felt she had calmed down enough, she opened the door. She suddenly realized that she had been wrong, mistaken: Körner really had left because of her, because he was afraid of her. Someone had been afraid of her, for the first time afraid of her rather than her being afraid of someone.

On the drive to Giza, she said to Martin in the taxi: He—she corrected herself—Jordan was never afraid of me. He was so sure that I would tell no one, that I would rather die first (as well as until death did us part). He never once displayed any kind of uneasiness. But I still have made someone afraid. One of them. Yes, that I have done.

Martin saw that her fists were balled up. He didn't understand her remarks, for the discontinuity of such sentences made it hard. In order to pull her out of her trance he took her hand and gently opened her fist and talked casually about something else.

When I'm outside the city, I breathe a sigh of relief, don't you? he said. We couldn't stay any longer, even if I don't have to get back. Holden says that none of us could stand the summer. The Holdens are going to Marsa Matruh this week, on the sea. That's near El Alamein. How strange. Good thing neither of us is sentimental.

He held her hand, and she looked at him with seeming attention.

I can't imagine myself walking around there with head sunk low, visiting my father.

Martin drove back to Mena House with her. There were fewer people there than at the Gezira Sporting Club. They could swim alone in the large swimming pool and eat lunch in the shade next to it. Often she had the urge and tried to tell him that an electric current moved through her head, a thousand volts strong. Is a thousand a lot? Because a bolt is running straight through me, all the way down to my feet. Despite this, in the early evening she got up and trotted along with him to the pyramids, a new hat on her head, since, as she said, I'm always losing hats.

She wanted to ride out to Saqqara and Memphis again, but then it occurred to her that it was the last chance for Martin to climb the Great Pyramid. Franza said, You've already missed so much, I'll wait in the restaurant.

She ordered a beer and carrots, took a couple of sips, and looked out across the entire city as far as the Mokkatam mountains, behind which the city disappeared into the sand as it did here in Giza. Martin came back once, finished her beer, and said that he couldn't find a dragoman and was going to climb it alone. If no one was around, then no one could tell him not to. How long do you think it will take? Franza asked, looking up searchingly.

She went as far as the pyramid with him, watched as he began his climb, and when he was about halfway up, realized how high the pyramid must be. He was so small, getting smaller all the time, moving always more slowly, though she still waved, for perhaps he could see her better than she could see him.

The evening was bright, only the piercing light of day having withdrawn. Franza walked the length of the pyramid and around the other side, and thought that if she walked the whole way round they would meet up again in an hour. From here she couldn't see him anymore. She waded through the sand, which required her entire strength, her hand running along the great stones like a bannister. Someone came toward her from the other corner. She looked at him quickly, a white man. She didn't pay attention to him, for at least he wasn't a genuine or false tour guide, or owner of horses or camels who were always calling out their prices to you between Giza and Saqqara.

When they both had almost reached the same point and she thought to herself, He will give way, she also thought of something else, namely that giving way only occurred out of instinct, which was just what happened. He had a stick in his hand and remained standing where he was and turned toward her. She saw him move the stick, reaching out to tap her. She stood there startled, receiving the light hit as if he had hit her with an ax, then for the first time she saw what he was doing with the other hand and what he wanted from her. She didn't utter a sound and didn't move an inch until he had walked past her.

She started to walk on, having seen how he had buttoned up his tight-fitting jeans. She walked further along, moving up the length of the wall as she walked higher, slipping away. There on the other side was her brother. She had to walk along two sides of the pyramid in order to reach him. She began to mutter to herself, Poor devil, he only wanted to frighten me, as she again grabbed hold of the large stones and pulled herself up.

And in Vienna, she continued, he too only wanted to frighten me. Still, I was pretty frightened already. They needed this.

She staggered along the rows of journals and reference works in Vienna, walking the length of the library and leafing through books, holding onto the stacks with all her strength. Exhibitionism, satyriasis—she should have seen it even then and thought about it, but she was stuck there in the library, averting her eyes and saying to him, No. No. Let me go, and yet when she wanted to escape he had shoved her against the hard edges of the shelves and done it, not in order to embrace the Franziska who, there in Vienna, was his wife.

How had she been able to forget that, the shove, and above all that he had done it to frighten her with a thousand volts of fear, and then the repetition meant to kill her. He must indeed be sick, but I am the one who became sick as a result.

She heard the sand rustling behind her. She turned around and knew already, before she even saw him, that the man had come back. She wanted to run in the thick, heavy sand and did so for some fifty yards. There was no one tending camels there, not one person, not a single one, and there was no Frau Rosi in the back room, sleeping already, or with the day off. The man grabbed her from behind, at first gently, she noticed, before she fell against the stone wall. He clung to her with weak arms, and then shoved her head against the tomb again.

She didn't hear herself make a sound, but something in her said, No. No. It was happening again. The same thing. She lay there, hanging from the stone, her head tipped to one side, and when she turned around she saw him slowly walk away in the direction from which he had first come. He's getting away, she thought. Perhaps she should yell for help. She only had to let loose a scream, but why call for help? He was already at the corner. What was the point of screaming, why do it? The poor devils, they need to do it, to frighten someone.

She smoothed flat the linen dress behind her. It's nothing, nothing happened, and even if it did, what did it matter? It doesn't matter. Her thoughts raced, and then she hit the wall, smashing her head, slamming it with full force, her head smashing against the wall in Vienna and the stone wall in Giza, her voice returning, herself saying aloud, No. No.

She could open her eyes and make out something as she returned to consciousness. She listened and was lifted up. It was three muscular, older Dutch women. Always when my brother is not around, she thought. She let herself be half carried, half dragged, and tried to tell the strong women that she had only fallen, but it was more important to tell them where she wanted to go. Yet it wasn't necessary, for they carried her in the only direction possible, back to the restaurant. She calmly closed her eyes and thought with some satisfaction, Perhaps we won't be able to leave now.

As someone shoved together two chairs on the terrace and tried to lay her down on them, she shook her head, pointing to the floor with her hand. She then lay there, sensing the fine grains of sand biting into her naked arms, in her hair, and at the back of her head as she waited. Why doesn't he come down? He can climb the mountains at home. Why did he have to climb this pyramid? Everything was going black. Why does he have to be so far away? Then he was back with her again, after such a long time, some ten years, more than ten years having passed between Galicien and when they were in Galicien again.

In the taxi he held her head in his lap, her legs crossed as she stretched out next to him. As they pulled up in front of the Semiramis Hotel, she woke up again. She tried her legs and found she could stand, and walked with Martin through the lobby and up to the room, since the elevator was not working.

Later that evening she was full of life, happy, having taken some pills. The headache was nearly gone, barely there, muffled. She didn't want to eat in the room, so Martin took her to the dining room. She ate voraciously and also wanted some wine, but left the glass standing half full. She talked and talked, just as she had in Galicien, making remarks about the waiter who never came, or that they had forgotten the forks, as Franza ate from the bowl with her fingers as she had in Wadi Halfa. She then laughed and said, Just like in Wadi Halfa. That was the best meal, I can't imagine a better one. She griped about the hotel food and then laughed again about the servants in the long red, decorated robes who started to sweep the room with brooms and then abandoned the brooms the moment the headwaiter was out of sight, then apathetically, without effort, began to swish the brooms around again when he returned.

Then she was suddenly quiet and made no more remarks. It had already gotten late and they were the last ones to leave the dining room. In the room she lay down without undressing herself entirely. Martin was falling asleep as she said wearily, I didn't want that. Not here. This is no place for me, nor this room.

Then, after he had turned out his light, she added, At least I've been in the desert.

She turned her head toward Martin and looked at him in the weak light of the lamp on her nightstand. Hopefully he had not understood what she said. Then she saw that he was not upset and hadn't understood anything. He, who had so often lain awake with worry, hadn't noticed at all that she was beginning to die from having experienced a genuine death.

Martin.

Among a hundred brothers.

The desert is something.

The edge of the Arabian desert.

With shattered, shattered, shattering.

All visions shattered.

The whites.

My head.

The whites should.

They should be damned. He should.

She moved her mouth again as if she wanted to say something to him, at last say to him what she had never yet been able to say. She didn't want to hold back anything secret, any enigma, but now something remained secret.

The whites.

In the morning an Egyptian doctor came. She was still unconscious. The doctor from the embassy, although considered incompetent, had the skills to diagnose her condition, but not to do anything about it. He waited with Martin in the room and spoke quietly, speaking English since he had studied in London. Martin extracted from his English a couple of words about a serious fall: pressure on the brain syndrome, an extended interval between the fall and unconsciousness were mentioned, often mentioned as he heard him say bleeding of the ventricle, arteria cerebralis media, the central artery of the brain, bleeding caused by the fall.

Martin felt it simply couldn't be true. The doctor from the embassy stood next to him. He no longer had to speak English — it was over. The doctor said quietly, One could have still operated, but only if something had been known about the fall. This "one could have still" caused Martin to shake his head. Perhaps one could have done something, but how had she fallen to her death after she had lasted so long in her illness, which he had begun to grasp, or at least more than the Fossil would ever grasp. He could not stop thinking about the senseless fall, and as he went to pay the doctor, the three hundred dollars turned up that he thought he had lost or that had been stolen. Astonished, he pulled the money out of his wallet.

Before he informed the front desk, he called the consulate, and a short time later a Herr Nemec appeared who was noticeably upset and surprisingly well versed in the questions surrounding the death of a foreigner. This Herr Nemec (why did he have to be named that, for it only made Martin remember someone else called Nemec, namely Elfi Nemec, who held her head high, but who most likely felt hurt and offended by now, and why did thoughts of death have to mix with thoughts of life?), this official from the consulate helped him with all the formalities and devoted all his energies to the situation, even after Franza had been taken out through a rear exit of the hotel at an hour of the night when no one except the hotel manager and two employees, and above all no guests, would be disturbed by the quiet, secret transport of a coffin out of the Semiramis Hotel.

The authorities were the facilitators of the darkness. Martin never figured out how he had managed to fly home a few days later, despite how much Nemec got on his nerves. In the airport bar he waited, finally alone. He ordered a double whiskey and spit the first mouthful on the floor, shoving the glass away, and then ordered a Fernet Branca, which he left standing there untouched. He then paid for the drinks so that the bartender wouldn't become suspicious and ordered a Coca-Cola, which he meant to drink, but Coca-Cola was suddenly no good either, and he didn't even want to look at the glass.

It dawned on him that there was a word he was looking for, the floor beneath him burning his feet. In the back of the plane lay the coffin. Or was it, like his luggage, loaded onto another plane? They would fly over the sea toward home and he would take her to Galicien. But that was not where he would lose his sister as the coffin sank into the open grave. Instead, he hoped that she had been lost earlier—in unconsciousness and from one point of pain to another, also in the moments of triumphant resistance, during which he had helped her grow stronger in those attempts at encouraging her, such as with the hashish, the embrace at the Nile, next to the rapids, and also in the red Arabian desert.

He hoped that she had not resented staying in the room at the Semiramis or his lack of concern about her condition, and that she did not die conscious of any of these. Wadi Halfa would soon be flooded. That's where she should lie, because that was where she had been the happiest. The Nile would soon overflow its banks, making the desert fertile and taking away the floor of sand on which she had stood. Apart from that there was not a single square meter on which he would have liked to bury her. It was only a matter of time before Wadi Halfa would be destroyed.' And it was already time for the pastor to stop his collection of phrases and his Latin sermon colored by dialect. Franza had forgotten to officially leave the church, and Martin did what was expected of him in Maria Gail: to throw a shovelful of earth into the grave; to lay down an expensive, formal wreath; to put on a serious face. To shake hands, remember names.

A couple of months later he was invited to the Altenwyls in Döbling for dinner. Antoinette and Atti reminded him that they had chosen the evening because there was a program on television that they knew he would love, and because he had put off a couple of times already telling them about his trip. Together they watched the program, though after the first few minutes Martin wanted to ask the Altenwyls to turn off the set, but instead he looked on with his head leaning forward in order not to see the two of them in the room or to feel them next to him.

That's Aswan, that's Abu Simbel, there's Cairo again. But as he tried to match up the images with those he remembered, it simply didn't work. There was nothing in the rolls of film of what was stored within his mind—most of all nothing of all the troubles, nothing of the sand and the bright sun, nothing even of massive Abu Simbel, which was shown from all sides. No film could depict his sister inside his head as she sat on the huge toes of Ramses in order to cool off, nor was there anything of him lighting up a wall with a flashlight in order to learn an entire history. He had already lost her then, and thank God Wadi Halfa was not shown, because it lay outside of Egypt, and for that he would gladly send the filmmakers a bottle of schnapps for refraining from filming it.

He continued to sit, leaning forward, his face pulled away from the others as he drank Atti's best Dürnsteiner wine. He had gotten used to drinking again in Vienna after many weeks in the red-hot zone where one couldn't drink. He had never felt at home among the petrified wood, the petrified forests, and the Nubian sandstone. Egypt had been a mistake for him, a magnificent mistake that was thousands of years old, but no worse than the present. Nor did the problem lie with the darkness that followed as the program finished, a dark interlude during which Antoinette quickly set down her glasses and Atti suppressed a yawn as the film came to an end before the face of a woman appeared to close the program, speaking in a tone that one could also take as an advertisement for darkness. Rather, it was the darkness after the film that did not want to reveal anything, and that remained as Martin gave the Altenwyls extended explanations and accounts, considered various aspects, lost himself in details, cited costs and percentages, and explored the economic situation of northern Africa.

What had happened. How all-consuming it was.

Yet how could he explain it all in Döbling, there in an apartment among trusted friends, a white among whites, how could he explain why someone had said that whites should be damned, or how could he even capture something of a desolate desert which in the end he had only experienced through another's desolation?

What had happened. On the last night we drank. Otherwise not at all.

The Arabian desert
is surrounded by shattered,
shattered . . .

It was late when he stood up, although he had already seen Atti Altenwyl suppress a couple of yawns. He thanked them and said good-bye. He staggered somewhat, but managed to make his way down the stairs without making a fool out of himself.

How all-consuming, for what had it all been about? Galicien? How all-consuming the desert is. Ah, the desert. Love as well is all-consuming. What was the matter with him?

If he was this drunk, then he had better find a taxi. He leaned against a lamppost and the swaying, as well as the sentences that passed through his head, stopped. He waved down a taxi. He paid a little under thirty schillings for this bundle of unintelligibility to be taken home, where he felt at home once again, there in the third district, and went to sleep and never thought this way again.

At that moment Wadi Halfa was being flooded. A military coup caused all of the paintings of General Abboud to fall from Sudanese walls, as well as from the walls of the ship. The rest was not reported in the Viennese papers.

But one can assume that the post office ("telegrams are delayed") was evacuated on schedule, despite an unscheduled delay, and that the brown and black hands would find themselves together again, reaching into a dish of beans in a new settlement further south. But Franza's white hand could no longer reach into a bowl in search of another morsel, and the silent woman near the wall would never learn that she had prepared the meal that had tasted better to her than all others.

Even if it were forgotten by the departing refugees, there was a light in Wadi Halfa that the Nile would rise above. It wouldn't be swept away, for nothing can be swept away. It couldn't be dragged under, for there was no current. Instead, a great flood. Rising.

The Egyptian darkness, after all, is absolute.

requiem for fanny goldmann

Why does Malina write? He no longer knows. He began when he was young, that's what he says when asked. And how does Malina write, and when? Magazines such as *Saturn, Prospect,* and *Antenna* want to know, but since Malina has missed an appointment, he runs over the usual set of lies inside his head, telling himself that he simply wasn't up to it, etc. But it's all so ridiculous. Discipline is what's important, discipline like Marek's. Yet Malina doesn't recall any period of discipline. In fact, he doesn't remember a thing about how he worked, rather only meaningless details. Sometimes he goes to the typewriter, but then he remembers that in interviews he says that he writes the first draft by hand. Then he wonders why he even said that, and then he types half a page.

Malina also has no opinions about things in general, only opinions that he uses in front of other people. In front of the typewriter he is without opinions. He makes no judgments, and he is emphatically indifferent. He needs to pass on this quality to Martin, his character, although he had never spent time with a stranger person than Martin, nor did he know the slightest thing about geology.

Slowly it dawns on him, as if a shadow were creeping over him from behind, himself wondering who prods him and makes him think of Martin Ranner. He stands up and paces back and forth in front of the typewriter, talking with him, dressing him and undressing him, picking out ties for him. Malina bends over the world atlas and looks for a route to Accra for Martin, then to Port Gentil, since he knows who is there, as well as someone else who wants to go there. Malina packs Martin's suitcase and then stops thinking about its contents. First he tries to think of an apartment in which the suitcase might be packed. This is the kind of thing Malina worries about as he writes.

Martin is already in Accra. Then it occurs to Malina that he ought to read up about the concentration-camp doctor, for he'll need to use him elsewhere. Also, it's too soon to leave Martin in Accra, or it could be too late. In any case, he needs to be twenty-nine and living in Vienna, not in Ghana, so he shifts him back to Vienna and throws the world atlas back on the shelf (who do you think you are, Malina?).

Malina doesn't stop thinking about it all, but as he cuts a slice of bread from the loaf and boils water for tea, he knows that he must avenge his sister's death. That's his new motive: revenge. Malina doesn't eat the bread but instead thinks about the shark, about the pool of blood, about his devoured sister, and then he realizes that Martin will not be able to exist without a sister. Like the steady drip of an IV, thoughts of revenge continually infiltrate him, causing him to become obsessed as he thinks to himself, anima, he cannot bear the thought of Martin without his anima after the loss of his own sister. It will be easier if Martin loses his sister, if vengeance is complete.

At the start of the Frankfurt Book Fair in 196_, shortly after the arrival of the flight from Vienna, several people crossed paths. None of them noticed each other, nor did any of them know that an entire novel could be written about them all.

Leaving customs, two men walked along together, a forty-year-old and a funny-looking twenty-year-old with black hair. In order to properly introduce them, let us say that one was the young genius from Styria, Jörg Maleta, whose photo could currently be seen in numerous magazines and on TV, and the other was Malina. As Malina waited with Maleta by the conveyor for their luggage, he saw a wheelchair a ways behind them. He stood there a moment somewhat distracted, for he didn't know if he should go back and say hello to the woman or simply pretend that he hadn't seen her. He also recognized the young woman who took something out of her purse for the woman in the wheelchair. After that a stewardess walked up and stood poised and ready to assist the two women as Malina saw the suitcases appear and decided not to go over to greet them.

At that moment Maleta looked at him and said, Did you notice, I think that was Goldmann. I could be wrong, but it could be. He's flying to Tel Aviv. I heard that's where he's headed. I mean Goldmann's husband. Malina then surprised himself by saying suddenly, Goodness, how much he's changed. To see him now you'd have no idea what he used to be like. He was actually good friends with my sister.

Malina wasn't sure if that was the right way to describe the relationship between his sister and Goldmann, which was none of Maleta's business. Meanwhile, at the mention of the "sister," Maleta was trying to yank his suitcase off the conveyor, his face turning red since his suitcase felt like lead. Either that or it was the thought of Maria Malina and of Fanny Goldmann and a day in Salzburg for a young student about to graduate from high school. But then it occurred to him that he didn't know what a person was supposed to say to express sympathy, especially one who was not a polished professional but rather a young rebel (he being so ironic about himself that even he would call himself that).

Naturally, at the mention of Maria Malina he felt he had to lower his head out of sadness, but as he looked at Malina he thought, It's not necessary, not any longer. It's been a couple of years since Malina's sister was devoured by a shark in Greek waters and, as Antoinette Altenwyl always stressed, in the presence of a man from Switzerland who informed us that he was very close by in the boat and yet noticed nothing, though whoever believes that is a fool. After that this Bünzli or Stünzli never showed his face again in Vienna, and that was the most sensible thing he could have done, for most likely he would have been lynched.

The director was named Wabbinger, not Stünzli or Bünzli, and after his first success at the Theater-in-der-Josefstadt he had the misfortune to go on vacation with Maria Malina and not return with her. The remarks about him had interested Antoinette so little that, even though they were meant to spark her interest, she could think of nothing else except that it was terrible and how one day at the Altenwyls' house Leopold Jordan made an ironic comment about the person who had "accompanied" Maria Malina, making it obvious that he had believed such misfortune to be accidental. At that another guest thought to himself, Why does this Jordan find it necessary to make such pointed remarks?

At the party in the Frankfurter Hof given by Gernreich, who owned one of the largest and oldest publishing houses in Germany, and who was giving the party in honor of the marriage of his only daughter, which he was only somewhat sad about, Gernreich had already received the guests with Barbara Wahl, his future wife, and found her to be far more charming than the deceased Frau Gernreich, even though she was also more pointed in her remarks, and more spiteful, and thus to be respected more so even before she took his name. There was nothing unusual about the party, only the usual shoving, the whispers at the bar, the talk about who would be there, Flamand from Paris, a representative from Harcourt Brace, and without a trace of embarrassment concerning this risqué locale, the man from Aufbau Publishers whose name had not entirely made the rounds since the peons took more notice of the writers than those attached to power and influence, since the writers were the ones who conveyed prestige and pushiness and large egos, which the agents couldn't set a value on.

Nonetheless, considering that this was thought to be one of the highlights of the Frankfurt Book Fair, nothing special was going on. Only one person stood out, a twenty-two-year-old Austrian who at first glance could have been taken for someone's son or a wayward student with what they used to call dark kinky hair and soft round eyes. But he was already known by almost everyone there and as something more than just the newest hope for the fall, there always being one of those. Instead he was seen as a clever and graceful young man, or as Frau Wahl, soon to be Gernreich, remarked three times with a hoarse laugh, "the young poet out of lush, green Styria," herself having read something in a travel brochure about Styria being lush and green.

This, however, soon got changed to "the young rebel out of lush, green Styria," and for the next few days someone only had to mention the "young rebel" to provoke an ironic smile and inspire good feeling all around. Some disgruntled people who had been neglected by the literary world for years mumbled something bitter about the young Rossegger,˙ making pathetic allusions to the only literature Styria had ever given to the world. Meanwhile, none of this bothered the elegant young man who had turned the literary establishment on its head six months before and then been accepted by it. He simply stood there for a moment by himself and drank a Coca-Cola ostentatiously rather than reaching for the trays of champagne and whiskey.

At this moment—which in its essence is hard to describe—a young man whose desire for fame and notoriety, contempt and trust, involves him in a secret battle out of which no soul or any advice can lead the way—at this moment a glance from the young Jörg Maleta fell upon a man who for the moment was standing alone and with whom he had traveled on the airplane from Vienna three days before. He looked at Malina, forgetting the book fair and his young, fledgling career as he noticed a glance from Malina and a vague smile, which suddenly caused him to feel transparent, though not uncomfortably so, since its source was also transparent. He had the feeling that he had to go over to him if only to speak to someone from his own native parts about something completely ordinary. Young Maleta would have loved to speak to the older man about Frankfurt and lush, green Styria, knowing he felt the same about all that, knowing that despite the age difference and there being no common interests between them, he wasn't disturbing him (though that wasn't entirely the case), for wasn't it true that the Germans made one gag.

For the young rebel naturally didn't think for the moment about his contract with Gernreich's publishing house, nor about how he would grow anxious about his next project, nor about how the anxiety inherent to this society would invisibly corrupt him. Instead, he still thought like a child, like a bird fallen from the family nest, having fallen out of time and into this smattering of sadness and confusion which had no use for his cynicism and common sense, nor for something as simple as Mother, or please turn out the light, or please be more precise, quiet please, settle down, be more discreet, please.

Meanwhile, the way Malina's lips were strangely pressed together invited him to come over and say with an audacity he was not only used to, but which he felt was his calling, What a farce! He said it as gently as a bleating sheep, for he himself was that tender, since a twenty-year-old is able to be so many things, especially when his elfin side has not yet disappeared, when his rebellion is still genuine, along with his ambition, his cynicism still possessing a certain flash missing in people jaded by experience. And so he stood there, suddenly next to Malina, feeling as if Malina understood him, although he didn't say a word but only handed him his glass of champagne, which the young Maleta drank straight down.

If one were to say that these two men shared no common interests, that would be incorrect, for the young Maleta knew full well what the relationship was, although he made sure not to mention a word of it to Malina. For him Malina was almost a writer, the reason why being that he had published a book ten years ago that had neither made him famous nor damned him. Rather, it was a book that hardly anyone remembered except other writers, all of whom had read it and found it remarkable. Nor did it make waves, for it was published in Vienna, and yet it was still translated into five or six languages. But it had changed nothing in his life and brought him no renown except good reviews, which led to nothing more, for he had nothing else to present in order to stay in the limelight, and indeed did not want to.

The last time Malina's name was heard in the news was in relation to his sister's death. The stories about Maria Malina, etc., mentioned that present at the funeral was the famous writer, Malina, brother of the deceased. Indeed, this in fact was the link between Malina and Maleta, even though they were separated by more than a generation, since Malina was thirty-nine and his being "famous" was only a sort of euphemism, for he now worked in the Military Museum of Vienna and had never published anything since, even though he still wrote, no one knowing what he wrote and no one daring to ask. However, young Maleta, the prototype of the rebellious young genius, also had a story from his past that he would not have told anyone.

When he was still in high school in Graz and went on a class trip to Vienna in order to see the Albertina, the Kunsthistorisches

Museum, and three theater performances, he saw Maria Malina. For the first time this seventeen-year-old, who would soon crawl out of his shell and shed his sentimentality, for the first time in his life, despite his life having consisted of nothing more than books, a bit of rebelliousness in school, and the usual mischief, for the first time and perhaps for the last time, he sat for two and a half hours in the Academy Theater, not knowing how to hold back the tears because Maria Malina, whom he'd never heard of before, had struck something which later a book, a catastrophe, a voice, or a piece of music would strike, though no one else could see what a cataclysmic effect it had, and always would have, her having struck him that day as he sat in row 16, seat 34 of the Academy Theater, though they weren't numbers that struck him like they would people who are superstitious and obsessed with such things.

Maria Malina became an actress shortly after the war and was soon discovered, then celebrated, then praised halfheartedly because she had nothing to do with the usual style of acting in Vienna. She had been in the city only three or four years when the young rebel from Styria saw her, having arrived in a place where one left certain words behind when entering, herself a young girl from the provinces who reminded people neither of the "provinces" nor of anything else mediocre, but rather of a touch of historical greatness. And so during these few years Vienna had an actress who was not merely good or prominent or enchanting, or whatever else, but rather was considered to be first rate, miraculous, indescribable.

Although some people outdid one another in searching for inadequate superlatives, this young schoolboy felt the jealousy of a madman as well as the suffering of a child who was moved by feelings beyond his comprehension. The young Maleta said nothing to anyone, and when the others chatted on and raved about Maria Malina, Maria Malina, he was stone still. Because it's not true that today deep feelings no longer exist, but rather that one simply keeps quiet about them when one really is at all intelligent, which he certainly was.

He wrote and continued to experiment with language, but the thorn in his side was Maria Malina. She is the absolute, the incomparable, he said, and I don't know how she does it, and in a hundred years I still won't know how she does it. If the boy had not been so innocent, and if he wasn't still so in a certain paranoid way, he would have said to himself that she had genius, that's what it is, what genius is, but he knew how he was molded by his times, and "genius" had become a hollow-sounding word.

A year later, just before his final exams, the young Maleta traveled to Salzburg in the hope of seeing Malina again in Hofmannsthal's *Everyman,* which he despised and sneered at before he'd even seen it. This contempt would be useful to him later, whether it was justified, as in the case of *Everyman,* or not justified, as in other instances.

But Salzburg was not about to make special concessions for a schoolboy, for there were no more tickets. He happened to hear in Café Tomaselli that Maria Malina was living in the Fondachhof located in Parsch outside of the city. So he walked twice to Parsch and stood before the Fondachhof. The second time he noticed that there was no barrier across the entrance and no tickets were being sold there, so he went in. At a table in front of the house sat a number of people. Then, as if in a scene where such things just had to happen, a woman approached in a terry-cloth robe, having just got out of the pool. He stared at her, for it was not Maria Malina whom he had seen, but rather the most beautiful woman he had ever encountered, though between Graz and Salzburg that was not saying much. Yet she appeared to him to be so much more beautiful than all of the Bardots and Lorens of the era who were talked about in school, even though her hair was all stuck together from the water and she herself spoke a bit too excitedly to seem completely natural. Nonetheless, he stared at her despite her age, for she was none other than Fanny Goldmann.

Everyone in Graz knew that Goldmann was marvelous, even fantastic, yet she was much more than fantastic, a work of art in the way a young Greek would speak of Venus still today. Since then, not only had ages passed, but also unfathomable times that had nothing to do with any specific era, yet he thought to himself, I have seen the most beautiful woman who ever lived, as men approached who brought Goldmann a bath towel, not as demigods, but rather as miserable creatures.

Otherwise there was not much remarkable going on around Goldmann, except for the chatter that was rather pedestrian as one of them said to the waiter, Bring Frau Goldmann a coffee, and Goldmann said, I have to dry my hair and then I have to change. And as he stared at the seventh wonder of the world in all her banality, a second group approached who wanted to drive off in two cars. He then noticed Maria Malina and began to see her for real. She had very large feet, size 10, said the future poet from lush, green Styria, and arms that were too long and big hands, which he began to doubt were beautiful, the hands being too big and connected to thin wrists.

He then realized that she had hands like a man, though later he no longer knew how he could have observed that. She had a pullover and a white blouse with an Eton collar, and she neighed like a horse that had escaped from the riding ring and was out of step. Then there were those hunched shoulders and large feet, and her nose was much too thick. She had no makeup on and had bad color and a thick nose and wasn't thin and wasn't fat, but of middle build, not a frail body, though the hair was greasy, stringy, and dirty blond.

That was Maria Malina. Later he didn't know how he had even recognized her. Meanwhile, he drew back, but not out of disappointment. Rather, as he returned on foot to Salzburg where he couldn't see Maria Malina onstage, he wondered how it was possible that a woman who plodded along could, onstage, be such a dream, an animal, possessing such vehemence, silence, crying and laughing, perhaps the greatest wonder since the Duse, and who now walked into the courtyard of the Fondachhof and got into a car with a couple of people.

And then nothing more happened. He went back to Graz and said nothing about it. The next thing he heard was the news of her death. And that was it. Maria Malina had traveled with someone to Greece and around an island with someone in a boat. And then she had jumped out of the boat because she was a good swimmer, or at least that's what it said in the papers. Whoever she was with turned around and she was no longer there. Then the water was red with blood, a pool of blood, and Malina had been devoured by a shark. She had been devoured before her star had faded. She was thirty-four years old and had been devoured by a shark.

And Vienna, which hides away all of its dead, but not its actors, gave Malina the largest funeral one could ever recall. Young Maleta read the newspapers just as he had after Kennedy's assassination and couldn't get over the shark. He also didn't know that after the funeral (which the Minister of Education attended, as well as the common folk who marched to the cemetery, accompanying a body that was not there) one would one day begin to speak about it, only fleetingly, when the renowned psychiatrist Jordan suddenly said at an evening gathering at his house: Wasn't there a third person there who could say what really happened, or was there only this one man on the boat?

But officially there was only the shark, and the shark is still alive.

In a time long past that has no meaning in itself except for the way in which it touched the lives of all who lived then, there lived Fanny Wischnewski, daughter of the wife of Colonel Wischnewski and in name the daughter of a colonel of the Austrian army who one day in March 1938 stuck a gun in his mouth and pulled the trigger. Then, in 1945, as Fanny took off the uniform of a German flak gunner's assistant (later it will be explained how Fanny and the German antiaircraft defense came to work hand in hand for a spell) and put on her Aunt Paulette's black dress, she could have claimed that she was the descendant of a patriotic suicide while filling out a questionnaire or applying for a job or further education. But since she didn't do it—such an omission having certain consequences—she not only crossed paths with Mr. Goldmann, the cultural attaché of the American occupation troops in Vienna, but also became his wife, appearing for some years after on theater programs, posters, and in newspapers as the enchanting, the incredibly beautiful, and what became an accolade in itself, the actress Fanny Goldmann.

Whoever saw Fanny Goldmann as Iphigenia, or in some long since forgotten drawing-room piece like *Thank You for the Roses,*˙ would perhaps only remember her as a decorous young woman swaying back and forth slightly, striking a pose onstage in half-light, in a circle of light, releasing a melody of sentences that seemed not so much the mark of a gifted actress but rather a mastery of speech as she unrolled sentences, blank verse, and free verse. Even when she spoke in prose during a party, people still felt that she didn't speak German but rather something lofty, something that always had class, something that simply was a gift. She spoke with a golden tongue, but not just what was written, and that was why no audience could remember any particular performance, but rather an overall tone, the public's good feeling toward her being best summed up by the assessment that she was beautiful and she spoke so beautifully.

But before Fanny stepped onto a Viennese stage and revealed her bare shoulders, she lived during the winter of

1945–46 with her mother and two aunts, Paulette and Lilli, who also shared the colonel's title and the distinction of his suicide as if they themselves had taken part in such terrible events, the aftermath passing from one to the other, three old women who never knew what Fanny knew and how near she had come to the truth.

In July of 1934, Colonel Wischnewski was linked with Minister Fey,˙ and after the murder of Dollfuss˙ the rumors never ceased that Fey knew about the assassination plot. When Fey shot himself in March after German troops entered Austria (and Fanny had gotten that far in the history), her father shot himself that same evening after he heard about Fey's suicide. Even if it couldn't be historically proven but instead reasonably concluded that Planetta˙ had not fired a shot, it was also reasonable to think that Fey had killed himself in order to prevent his double-crossing betrayal from being disclosed. Thus Fanny had also, as a result, the justified suspicion that her hero-father was not a hero at all, but rather someone depressed, frightened, mistaken in his reasoning, full of shame and hopelessness. Whenever she prevented the wife of Colonel Wischnewski from doing something to rehabilitate the hero, she declared that there were other things to worry about, that the Allies certainly could not understand what had played out in Vienna in 1934 or 1938, or slyly said to her mother, "Mama, please, they are all just too ignorant to understand, for I have spoken with a number of them," thus causing her mother to turn her head back to cooking or feeding the furnace.

But in fact Fanny had spoken with no one. She only knew the name of Mr. Harry Goldmann, whom she had to see to apply for a job, but she didn't bother to see him since a friend of Aunt Paulette's got her a position at the writer's union. There she sat in a cold room handing out red tickets to people who were not writers so that they could claim they were and thus would have a right to a room. This was Fanny's first contact with the literary world of Vienna, though she would never have linked any of these men who got their papers stamped by her with the writing of a book. It also seemed hardly possible that these miserable creatures, who would later be joined by younger writers, had ever written a book or ever intended to do so. All they wanted was a room and official papers. From these first writers there emerged two or three at the most whom she knew in later years, the others having saved themselves through more lucrative occupations or come to nothing or transformed themselves into sports editors or writers of obituaries. But after Hiroshima was turned to ashes, one could hardly be concerned whether a writer was really a writer at all.

Fanny thought "Harry" was an awful name. It sounded like "Tango" or "Jimmy" or something from the 1920s or 1930s. Fanny's sensitivity toward names was also put to the test in other ways. Goldmann was born in Vienna and had returned via California to Vienna. When he met Fanny for the first time he was in the middle of an affair with Maria Malina, who knew that such a liaison was the kind of thing that could change a person from a nobody into a somebody in certain quarters.

Meanwhile, Fanny, who was as noble as Iphigenia, as classy as Clarissa, and twenty-five and beautiful, had an unbearable and, even to her, monstrous hatred for Maria Malina. Little Malina, as she was known then, was nineteen when she left Klagenfurt. This only fanned the flames of Fanny's hatred, for she couldn't stand her stuttering, her plainness, and her being so tiny, wispy, and unclean. Much later, long after Fanny was able to articulate her hatred, she understood nothing of Maria Malina, nor why she had slept with Goldmann, then with every director with whom she worked. Long before others would have said the same, Fanny's incredible and senseless hatred helped her to perceive that little Malina didn't have to do such things. In fact, it became clear that she could do just what she wanted, for within a few years she needed no one and nothing more, for she had it all, namely what Fanny and the others didn't have, something that couldn't be learned, that was untouchable, along with her ample abilities and passions so deeply entwined with her own ugliness, all of which she could so easily present onstage.

By the time Fanny was reduced to working as an extra onstage and twenty talented little actresses had turned up in her marriage and had disappeared as extras onstage, no one doubted what Goldmann had noticed from the start, namely that there was only one great actress and that was Maria Malina, though in reality it had been Fanny who had noted it way back when no one would have paid even a penny to see Malina. And in reality Harry Goldmann probably kicked himself as well, for he could have "captured" at least twenty lovely-looking actresses, though no matter what he would have married an actress.

When Fanny asked Goldmann, though rarely enough, what he had found attractive about Malina, he gave her a resigned look or laughed like a boy. Once he said to her, You don't understand. She's beautiful in bed and beautiful onstage; otherwise she's nothing. Oh, I see, Fanny would reply with mock surprise, asking again, What did she want from you? Nothing, said Goldmann, that's just it, nothing, just like you, although he saw that this made her angry. It's true, neither of you wanted anything. Don't get angry, but don't you see the similarity?

Meanwhile, Fanny protested loudly and inside even more loudly against having her similarity with Malina pointed out. She looked and looked for something awful about Maria Malina that could also convince Harry, saying amid the white heat of her hatred, This person simply can't love anyone. Have you ever noticed that whenever she likes someone she is always upbeat and friendly? She is only an empty shell with nothing inside of her own.

But I disagree, said Goldmann. She told me, and probably no one else, that she loves someone, but that person doesn't know it. I wouldn't say that she loves like Juliet, for that seems cheap and not quite right. But she has the potential to feel love, hate, patience, attachment, though in reality she's never able to bring them to fruition. She has no time for it, and if she had time it appears that there is no one to instill in her what she could bring forth, for it's there already as she lies in bed with her eyes closed, loving someone, though I'm convinced it's someone who doesn't exist. That's what makes her seem so cut off, for she is open to no one, and you, my dear, you seem radiant to me and to everyone else, at which he laughed.

I hate it, said Fanny. I hate it when someone is so cold. That's what she is.

Fanny's stale rancor against Maria Malina, which never found a genuine reason to exist, was for Fanny herself her first lasting pain. Goldmann thought to himself that it was unfortunate that Fanny was never able to mix with people who threatened her, for she wanted to be beautiful and innocent and generous. She could stand for nothing less than the ideal Fanny, and she couldn't stand to be accused of jealousy, nor could she forgive Maria Malina for being a living threat.

Is that Christian love of one's neighbor? asked Harry ironically when he saw that Fanny had thrown a gift from Maria Malina into the wastebasket. She trembled with shame and fell into his arms as she said, How stupid of me, please don't think me atrocious. I'm really not this grizzly. Forgive me, then everything will be all right. You must forgive me.

Three years later, after the last performance of *Thank You for the Roses*, Harry invited their best friends to the Three Dragoons, the best restaurant in Vienna. There he held Fanny's hand openly at the table, something he hardly ever did. Finally she beamed at him and the others as she took hold of her wine glass and said, You can congratulate us, for today we got divorced. No one believed the news as Harry said with embarrassment as he pressed Fanny's hand, Yes, that's the way it is. She's telling the truth.

He kissed Fanny's hand and she hugged him demonstratively in front of the others. Because such excess had never before been seen on the part of Fanny and Goldmann, at last the others believed them and began to laugh hysterically, each of them hamming it up, even those who were not actors.

Frau Gebauer said, You are both fantastic. Someone then drank to Fanny and Goldmann's health, and the two of them laughed as they continued to hold each other's hand.

Klara then asked freely, And will you two still live together?

Yes, for the time being, replied the divorcés, which only made everyone more curious.

A cabaret performer returned to the subject at hand and said that he thought it was the most marvelous Viennese divorce he'd seen in a long time, a superb example for an old, cultured city, something that could only happen in Vienna, and that Harry had to agree that it had been worth the return to his birthplace, for he had married the most beautiful woman in Vienna and happily divorced her and again envied her, the performer's voice hitting each note with great skill as he sang "When It's All Over." Meanwhile, Fanny continued to beam until she sat with Goldmann in the car and he slowly tried to insert the key, missed, then tried again. Don't ever leave me, said Fanny quietly.

But Fanny, said Goldmann.

Never, please never. She suddenly sobbed and laughed, and by the time they were home she was shivering and let him put her to bed. It's got to be the flu, she said, I know it's the flu. Meanwhile, I've forgotten to call my man. I'll ring him, said Harry as he went to the phone and called Milan and let him know in detail about Fanny's condition and temperature and then arranged a later train to Salzburg for her and Milan.

In eight days we'll be back, said Fanny. Try not to look too happy.

I feel more cause for celebration than I did on our wedding day. Do you remember?

He tried to joke. They began to tease each other. Do you remember? She remembered. He remembered. One always remembers.

Don't betray me by sleeping with Malina, Fanny murmured as she fell asleep.

Goldmann and Fanny were seen together for about another year. Then Goldmann went to America, and after that to Israel for even longer. One got used to seeing Fanny with more people than usual as she got used to eating without Goldmann and sitting in a café until midnight knowing that he wouldn't call. Klara said in passing, Fanny has an apartment now, a lovely apartment in the heart of the city. Everyone said that Goldmann had behaved like a gentleman, but no one seemed to know just what he had done, perhaps something about the move or the furniture. Soon after people stopped asking Fanny about Goldmann, and he, who had never missed a social evening, was no longer missed, and the newly hired actresses and the guests no longer even knew who Goldmann was.

Fanny had Klara visiting and at one in the morning didn't want to answer the phone, so Klara picked up and spoke a gruff hello. She then turned to Fanny in astonishment and said, It's Harry. Who? asked Fanny. Oh, I see. She slowly went to the phone and stood there, speaking in monosyllables, though Klara couldn't understand what it was about.

Later Klara waited for Fanny to explain, but Fanny only smoked and said, He's changed so much. No, I don't mean anything specific. And yet I have to say that he's changed so much. Naturally that has nothing to do with me.

She then lost her temper. It has nothing to do with what all of you think.

Don't say *all* of us!

Indeed, all of you think something, but it has nothing to do with that. We were both completely different. Everything was different than what you thought. Yes, I say all of you, for that's what feels right and that's the truth. We were good to each other. No one understands that. To be good, one has to be good, but one can't do that amid complete Hottentots. Harry is no Hottentot.

Fanny visited Goldmann. He now lived two houses further down the street near the Altenwyls. They both laughed, though she didn't know how to make her way through the suitcases, books, and folders that lay on the floor.

She sat down like a visitor in a chair and crossed her legs. Goldmann quietly walked around, always looking for something. Once it was for an ashtray, but it made little sense to get up when you didn't know where a man kept his ashtrays or if he even had the same kind that he used when they lived together. Fanny sat there as if someone had buried her alive. She could no longer move, for so many sentences were running through her head, so many considerations, that she was ready to say, It's simply not working, let's live together again, it's simply no good. But just as she had finished working through her elaborate thoughts and was feeling tender as a result of the memories and the emotions she felt, Goldmann began to talk, having found the ashtray, himself tired and tiring to listen to.

Fanny could barely stand to listen to him, feeling that everything always had to do with her. But this time it had nothing to do with her, but rather with his work, specifically his new field of study, which she knew nothing about. She felt as she once had in school when she had changed schools, the other students on a completely different lesson plan with completely new materials and methods. She began to forget her tenderness and to listen, staring at him. He wanted neither to start a film company nor to operate a theater agency. She glanced at the books and maps, and then at his face. She wanted to ask him what had happened, but he didn't seem to notice at all that what concerned him was strange to her, namely Judaica, for she had never known a Harry Goldmann who had ever been concerned with the history of the Jews. No, certainly not one who felt any responsibility to the Jews or had anything to do with them. And now here he was about to attend Eichmann's trial, nor did he ask, Do you understand what really interests me? Instead, it was something way beyond her, something that she could not embrace, such as his emigration, the return to Vienna, it had nothing to do with the most beautiful woman in Vienna and their nights together in Nussdorf.'

Three times a week Fanny visited the colonel's wife, who always made her nervous. When she returned to Goldmann before their performance she said, If it weren't for you no one would understand me. He'd then ask, Why no one but me? She laughed. Because someone once told me that Jews love the family so much, and I'm related to Mother and Aunt Paulette and Aunt Lilli and all the other crazy old bats. What you know about Jews is overwhelming, he said. Let me think for a minute whether or not I like my family. I don't know, I don't think I do.

But does it bother you if I visit the three crazies?

They are the nicest old ladies I can think of.

Fanny ate herring and sandwiches at her mother's place and salad with her Aunt Paulette, since the latter was a vegetarian. With Aunt Lilli she looked over dress patterns, for Aunt Lilli occasionally shortened or lengthened dresses and monitored how the sleeves hung, especially when Fanny had bought something on a whim and the front or back did not "sit" properly. "It doesn't sit right," said Aunt Lilli. "They simply don't make things like they used to, child."

The colonel's wife got on Fanny's nerves most of all. Once she gave her the family's dessert cutlery, but Fanny had to give her a schilling since there was also a set of knives, the superstition being that a gift of a knife threatened the love of a mother and daughter. Fanny also had to check all the door locks, or make sure that the gas was turned off, for the colonel's wife was always afraid of something, be it burglars or leaking gas, or creaking floorboards or drafts. Her mother said, Don't you feel a draft? It's blowing straight over the bed. Fanny would then have to lie down on the bed and sort out which window the draft was coming from.

On Sundays the three old ladies sat together and both criticized Fanny and praised Fanny to the heavens, asking her if she wore warm underwear, whether it was true that Maria Malina led a slovenly life, whether Siedler' had children, whether Holzmeister' really was as beautiful as Aunt Winni (a cousin of the Wischnewskis) said she was, and whether the little Swiss girl who played little Kathi was really talented. Secretly the three old ladies were convinced that no one except Fanny was talented, that no one could be as beautiful, and that all actresses got their roles by sleeping with someone, although this didn't stop them from nagging Fanny by asking why she didn't wear a hat, why Goldmann didn't buy her a fur cape, why was she so good-natured instead of furious with those who used her, and why she had a maid but no cook.

Why didn't she have a vacuum cleaner yet, and why no car and no pressure cooker? Many Sundays ended with Fanny at the end of her wits, edgy, and an irritated tone having come into her voice that no one had heard before, until finally she closed her ears and forgot her upbringing and slammed a door, the colonel's wife then scolding her, saying, Fanny, you come back here immediately and apologize or that's the last time you can come here. Fanny would then kiss the hand of the colonel's wife and promise to behave herself, after which she returned to good standing.

She then had to hear how Maria Pilar was behaving terribly and had changed for the worse since last summer. The count, who worked for an American news agency, had a terrible influence on her, and why couldn't Fanny care a bit more about her sister and talk to her. So Fanny promised to talk with her sister, even though no one really knew where Maria Pilar was living now since she continually moved, together with Kaltenbrunner, who supposedly wrote poetry. Fanny meanwhile felt flattered that they relied on her and that she was the only source of joy and honor for her family, even if she was a woman of the theater, though one married to an honorable man. Although the ladies never spoke about Goldmann in front of her, they remarked from time to time for no particular reason that he was a fine, upstanding man. Privately they loved it when Fanny was picked up in the large American car driven by a chauffeur, or by Goldmann with a chauffeur, she being picked up as the wife of this man who arrived in such an ostentatious and tasteless carriage (Terrible, said the three ladies, tasteless and terrible), which they spoke of in the same way as another man having too much nose hair or a lame foot or squinty eyes.

When Fanny divorced Goldmann, she decided after long discussions with Goldmann not to tell her mother and the aunts. Goldmann also called now and then, and picked up Fanny once during the following year. Fanny meanwhile never forgot to pass on greetings from him, and at Christmas she made sure to bring along a gift from Goldmann during the years that Goldmann was no longer regularly in Vienna and had begun to forget that Fanny had been telling her three ladies a white lie for years.

Meanwhile, the colonel's wife, who had grown so farsighted that she could hardly see anything that was up close, had begun to take up needlepoint. In fact, it was on July 3 that the colonel's wife had begun, for that was the day that Fanny first met Toni Marek in the countryside outside of Salzburg. Fanny was wearing a dirndl, which made her look ridiculous, for one looked at her and imagined her standing buried in marzipan pigs and chocolate dungheaps on a postcard with deep blue lakes surrounding Salzburg. Indeed, summer was Fanny's favorite backdrop for wearing a bodice and bare shoulders in Salzburg, along with a fringed shawl. She had never traveled to St. Wolfgang* this early in the year and returned thinking only of the confident young man who sat with an arm draped over a garden bench at the Altenwyls. Antoinette had cultivated him, though he said two sentences about Fanny that she heard about later in Vienna when Antoinette informed her on the telephone about the two witty, somewhat dubious sentences that were also flattering, but which she then immediately forgot.

Three months later, as Fanny was invited to a theater club and saw a very weak play by one Anton Marek, she remembered the young man she had met outside Salzburg. She went up to him after the performance, along with the Altenwyls, and congratulated him hesitantly. She was now of an age where an encouraging sentence from a renowned actress could seem like soothing balm for a young playwright who himself had the feeling that he had achieved something neither great nor revolutionary and that he had to rely on a couple of friendly sentences meted out by people with names.

That evening Fanny was not driven home by friends but instead decided to walk through Vienna accompanied by Marek. The city itself seemed wonderful as she rediscovered it, seeing it as if it were just restored and no longer the run-down, ruined Vienna, but instead a city in which one had to stand on every corner and breathe deeply in order to appreciate the facades and the quality of the stone.

In the Burgtor⁺ he embraced her for the first time, and close to three in the morning, as the sky began to brighten, as she reached her apartment with trembling knees and a washed-out face, she sent him on his way, saying, I will never see you again. No, don't think about it, just go. As she sat on her bed, the telephone rang, and a voice she already knew said that he couldn't go home. He was in the phone booth on the corner, looking up at her window. Fanny answered, But you don't know my window, as he said that it would be horrible if she let him look at the wrong window. After they spoke for an hour on the telephone and Fanny had the feeling that she was about to collapse, she finally went down and opened the door and held her hands in front of her face and kept murmuring, I look ghastly, please don't look at me.

A short time later she was his alone.

Anton Marek, who was called Toni by his friends as well as by Fanny, grew up in Mattersburg in Burgenland.⁺ He often took some ribbing for this, like most people who are born somewhere but who can't ever say that they are related to so-and-so or that so-and-so is a friend of the family. Like many young people who come from the provinces and from a small-town background, he tried to maintain a mysterious silence about his family in order to speak more about Burgenland and such local specialties as bird hunting, the melancholy of the plains, or the Danube's slow current. He had noticed that there could be advantages to being able to speak about longing for a paradise while in the city, best of all a lost one that one feared returning to, though Marek was afraid of nothing but once more being stuck in anonymity and missing a day that could yield a "relationship." He kept track of every relationship, and any invitation he made was a selective one, for it always involved a brief chaotic time during which he had to run through his choice of women.

Through his success with Fanny he experienced his first great illuminating triumph, for she appeared to him to be the key to a Vienna he had never been able to enter, having done so only occasionally without ever achieving a sense of belonging to the kind of society that no one could doubt. He was in some respects what Martin Ranner said of him, a shy, small-time criminal possessed of an unscrupulousness that incorporated those scruples and dogmas adhered to by high society since the best of them suited well a man from the provinces.

Marek was capable of feigning an interest in politics that he didn't even have, or feeling the pangs of the German and Austrian past, though it meant nothing to him, meanwhile accomplishing great things as a model pupil of the times by holding forth on a wide array of subjects as he interested himself in the right books, failing only somewhat later on when he was in Germany for the first time, the lessons he had learned no longer applicable, though he rose to the challenge of the new situation and learned a whole new set of expressions to drop in regard to what was in and what was out.

From September 30 onward Fanny became interested in literature more than ever. She had certainly read the classics in the Wischnewski household, and the position at the writer's union and helping at the PEN Club had also introduced her to many books. Now and then she resented Goldmann, for he had no influence on her reading but rather more so on how much she hadn't read. But now a new life began for her, for she read and carried home books and told Marek everything about them, since he had less time to read, as well as specific passages she had come across, he now and then wanting to see a page himself.

She suspected him of being lazy, but she was immediately convinced by him that his work kept him from reading, and so she told him everything. When Marek gave a radio interview, she was proud that he spoke about Italo Svevo as if he had read him, never daring to bring this lack of honesty to his attention. Toni was so innocent, thought Fanny. He probably no longer knew himself what he had gotten from her, and this only deepened the sense in which it was hard to say where the thoughts of the one began and the other's stopped.

That's what Fanny wanted to believe, and when Fanny wanted something the world responded, for whatever Fanny thought was valid. And so, undetectably, Marek's entire person was drawn into a process from which it could only have emerged more meaningful, more pure, more mature and marvelous, or more adorable. What remained of the former Toni were a few bad habits about which she kept silent for the most part, since they couldn't be removed, while now and then she allowed herself to joke, to make a Fanny Goldmann joke from the old days that was ladylike, charming, and made people smile.

But it was not easy to get Toni to smile. Instead, he huffed and said he didn't want to see her for two days. Fanny, trembling, agreed to this penance and implored him over the phone to at least come by for dinner. She was afraid that he would starve or that he wouldn't be able to work because of his anger. Indeed, he came to dinner a day early and informed her that he had not been able to work because of her and that he had drunk himself into a stupor, sitting around with these people the whole night long. Wounded, Fanny looked at him and promised herself and him to always think about his work, come what may, since Toni was so unstable, having set aside the novel again because of his serious instability, Toni himself also being in danger. Fanny was his protector, guardian, and shield, as well as his source of confidence in the future.

The main source of his confidence, however, was the fact

that she had spent a weekend in Salzburg with a German publisher many years before whom she was now writing in order to
push Toni's genius. The reply was that an Austrian genius from
the land of geniuses would be most welcome, as well as something obscure in the tone of a sentence that said from time to
time one still thought fondly of Fanny amid the glass and con-
crete palaces of Stuttgart, as well as of Salzburg.

Soon Marek himself received a formal letter signed by the
publisher's secretary in his absence. This gave rise to his spiteful
remarks about German manners, which made a thank you to
Fanny superfluous as she apologized for her weekend friend
in utter embarrassment, she also finding the letter to be unac-
ceptable. When a year later Toni gloomily announced that it
was time to think about getting a publisher (the novel having
been restructured), she nonetheless wrote back to Stuttgart and
portrayed this genius from Burgenland as difficult and over-
powering, herself trembling with fear, in order to preempt any
problems so that this German and Toni didn't get off on the
wrong foot.

Her trembling, however, turned out to be needless, for Toni
would have taken a contract from a German hippopotamus or
monster. His touchiness about Fanny's renewed "acquaintance"
lasted only as long as he found it necessary to look sensitive.
Marek was not indebted to her for such a letter from a German
illiterate. On the contrary, he accused Fanny of a lack of tact and
being crude, leading her finally to conclude that he suffered from
having to sign such a contract, which was obviously a reason
why he was incapable of even a friendly word.

She needed months to come to terms with the fact that he
had become difficult. She became more fearful and older each
day, worrying that the lover who could not live without Fanny
Goldmann would become a novelist who could not live without
his work and his appointments, whose telephone bills climbed
ever higher, who spoke to Fanny more and more in monosylla-

bles, who treated Fanny's friends as if he had known them forever, meaning that he would go out to eat with the Altenwyls
alone, or would meet people from radio and television whom
Fanny had introduced him to, such as directors who were
impressed by his criticism of his first play and who no longer
waited to bump into him with Fanny in a café.

Toni talked about Karin Krause for the first time while Fanny
and he sat three yards away from each other in her living room,
Fanny herself upset over some detail about Marek having stayed
until 2 A.M. at the house of an aspiring female poet who had a tin
ear and whom Fanny connected with Marek's frequent absence.
Toni overreacted to Fanny's query about whether or not he
would be seeing the lady again by standing up and shouting that
the lady's name was Fräulein Hobaluek, she was called Helga
Hobaluek. Fanny concluded for herself that she was certainly no
lady, not with a name like that. But Toni, who was clearly determined to discuss Fräulein Hobaluek further and to come to the
issue at hand, suddenly broke into a grin. No, Fanny thought,
this can't lead to anything good at 2:30 A.M., because he wasn't
laughing, but rather grinning. He then set Fräulein Hobaluek
aside, bent down, and said, Okay, Fanny, my dear Fanny (she
noticed then that he was drunk), how many times do you think
I've betrayed you, guess, how many?

Fanny, who was suddenly speechless and quickly changed
from Fanny Goldmann to the colonel's daughter, said quietly
and indignantly, It's very late. Let's just go to sleep.

You just want to ignore it, you don't want to listen. But your
throat is already wrinkled. Don't be so haughty. It will make it
easier to swallow what's still coming. What do you think I'm
supposed to do, carry Fanny Goldmann's wedding train forever? I'm not a fool. Is that what you think?

Toni, said Fanny as she opened her purse and closed it again.

She didn't know why she still had her purse in her hand. She wiped her nose with a handkerchief tucked in the arm of the chair and stuck it back in her purse. If you have something to say to me, then please say it tomorrow. I'm tired.

Ah, the lady is tired, and yet always still so ladylike and uppity, of course uppity when someone says to her, I have betrayed you, continually betrayed you, always betrayed you. Do you hear? Betrayed you.

But of course I hear, said Fanny. I hear it. But it's really late.

But I will not betray you again. Not again, do you hear? For it's over now, simply over.

Toni, please, said Fanny as she strained to get up from the chair. She thought for a moment that she had had too much to drink, for the room went dark. Then she found herself still standing there, holding onto the back of the chair, Toni no longer standing next to the other chair but instead lying there at her feet as she thought, How awful.

She said, Please, Toni, I don't understand.

Toni was kissing her feet, kissing them in earnest. No, he was kissing the carpet, kissing the Persian rug, though he was probably not kissing the rug but instead had tossed himself onto the floor and said out loud, She is so lovely, lovely, if only you could know how lovely she is.

Fanny stood there somewhat perplexed and said with irony, But who is so lovely? I'd simply love to hear.

Toni sobbed. That was something completely new, or at least something new to her, for she thought of him as being very reserved. Someone like Martin would say that this man was reserved only when it gave him a tremendous advantage. But now, amid his sobbing, Fanny could only hear Karin's name.

She couldn't take it seriously. In the language of the Wischnewskis that meant, roughly, this was simply not possible, for Fanny didn't think about Karin Krause, whom she had seen several times and with Toni as well, but rather about how ridiculous the name seemed to her. And then it occurred to her that she was *very* German, something that seemed a matter of bad taste she had never thought Toni capable of, for she thought that she knew him. She stood there like Iphigenia with the immortal shoulders of the 1950s, reminding one of Medea from upper or lower Magdeburg or Taunus* (Taunus, Taunus, it's no good for us, we sang in high school during the Nazi period whenever we had German geography, Taunus representing on the syllabus the epitome of that land of the Huns). Karin Krause was certainly from this land of the Huns and what they called mountains, but which were really hills. No doubt she also spoke at too high a decibel level, gesticulating as if she were the only one at the table and in the world, and did modern photography and had no education, certainly no formal education, but nonetheless talent with a camera and with Toni.

Ten minutes later, after she had missed Toni's explanation of where he'd first slept with Karin and how it had all come about and that he wanted to marry her, Karin, Fanny realized that her purse had fallen from her hand to the carpet where Toni sat, everything having spilled from it, including her lipstick, notebook, pen, many cigarettes, and some coins. Meanwhile, Toni, thank goodness, just sat there and talked, and then together they gathered the coins as Fanny said, No, just leave it, I'll take care of it.

Toni, it's late, she said. We can talk about this tomorrow. No, she corrected herself as she turned red, for a Goldmann-Wischnewski didn't say that, no, nothing about talking. We will see. Everything will work out, said Fanny, smiling. Come, Toni, you're very pale, you look terrible. You must have been very worried, and about me as well, said Fanny. Let's go to sleep.

When Toni was asleep beside her and outside it started to get bright, Fanny quietly got up and went back into the living room.

She rested her head in her hand and thought clearly to herself that it was true, it was over and he would marry Karin. However, this wasn't the only thought that traveled through her head, for there were snide remarks as well, such as Karin, what a name. Maybe she could suggest to Toni that he call her something else, for maybe she had a second or third name like she did herself. Karin simply wouldn't do, and she'd have to tell him that straight off.

As for Karin herself, she was the child of a "thousand-year Reich," a child for the "final victory," a child of a nation without space, a pretty child, the child conceived beneath a picture of Hitler, though that was not her fault. She would soon lose the name of Krause and become acceptable. And if instead of manners she had charm or something else that would pass, then Fanny could live with it. Hopefully she will behave herself, sighed Fanny. Not knowing what right she had to sigh, she lifted her shoulders, which had become heavy, and said to herself again, Hopefully.

Then it dawned on her that Maria Malina, her archenemy, was as similar to Karin as the lizard is to the dragon, for Maria Malina and Fanny were from the same country and knew the rules of the game. What one could expect from a Karin Krause, God only knew. Fanny trembled as she slept, a child who was old and big who had to face the unknown (German) danger of Taunus and Krause and Karin and the indecency of it all, though Toni was always there, she sighed, my Toni, my love, and then she slept.

The daughter of a theater critic who found it easier to live in Vienna after being somewhat cleared of his Nazi past, Karin Krause revealed herself to be not in the least off-putting on first meeting.

This is Karin, said Toni, beaming. In Fanny's living room he said to Fanny, Please, everyone have a seat, and this made her feel ill. Fanny stood, feeling her own resistance, but because she didn't want to scold Toni, she sat down, though at the moment she thought for the first time that Toni had no manners. But then that felt like a sacrilege in the face of who he was, so she put down his odd suggestion to the fact that he was tense.

Fräulein Krause kept smiling and was so charming that one could suspect that she had glands that exuded charm. She was so charming that it flowed out of her like a surplus, as she said in a lovely, cloying voice, I know what you mean to Toni and what you've done for him. Fanny felt a knife twist in her heart as she smiled like she once did in *Thank You for the Roses* and offered up an answer that seemed like something from the second act as she said, Men always do more for us in doing nothing than we do for them in thinking that they have done something for us, while we in the end think that they've done nothing at all. After that the second and third act deteriorated from such pleasantries into bitterness as the curtain fell. Fanny noted, as the door closed and she heard them take the elevator down, that Toni had not left but rather that Toni had left with Karin.

Later she saw Karin alone only once, though because of the German's tendency to be vague Fanny missed the point of the conversation. In fact, an hour afterward Fanny couldn't recall what she had talked about with the young woman. She only remembered gesticulations and words like "Toni," though it seemed that Toni was not the most central topic, but rather words like "marriage" or "literature" or "photography," since Toni was writing the text to one of Karin's series, all of which would have nothing to do with Fanny.

Toni called every day and said that he was working and wished Fanny could see what he'd done. It would only take a couple more days and no one but Fanny could see it. "No, Fanny, what can you be thinking. Karin won't see a single line of it. You are the first. It's simply taboo, for there can be no one but you, and I swear to you that you are the first. Only your judgment, you know, only your judgment is all that matters to me. Fanny, you know what? You are still my guiding spirit. Speaking of which, have you written the publisher? Listen, if you think the book is no good, I'll abandon it. You know that, don't you? Everything depends on you."

The rise in Fanny's spirits was attributable to the fact that she had never felt like she did at the time of his appeals to her. Without her approval Toni would never release his book, and such happiness humbled her completely. One night he called and said, I think I only have five and a half pages to type. Do you know what that means?

Fanny breathed, Toni, you're kidding. That can't be true, you can't be done. My dear, that would simply be unbelievable. No, I can't believe it. It will be much, much better if I don't believe it.

Toni replied, Are you still there? You're whispering so quietly. It sounds like the old days, you know. Don't whisper so secretively. You know how that makes me love you all the more.

Toni, said Fanny, and then much louder, But Toni, stop saying that. You know you shouldn't be saying that. How is Karin?

Please, let's not talk about that, it's not important. You know that it means nothing, not to us anyway.

Fanny was quiet. She suddenly grew sober. I don't understand, she said. But he had already said goodnight and she still didn't know what to do.

She ran through the center of the city again like she did on the first night they met. The dark shadows in the Burggarten engulfed her, at the entrance to the Hofburg Palace she met a group of drunks, and as she neared the church across the street she stopped at its door and rattled it. Someone had to open up for she simply had to get in. When would a person want to get into a church more than at night?

She walked along the Kohlmarkt to the Graben.˙There she stood on the corner, not knowing what to do, and slipped around the corner. Things went so quickly; she came to Kärtnerstrasse,˙ where people were still walking along, one voice talking, then three voices, then again nothing. She leaned against a storefront and cried helplessly. I have to call someone, there has to be somewhere I can go. It then dawned on her that she could still find a place to sit in a café, but as she entered one near-by the woman in charge of the coat check said, Dear lady, every-one has all gone already. Could I call you a taxi? Fanny shrugged her shoulders and said in a snobby voice that her watch must be wrong. She really thought it must be around midnight. She then shook her head, amazed at herself, asked for a taxi, and went home, feeling as if she could never again show her face in public or burden her shoulders with one thing more.

During this night something happened to her beautiful Goldmann shoulders. They had fallen like the front line of an army laid low by the enemy, and there was no one who could say who this enemy was, by what means he advanced, and what he was planning. Like the symptoms of serious illnesses that still conceal the connection between them, much like mysterious visions preceding death or disaster, something dawned upon Fanny between St. Michael's˙ and Kärtnerstrasse, her eyes grow-ing wide, though she saw nothing, glanced at nothing, grasped nothing, but rather understood nothing and simply stared, unable to focus on anything.

When she got home she put on her favorite Schubert record, a copy of which she had also given to Toni so that, even though they were separated, they could both listen to it. Her eyes still wide, she then thought to herself, The only records he has are those I bought for him, and even if he plays them at home for her they are still my records. She then ripped the needle across the record, scratching it, and then stood in front of the record player, unable to play a record. She suddenly realized that he played her records with Karin as well.

Then she settled down again and thought, No, he would do it completely differently. She would speak with him, no, he with her, and it would be made clear that this border couldn't be crossed. Toni was too sensible, too wonderful. He would realize what would hurt her even more than any split could do to her, and so she stared at the Schubert record in horror and thought, How terrible of me; how could I have ever doubted you, my dear. She really must be no good through and through and a victim of her instincts, for Toni simply couldn't do that. What they shared in common meant too much to him, even in the face of Karin Krause.

Pilar arrived in the afternoon with Burschi and Mädi, and although Fanny was determined to spend her last penny to put her sister and the two kids into a hotel, she didn't get anywhere with Maria Pilar. Instead, the two sisters moved mattresses and blankets around and put the kids to bed that evening, after which Fanny sank down on the sofa in the living room and asked Maria Pilar to get the wine.

As she sat there Maria Pilar told her how things were in Leoben and about her last move and how Erwin had gotten a raise. Fanny responded, exhausted, What a fool, he should have gotten it earlier. Then she thought how sad it all was. Here was her sister in Vienna, this sister always on the move, married to this mercenary, having raised these two dreadful children with whom, tomorrow, she had to go to Mama, whom Fanny knew was not in the least happy about it, but on the contrary insisted she was a terrible grandmother who wasn't going to change just for Mädi, who had ripped her lace scarf, and even less for Burschi, whom she thought a devil as he fingered his food and spoke in a Styrian dialect, something that meant expulsion from the Wischnewski clan and made him unbearable.

Burschi and Mädi, as the brats liked to be called, were the product of a new kind of upbringing that was much less inhibited, and this in a place like Leoben. That same night Burschi was so uninhibited that he wanted to suffocate Mädi with a pillow. Then he wet the bed, then cried because he wanted some Turkish honey, and finally, whimpering with exhaustion, he remembered that he had not been taken to the Prater.

These kids, said Fanny, I don't know how you manage them.

Maria Pilar gazed down at her lap, as one used to say, but she only stared at her stomach, feeling embarrassed for the most part as she mumbled, Mädi is so difficult. She hits me constantly and there's nothing I can do.

Fanny stopped herself from saying something, for she had no kids and no right to meddle, but she could feel a slap meant for Mädi resting in her hand.

I don't know, said Fanny, I think your family is abusing you. Then she went silent, feeling ashamed, for the Wischnewski daughters were not so dissimilar, even though one paraded across the stage and the other wasted away in Leoben.

Pilar, Fanny said suddenly, for she was overwhelmed by a terrible fear. My Pilar, she said and embraced her younger sister. How do you manage it? What's the matter? Tell me, I beg of you.

And Maria Pilar embraced her, her cheeks wet, and said like Goldmann used to, Fanny.

Fanny no longer heard what she said as the telephone rang and she stretched out and lay there rigid as a corpse. Pilar picked up the receiver and finally said, You need to call information for you have the wrong number.

Fanny knew that he wouldn't call, and so she lay there stretched out, listening to Pilar tell the silly story about the wrong number. She took her sister's hand and said, I feel better now. It would really help if you were always here. I feel so alone.

And Goldmann? asked Maria Pilar timidly.

Fanny made a dismissive gesture with her hand. It has nothing to do with him. We were divorced long ago. There's no need for Mama to know. It's been seven years. Please don't cry, it's much too late.

Oh my God, said Pilar as she cried, you must be miserably unhappy!

Yes, but not because of that, said Fanny.

Didn't you love him? asked Pilar.

You silly goose, said Fanny, that has nothing to do with it.

Karin said, And so after a while Fanny had the impression that Austrians had something in common with Germans, from car models to fashionable drinks. In many respects, everything but the same language, and a commonness that had rarely existed.

Yes, they have taken over entirely, said Fanny as she pulled on her half-length gloves, though it was not clear why she was doing that, for normally she knew what to do with her gloves.

She then said to Dr. Ritter, You, you make me nervous, for you always think that one can simply do this or that. But it's not that easy. One can't drink a certain drink at a certain time, nor can one simply walk through the Kohlmarkt. If you expect me to walk with you through Josefstadt this evening, my teeth will suddenly begin to hurt, for today is simply no good at all. One simply can't walk through that neighborhood, though there's no way to explain to you why. At three in the afternoon you'll only find me at Gerstner's if you drag me there. Nonetheless, there's no way I can explain to you why all this means nothing to us but it means something to you, meaning that there's some apparent conflict, right?

Fanny looked up at him so that he could see her in half-profile, for she knew how good she looked in half-profile and from this side. But since Heimo Ritter would have been unable to appreciate even a piece of furniture, and since he was in fact not easily infatuated, he recognized that Fanny was beautiful, but certainly not because of the half-profile. For him it was enough that her legs, as well as everything else, were lovely, and Fanny herself knew that he noticed nothing and never would notice anything. She spoke her monologue and acted her part for the stones and the shadows and the sun. She loved to walk along the streets and to set her feet down elegantly as she passed the Stock im Eisen,ʼ though this fleshy flounder walking beside her couldn't possibly appreciate a jewel like her. Instead, for him she was certainly a marvelous woman with lovely legs and breasts, while in reality the source of her loveliness rested mainly in her shoulders, which were incomparable and the likes of which probably had not been seen in a decade, if not a century.

For even Harry Goldmann had looked at paintings and wondered if she belonged in a Watteau or Boucher, or the Settecento or Ottocento, though they finally settled on the Settecento. At least once a week Goldmann was overwhelmed and suddenly lowered a dress or a nightgown with a neck that was too high, despite her protests that she couldn't stand to sleep with bare shoulders, since it made her sneeze. Then put on a nightgown with sleeves, he'd say. You're like the people who keep their furniture covered, except for special occasions. Just imagine someone putting a nylon sack over Karlskircheʼ in order to preserve it.

He designed clothes that he wanted her to have made by a tailor near the Prater, and he went along with her to make sure that, as he said, someone paid attention to the shoulders. I can't stand it when someone defaces you, even if it's you yourself.

Fanny realized too late that Klara was right. She was completely bloated and naturally it was because of the drinking. She was already drinking by eleven o'clock in the morning. Around noon she took a little break, the coffee helping a great deal, after which she drank more. And since she still didn't have enough money and still had some bills to pay for Toni that now and then came in from their time together (a round-trip ticket from Vienna to Munich, another from Stuttgart to Vienna, or the rent for Toni's "studio"), she was not only reminded, but also made to notice what she had never noticed before. Once she was so angry that she thought of sticking the bills in an envelope and sending them to him, but the thought that he would think her mean-spirited held her back. She couldn't be mean-spirited, ever, but she could be something else. What then? Resentful, contrary, or she could simply find him contemptible.

For hours and hours she paced the apartment, and after many hours of this she discovered that she was capable of hate. This discovery was as amazing to Fanny as was the gold rush in California to the settlers, or a water or oil strike to an Arab. It was as if her entire existence had become petrified and then sprang to life again. Yes, that was it: She felt hatred.

She was forty-five years old, had never hurt a fly, not to mention a man, never hurt anyone or done anything, the struggle for existence having been reduced to a couple of graceful taunts and a bright laugh when someone told a story, for she only laughed because she laughed so well and never at someone's expense. If, in order to examine her soul, one were to have brought Fanny before the Inquisition,˙ that terrifying institution which had more to do with sinful thoughts than with actions or crimes, they would have recommended that she go straight to heaven. A minute later the cancerous tumors would then set off, continuing to spread through her, influencing her every thought, her every action, her every glance.

However, it's difficult to say from where hate emanates. This is what allows one to compare Fanny's hate with a cancerous growth, the discovery of which seemed to her like a death sentence. She would then be only a person, ignored completely and utterly, no longer operable, no longer able to be radiated with happiness, no longer guided by a Heimo Ritter to safety. Her entire body had been consumed, her brain and nervous system completely full with hate, her entire body consumed. If Fanny wanted anything it was, at least in the beginning, that this hatred could be removed from her, since she saw it as a sickness unto death. Since she realized this she had wanted Toni to come, not so much to settle accounts or to sort things out, but rather to have the hatred from within her removed when he lay his hands upon her. There had to be something he could do (who else was there?) that could free her.

Fanny opened all the windows, and though she was quite drunk, she didn't think it possible for her to plunge to her death. Nor would the hatred plunge with her, but only a once lovely, now bloated Fanny Goldmann would hit the ground and break her back, but never her hatred. Nor could she leave behind such hatred and embrace the world, separating herself from his amniotic fluid and the memory of this Marek drama, for it floated within her and grew like a tumor.

During this time Fanny stopped using the word "monstrous," for she realized that the name Heimo or Karin or bad manners or stupidities didn't do justice to the word. However, she had discovered something new which no word adequately captured. Fanny finally went to sleep when she had drunk enough, Toni's name disappearing from her thoughts as she nodded off.

She stood there in the kitchen without moving. Then she moved her hands. She cut off the stems of the flowers, swept them up with her fingers, and threw them in the garbage can. She washed a couple more bowls and glasses. She wasn't tired, but every movement made her feel as weary as one could possibly feel. Then she went to the bedroom, having already made the bed onto which she now threw herself. She then grabbed the book and began to read again. She was already familiar with it, having read it before, though still she read it again. Indeed, she was no longer reading it, but rather just scanning it with her eyes.

She chewed on each individual word, then read some sentences quickly in order not to choke, and then again read one word after another. He wrote and she read, and that's the way it would remain. She was over forty and reading from a book.

The book was about her, she told herself. He had known her for two years and then no longer after that, but it was still about her. Here she could read again, chew over again how she had lived with her husband, as well as what she had done as a young girl and what she had not, all of it from stories she had told him. She had told him things at night as she lay beside him, or while walking through a forest together, riding a bike, drinking their first coffee in a café. In two years she had told him everything that had happened to her. Yes, that's what she had done. She said to herself, it's your own fault, and then read on.

However, her life seemed entirely different in these pages. Although it was clearly attached to her life, it seemed quite different. On page 226, for example, it read as if she had made fun of his stepmother. But that had not been true, ever. She wondered if her ex-husband was also reading the book at this very moment, or if he had read it the year before, though it was also possible that he didn't know about it. With every sentence, however, it became clear that everything was there. Her sister, her friends, all of them betrayed by her mouth, and now by his mouth. No, that wasn't it. It was through his letters that they existed on the page. She felt robbed, stripped of all her sentences and judgments, and herself in pajamas or on a bicycle or at a concert. Where was her life? Here.

At first she thought, amid her boundless naïveté, that now he had written the book it would only be three days before he would come to her on bended knee, though he was a person who never got down on his knees. Still, that's what she thought, believing as well that he would ask her to live with him again, for he had written down and gutted their seven hundred days and nights and numerous bottles of wine they had shared. Yes, it was called gutting, for that was the word she had heard someone use. He had butchered her, turning her into sausage and meat. He had sliced her up. She was sliced up into 386 pages in a book. She thought, Still he'll come, and then everything will be good again. He would be with her and for the rest of his life try to cover up this disgrace, namely the disgrace of her having been sliced up, boiled, and smoked like a pig.

Yet she also thought, You pig, he was a pig. It was the only word that she could think of for him. He had been ten years younger than she and was still ten years younger, living in another district on the other side of the city. He was her butcher whom she referred to as a pig, even though she was the animal that had been butchered. A lamb, that was it, the lamb of God, no, not the lamb of God, just a lamb. She had been his animal because she had never been an animal. At best a lamb, she thought. The lamb of God, my immortal soul.

However, she had no immortal soul that she knew of. She was only a poor woman, someone who cleaned carrots and made her bed at night and didn't eat regularly and now and then drank too much schnapps or bad wine while the butcher was with Karin, and not with Fanny, but with her, the other one instead of her, the smoked sausage, the raw blood, the drumstick on which Toni and Karin gnawed and fed.

He, the butcher, barely thirty years old then, and now over thirty, which she delighted in recalling, was also no longer immortal and incapable of being wounded. He lay there with the twenty-four-year-old Karin, an awful name that revealed her low ancestry, for it was a name that had been created in 1939 (under the thousand-year Reich), whereas she had been born with an old-fashioned name, such as Stephanie, that would last eighty years at best. Nonetheless, he lay there with this name in his district, which was the seventh district, a neighborhood that Fanny disliked and which she couldn't envy. He, however, had an acceptable name, this biblical scribe, this depictor of the Passion. He was called Anton Marek and had become famous as a result of the Mount of Olives and the sponge of vinegar she had squeezed over her head.

Sometimes she read his name very slowly, as if it belonged to a stranger, for yes, he was a stranger. It was not the name of the young man she had gotten to know one afternoon, a name she later couldn't recall, a name that didn't mean anything to anybody, nor to her back then. Two weeks later she no longer used his last name, but rather his first name, which by then she had said a thousand times and now kept to herself, her old name of Fanny having submerged into that of Toni, the name he'd used as a boy.

She had let him completely consume her, pressing himself into every letter of her name. His A had passed into her vowel, his consonants had wrapped themselves around her own, growing moist and wet, twisting into one another. He had softened her name, wrapping himself around it from F to Y. Her name had been sown so much with his that she thought he had also begun to grow inside her. But no, it was not so. He had changed her name. He had named her Stephanie in his book. My Fanny, my own dear Fanny was now called Stephanie, her consonants no longer entwined but rather pierced like a butterfly by this name that was not hers and that she now saw as her own in the 386 pages of this Bible.

And God spoke. As she turned around she froze into a pillar of salt. No, she didn't see this, but instead saw him, Marek, also known as Toni, also as Anton Marek, then herself frozen into salt, then herself once more.

And she thought, What is he thinking now? He's certainly on his way to me in order to fall down before me, weeping a thousand tears as he says, Fanny, forgive me (forgive me?), weeping a thousand tears for those 386 pages as he falls to his knees and says, Forgive me. I'm not worthy, he would say, I'm not worthy, I'm no good. But it appeared that Anton Marek, also called Toni, was worthy and wasn't on his way from the seventh district to the third, despite it being not very far at all.

This Herr Marek, who wasn't such a unique breed (but rather a butcher with blond hair and gray eyes), had something better to do, namely to sign a contract. Fanny had written the publisher herself before her heart had been broken. That was also before she had tried to kill herself a few weeks later, something Herr Marek simply couldn't comprehend, though nonetheless he recognized Fanny's efforts with the publisher and thanked her. That fine piece of German workmanship, Karin, also thanked her, but since it took such a long time, just as it always took a long time for Fanny to realize anything that had to do with her, it was only later that she realized that she had signed her death sentence when she had written the publisher, followed by Marek, and then the publisher and Marek, full of hope, began to write one another.

Eventually she realized after the usual delay that this Marek wasn't at all reluctant to sell her life to the public at large, but indeed had been willing to share part of the profits with her in the form of a percentage or a lump-sum payment, both of which she had declined since she didn't realize what was going on until later. Naturally, that was not what he had meant at all. What he had said instead was that, in the event of his death, all royalties went to her. Yet she couldn't understand why he spoke about his death, something that was so far away that it was barely imaginable.

Instead, death was something that was much closer to her, especially given her health and the way she juggled Seconal and Nembutal, both of which she had downed in the middle of December before jumping into the river from a bridge while half asleep. Afterward she was brought half asleep and half frozen to a hospital, where she was given the usual treatment, herself without a will and without royalties as Herr Marek, who wasn't ready to come to the hospital, made corrections to his manuscript and the changes suggested by the publisher (the nerve of him!), which had to do with altering genitive constructions and certain Austrian sayings.

Meanwhile, Karin Krause had married Herr Marek and let herself be convinced by him that it would be better to leave Fanny alone and not maintain friendly relations with her since she had gotten on his nerves, especially on Sundays when she had refused to come along on outings, and was unable to mix with his friends, and especially because of some hysterical phone calls, during which she made it clear to him that she was counting on him and waiting for him to visit. After that Karin Marek wasted no time in feeling guilty about the sheets on which she lay or the refrigerator that she used, which Fanny had given to Toni. Instead, she tried to get along with his friends and to laugh in the car on Sundays as they sped through Burgenland, the needle on the tachometer going wild as he passed car after car dangerously, everything seeming easy to her which had been so difficult for Fanny, for she was the ideal woman for Marek, who felt reborn, and who already was appearing in catalogues and book excerpts.

Fanny, however, had unfortunately seen each of these catalogues and had read each excerpt that depicted the history of the miserable enslavement of an older woman to a younger man, etc. As she read she licked her lips, telling herself, It won't be long, eventually it will get to me, only another six months. Then I will be butchered openly in public, a bleeding pig making small maddening shrieks. And so she lay in bed and released small maddening shrieks and drank and drank the cheapest alcohol she could find at the Bohrer delicatessen.

He has to come back, she said, trying to be brave. He has to come back. He has to protect me, stand in front of me, guard me, especially at night, so that nothing happens to me, and he has to do it himself. In order to assure me that I am not now what I once was to him, he has to take back page 66 and that part about the wrinkled hands. And then two pages later he has to change that part about bad breath and the first night that we spent together. He has to repent, and he will certainly do all that, rather than only make money, get good reviews, and cause an uproar. Naturally, he wants that as well, but he can also make sure that Fanny is not hurt in the process.

Although she had never been religious, one day she wrote to him, saying, Please stop at a church and light a candle for me. In return Herr Marek wrote back and recommended that she give up this idiotic wish, for he didn't go to church, candles meant nothing to him, etc. Though some months later this idiotic request would be lost among other idiotic requests, nonetheless what he thought the reason was behind this strange request he never revealed, not in the least. He only said ironically that he hoped all would be well with her.

Three months later, as she was doing her spring cleaning and had to stop vacuuming after an hour because she was crying so much, she wrote to him and asked him to at least take a record of hers that they used to listen to together, but which she now played too often while alone out of sheer despair. Instead, she thought he should play it now and then himself. But three weeks later he sent it back with an apology for his delay in doing so since he had been in Munich to meet with his publisher. He said that he didn't think that he wanted to listen to the record since he didn't like opera. Even she should have realized that in the meantime, for in some areas he was a purist. He referred to himself as that, and so Fanny unpacked the record and set it in the little cabinet with her other records. The third request she made was about two cups that she had given him and from which they had drunk their coffee together each morning at breakfast. To this, however, he gave no reply. Most likely Frau Marek had smashed them or they no longer were there or they stood there every morning during breakfast, along with numerous other things of hers that didn't belong to Frau Marek.

And as for Frau Marek, née Krause, one could not expect her to be a clairvoyant and to know everything about the nest in which she had bedded down happily. Meanwhile, even Krause herself was not so happy, for there were rumors about disagreements. One could imagine that the woman born as Krause had other worries than a couple of dishes from Fanny's time.

After two years Fanny was alone. Three or four of their old friends now saw Marek, whom earlier they had known only in passing or had known only through her, but who now stopped calling her altogether. The others at least stayed in touch at the beginning, felt sorry for her, understood, didn't understand, said it simply was meant to be, the usual, what a shame, etc. Fanny, however, was stubborn, for she demanded generally, since in fact there was little she could demand, that these old friends stand by her, and that they would still see her and let her know how sad they were about all that happened. But no such thing happened. These old friends, who perhaps had never been friends at all, but whom Fanny had thought were friends out of the desperate need for love, they were not against Fanny, but rather against the absent and sad Fanny so unlike the Fanny they once knew. They were such brave knights, Fanny said sarcastically, and rightfully so. They were against meeting a morose, teary, and frantic person, which is what they called her whenever they happened to speak of her.

Fanny was drinking less now, but she still drank every second or third day. The next morning when she tried to get out of bed, she realized that she couldn't do it. At seven in the morning she lay trembling in bed. She continued to lie there, a headache coming on by 10 A.M. After shopping she felt dizzy. After cooking she had to lie down, and after lunch she called Klari in order to say that she couldn't possibly go out that evening, that she needed to take it easy, saying to Klari as she always did, as if each day were like the day before, I feel terrible, I'm not up to it, it would be better if we didn't see each other, be patient, I feel like hell, please understand, I can't talk about it (and then she would talk about it, for nearly twenty minutes, and only about how it was impossible to talk about it!).

Meanwhile, Klari said, I understand, but really you've got to do something. What does the doctor say? Why don't you come over anyway, I'll see you tomorrow, darling. My dear, this can't go on, you're ruining yourself, it's just not worth it.

Fanny replied, I only need some time, please understand. I just have to think about something.

Then Klari said, Then for God's sake I should come visit you!

And Fanny said, For God's sake stay home, or go out. How is Fritz by the way? Why don't you two eat at Linde? Oh I see, he was there, but with whom? No, it doesn't interest me, no please, it can drive a person mad. Don't say anything about him, it will only make things harder, and I'm almost over it.

And Klari said, The best is not to talk about it. You should really go to sleep. Are you really not drinking anymore? You have to promise me that. No, please.

Fanny then said, I'm already half asleep, there's no need to worry, I already took a sleeping pill, please, please, don't make a big fuss, that's not what I want, I don't want to upset you.

Klari replied, But please, please, you have to talk some more about it. Fritz has just come in the door, do you want to talk to him? We're going out with the Zibaleks. They're here for eight days from Kitzbühel. I'll call you when we get home. No, I won't call you, for it's better that you sleep. I won't say anything to Fritz. No, of course I won't say a word, that's understood. Goodnight.

Klari said to Fritz, I don't know about Fanny. She says hello. No, nothing special. No, I'm worried, she's not doing well at all. Yes, I'll shut up, I just couldn't help myself. No, is it true that Trattner is circulating that story again? I think that's awful. You shouldn't put up with it.

Fanny is half asleep. Fanny cries. Fanny no longer cries. Fanny has her pride. She tries to read, then stops. Fanny walks through the apartment, washes the dishes, then cleans the tiles in the bathroom and changes the hand towels. At five in the morning Fanny wanders through the apartment without any slippers, her feet ice cold, looking for something. She is looking for a pencil she has seen the day before. She wants to write something down to send to her mother, but she can't find the pencil.

At seven in the morning Fanny lies in bed with a hot-water bottle in the middle of summer. She no longer is looking for the pencil, for she has found it, though she hasn't written anything down with it. She has covered her face with cream and it feels greasy against the pillow. She then wipes her face clean, saying to herself that there's no sense in having a greasy face. Nor does she know why she put the cream on. For life. Like a brave knight. I am not a brave knight, she says. Then she says, I only want to live for half a year more. If nothing changes by then, I'll kill myself. I will give—not for my sake, not for life, not for him, not for the others—this trembling, this restlessness at night, this catastrophe that is silent and has nothing to do with life, a chance to pass. After half a year is gone and I look at the date, today being the _____, then I will kill myself. Before then I must go to Italy, for there one can get medications without a prescription, and that's what I need to do.

Fanny is half asleep. Fanny dreams that he is her brother, that she loves her brother, that he comes home and doesn't say a word to her. Fanny knows for the first time that Toni and her brother (she doesn't have one) are not one and the same person, that she has to separate the two.

Fanny cries, for she can no longer separate her blood brother from Toni. She speaks with Toni, who wants to go to the Prater, who wants to ride on the Tornado, who wants to listen to the carnival music, the troubadour (and Toni never liked the troubadour or a thousand other things). It's clear in the dream of course that Toni has already heard the carnival music with Karin and perhaps has walked through the amusement park with her. In any case, Fanny knows that Toni has committed incest with her. Incest, my brother, incest, incest, I tell you, a disgrace, I say, I tell you a disgrace.

Fanny tries to talk and separate the two. She wants to separate the two, and that's why she speaks, but in the dream she has no voice, and he, her brother, is so terrifying. He says something, for he can open his mouth. She opens her mouth as well, yet every word remains unheard, a movement of the lips, a gruesome movement of her lips and no sound as she feels herself make no sound.

Incest, I say incest, and in my father's house. God, and the lamb of God. Though it's slain on the cross and the lamb of God, she wouldn't know what the lamb of God is, for she is innocent. Who placed within her a lamb and God and a brother and incest? And who gave her life, and this incest, and then did not hear her, her mother and her aunts not hearing her, nor any of the neighbors who all remained in their houses, for she didn't hear herself. She was explaining something incredibly important and yet could not even hear herself speak.

She wanted to rip the book to pieces, then burst into his house and rip it to pieces, then crush the bread basket and smash the cups to pieces, the ones that this man and this Donna (as she sometimes called Karin) had left behind, since he had mistakenly forgotten to return the bread basket to her, which she didn't want to have, didn't want at all, though she also didn't want him to eat from this basket together with that shameful name, that German. The young man had merely forgotten, being forgetful like young men are, to give back the bread basket and socks and flower pots. He simply never thought of them. He lived with a sense of quiet contentment, but he never thought about it. He was not in Sodom and not in Gomorrah. He was grateful to Fanny for being so quick to understand, for she always understood.

One day he had said to her, This is Karin. She would very much like to get to know you, and she said, I'd like that as well. She got to know Karin, she of a thousand-year Reich, and she knew immediately that someone who is forty is no match for someone who is twenty, or was it twenty-two? Such a child, she said. She is a pretty child and so young. And the young man understood as well that they could not get on with one another. Both of them understood, and it had been a long time coming.

After three months, the beautiful young thing not having disappeared from the picture, Fanny attempted suicide. Her friends thought it was because of the beautiful young thing and what's-her-name, but she steadfastly refused to respond, for it was not because of the "young thing." One couldn't talk about the book with the beautiful young thing, and Fanny had been able to talk about most anything for years. That's what was so wonderful about Fanny, that one could talk about anything with her, Fanny, who was so wonderful and knew so many people, dear Fanny, who could handle anything and could initiate anything, Fanny who would always be there, obviously, since one could always count on Fanny, dear Fanny, who was so much older.

She lay there for days and occupied herself with the Bible. Before long, months had passed, and she still buried herself in the Bible. At first it was only the Bible that interested her. Later it was particular things that suddenly occurred to her, such as the thought that Herr Marek was sitting with Frau Marek in the Linde restaurant, the two of them eating, and it not occurring to him to bring her some bread. He had never thought at all that she might be hungry because of him. Still, she told herself, using her own special logic, that he would know nonetheless, for she thought that he still calculated as precisely as he always did and that he would figure that Fanny no longer had anything at all, having lost everything, her position and her charm, the money and the men, in short everything.

But she forgot that Herr Marek no longer calculated such things, that he had only done so early on when he said it's cheap here, it's expensive there, or that's too expensive for us. Now it no longer mattered to him at all whether Fanny chewed on a crust of bread or drank bad schnapps, for he had clearly said to her that her name was Karin, saying as well, We will hardly see each other from now on, as he added, I have to save my money for Germany.

She had never saved, whereas Toni had always saved. She also knew exactly how much he had by the time he left her for Karin Krause and began saving with Karin. She asked herself how that was possible and why she had always given money to men, but it was difficult to figure out, for the simple fact was that she had always given away her last schilling, even when she tried her best to hold onto it, whereas men had a future and could plan for it. She had no future, but rather a man, which was why the last schilling meant something to her, but she gave it away nonetheless, never thinking ahead, for she had no future, since men promised her a future, something that she had never done herself.

Marek had also spoken about this when she had not so much as a schilling, saying, Now you make a big deal out of it, but you never said to me that you even wanted a future with me. She was completely taken aback, for she had indeed never thought about a future with him, for he was too young for such things. Still, she could have said, But I gave you everything, but she could not say that now. He would have had to agree, but she didn't want to say it. She would rather have died than say it, although it was self-evident. Yet he had no interest whatsoever in tallying up the past. If he did, he would have quickly realized that Fanny had given all of her money to him, but he had not given all of his to Fanny. The reason why, of course, was that he had a future that he wanted to prepare for, be it for Germany, for Karin, for the day he could buy an apartment, or for a child.

Fanny shivered, her entire skin twitching as if someone were applying electric shocks to her, the current running beneath the skin and up her leg, then another one entering the small of her back and traveling up her spine to her scalp. She was now ice cold, but the current flowed. She shook, she groaned, she lay completely still, unable to move at all. Amid her fear, Fanny tried to keep her eyes open in order to remind herself that she was alive and was in her room. But as she suddenly felt that she would die in this room, in this one and no other, she began to cry, the tears causing terrible convulsions, not because something was making her sad, but rather because the tears passing through the tear ducts relieved her of a terrible condition. She had heard from her mother that someone who was sick but could still shed tears could not die. That immediately calmed her and she cried some more as assurance against her death.

Then she stopped as she felt something being written on her body. She pulled up her dress and tried to look at her body on which something was being written, the stigmata appearing, and she knew immediately that it was his name that was appearing in spots on her skin, burning into her with upward and downward strokes. As his name flickered upon her skin she passed the time without breathing deeply and without smoking, breathing a shallow breath through her teeth, incapable of taking a deep breath, a person with no desire to do what was best for her to do.

Two months later a doctor said to her that she was stigmatized, that there was nothing that could be done, and that she had to expect that each time something upset her the condition would reappear. But she found that he was wrong, because she didn't even become upset again. When her rent was raised such that she could hardly pay it anymore, she should have been upset. But Fanny paid eighty schillings more and didn't get upset. Nonetheless, the spells returned, along with the shocks and the writing, and she knew that she had fallen for Toni, in fact more so, by far much more so than she had during the time when she first met him.

Fanny got the idea that perhaps she could hire two young men who would bring Marek to her, tie him up without hurting him, but tightly enough for him to know that she meant business, and that she had him in her grips. Thus Marek sits in her stiff wing-backed chair as she loosens the ropes on his hands and hands him the book. "Read it out loud," Fanny says and opens it to page 58. "Read that out loud and calmly, if you can." She knows that Marek is grinding his teeth and will refuse to read. She then has the two men with masks hit him in the face with their fists. Fanny is ice cold and in control. She only wants him to read aloud what he wrote.

Marek begins to read and stops after the first sentence. Fanny has to think of another way, for she doesn't know if the two men she has paid can keep their mouths shut. It has to happen without witnesses.

On a trip to Graz Fanny buys a pistol.

She invites Marek to her apartment, locks the door, shows him the pistol, and commands him to read aloud. Marek, however, doesn't let himself be frightened by the pistol, but instead talks to Fanny with contempt. He knows that she won't pull the trigger, that she can't keep him in check as long as she isn't ready to pull the trigger.

This is Fanny as one of the Furies, as the avenger of her

honor. In the apartment she walks up to Marek, telling him in three sentences why she has come, rather than with hundreds and thousands of sentences like she does during her nights alone. She is suddenly able to say it in fewer words. Yes, but able to say what in fewer words, for that means she must use fewer words, and what are those few words supposed to say?

Fanny pulls the trigger. She shoots but she doesn't know where she wants to hit him. She tries to aim for his abdomen, but she doesn't think she can do it. The head is easier to hit, but then she can't stand the thought of not seeing his head anymore. She thinks of crime novels and terrible wounds she can't bring herself to inflict. She aims at his chest, but that seems easy, too tasteful. She doesn't want to aim at his heart, no, she doesn't want to aim at that. Given what his body means to her, she'd like to find a different way to kill him, but she doesn't know what that would be. "Remove his soul." That was it, she wanted to remove Marek's soul. She didn't want to see Marek collapse and die of fear, nor did she want him wounded.

Then she suddenly shot, the gun going off aimlessly in his direction until the thing was empty of, what were they called, cartridges or shells?—for how was someone supposed to know who wanted to shoot but couldn't.

As it became apparent to Fanny that she was not prepared to shoot, she began to turn into a Fury (for in fact there was no question of doing anything else because of the seriousness of the crime, for Fanny considered it a crime that no judge could give a name to and which she alone could accuse him of having committed). She yelled at Marek, and as she looked at him sitting before her, she found herself saying words that she had hardly ever heard before, neither from Pingeles, who was such a distinguished person, nor from Marek himself. She spit at Marek's feet, she screamed for hours at Marek, who remained dumb, turning his back to her and calmly rummaging in her closet in order to look for a fuse, since a fuse had burned out and Fanny could never bring herself to buy a long-lasting fuse whenever a fuse burned out.

Fanny then threw all of the dishes on the kitchen table onto the floor in order to shake Marek out of his lethargy. She screamed and hurled more objects onto the floor until Marek lost his patience. He grabbed her hands and held her tight until her wrists were burning and her face was red and she began to choke. She then waited for Marek to kill her. In fact, that's what she wanted most of all. He should murder her and it should be plain as day that he was her murderer. It was the only way in which she could murder him. He should murder her right here and now. She would talk to him and hold up his crime to him until he no longer knew what was what and thus condemned himself, fully and certainly and demonstrably committing the murder that for her had in fact happened already, and in a different way, much earlier.

Fanny died in December* after suffering through a brief illness. It was not July. Fanny had said another six months and then, and when, and then. But it was in December. The holy sacraments were performed, for she had forgotten to leave the church officially the way she had discussed with Toni Marek for hours on end during their first year together.

At the time she didn't have many plans for the future. A few people were there to follow her coffin. There was the landlady of her building, Frau Melanie Pospiszil, her friend Klara Anna Theresia Schütz, along with Klara's friend Professor Friedrich Gebauer, her schoolmate Jolanda Nicoletti, her friend Hedwig Maria Abendroth, and her former boss at the PEN Club, Dr. Eder. There were wreaths from the PEN Club and her landlady, as well as a bouquet from her former husband, Harry Goldmann.

Marek heard the news of the death from Klara, who called him when he got back from Munich. She had tried to reach him a number of times, though when she finally did he was already disturbed after having ripped open an express letter from his mother that brought bad news. Because he heard the news that Fanny had died eight days ago while thinking simultaneously that he probably should go home immediately in order to see his mother, probably for the last time (which only made him think of the grisly details that only a funeral brings into focus), neither of the events really sank in.

He went back to the bathroom and lay in the tub, letting the warm water flow. When Karin returned from the city after an hour, he was suddenly cold, feeling drained by the news. The bathwater was now only lukewarm, and as he felt chilly and tried to douse himself with warm water and cold in order to get his body going, he said to Karin through the door that she should read the letter. Then he said that he was probably coming down with the flu, though he stopped Karin from calling Alda right away. Finally he said that, by the way, Klara had called about Fanny.

Karin sat down and began to cry, but then suddenly stopped as Marek said nothing, stood up, and got dressed. She looked at him and noticed that he couldn't stand to be watched like that, which only made him continue his silence. Karin, with her talent for upsetting him, would have liked to yell at him and ask what he was feeling, what he was thinking, whether he was at all upset, etc., about important matters that meant nothing to him, since he was extremely incapable of feeling and thinking as Karin wished. Since he knew her hysteria, he began to say out loud, It would be good if you ordered her some flowers, Karin, or even better, a wreath.

He had no idea whom he should really call. He thought of Dr. Harry Goldmann, but then that seemed totally stupid. One couldn't simply call up the former husband only because he happened not to be there as well. Instead, he would simply make his presence known through the flowers. He had finally spoken with Klara, and Fanny's mother didn't know who he was, and he had seen her sister, who was a real horror, only once. Now it was only a question of finding out where Fanny had been buried.

Karin saw Klara again for the first time at the premiere in Josefstadt, but no one said anything about Fanny. Instead they simply chatted with each other, some about the play, then about Degischer,˙ who was such a good actress, then about Alda, Eugen, and the glider championships being held in Seeboden. After the premiere they happened to end up at the same restaurant, though Klara and her professor sat at a different table. They waved and nodded to each other, and at the end Klara called out to Karin, telling her to call, but soon, though the professor seemed as intolerable as ever.

Marek and Karin were in especially good moods and were happy to have seen the two of them again. Later, as they undressed, they talked continuously about Klara and how Klara was looking well again, and that the professor had earlier lived with so-and-so, and that Klari had not changed him at all, though she herself had changed, and much for the better they both found as they went on to talk again about the actors and all the people they had seen and what they thought about them, although they already knew what the other thought.

As she turned out the light, Marek was already snoring. Karin lay there with her eyes open and her hands folded, something she had recently begun to do in the dark. Then she said to herself or to someone she addressed as God that it had been good that they had met up with Klara and not mentioned Fanny, and that Toni had clearly gotten over what had happened to Fanny. Then Karin suddenly started to cry again and thought, Oh God, as she said in the darkness, I know that she is buried in Neustift-am-Wald,* lying there dead. Oh, I can't believe it.

After this intense focus, Karin became ever less focused and started to think in more general terms about death, something for which she had a vocabulary only at night. Thinking about death, she thought of the reaper, and death, the monster, and all that darkness, and all that must pass into it, and so forth. She pressed against Toni, who lay on his back with his legs spread, which made her mad, though finally he turned in his sleep and lay such that she could press into him. Finally, she thought, she had to get him to stop drinking, and then she fell asleep.

When someone is referred to as the most beautiful woman in Vienna, naturally it's not meant as a slight against other women who are also beautiful, or who at the time were much more prominent. Instead, what is actually meant is that one cannot help but agree with this or that old man who, on hearing someone make exclamations about a woman, dismisses that person with a melancholy wave, saying, My friend, clearly you have never seen Fanny Goldmann, all the while saying it like someone who, without the right words to describe her, would nonetheless make clear that we will never see the likes of a Duse onstage or a Pavlova dancing, while one already had to be satisfied with being able to say in ten or twenty years, You will never be able to grasp what Callas was really like.

A beautiful woman is much more special and doesn't live as long as a distinguished woman, especially when she's an actress. There was a silent agreement that Fanny Goldmann should not be criticized, but also an agreement, if one were honest, that there could never be a more beautiful or noble Iphigenia, though her embodiment of a Greek sensibility was so ladylike that it made one forget Goethe altogether.

She was at her best in drawing-room comedies like *Thank You for the Roses* and other similar pieces where tea was drunk in English country houses, which appealed especially to audiences in Vienna where people drank Nescafé. It was a time when literary criticism emphasized catching up with the times, and so what was read and staged was often strange. While some student groups were performing plays by Horváth and Nestroy,* others were reading Catholic writers as if it were imperative to reinvigorate Catholicism, though it could not have disappeared completely in just seven years and had to be a different Catholicism anyway. On Sundays there were sermons that one could have called sermons for intellectuals or what could be described as part of an upper-class Vienna where one could talk about Rouault and modern art and even go so far as to talk about Picasso as if he were St. Teresa of Avila.*

In between there were endless disagreements about Heidegger* and Jünger,* as well as existentialism in Germany and Frankfurt. But that was reserved for the Catholics who flirted with such discussions and got involved, though they never took them seriously, while other people worked harder to read these articles and understand them.

Twenty years later it seemed ridiculous and improbable how people behaved in such historic circumstances or what it could have meant to continually play Claudel* or O'Neill or Eliot amid the ruins. Yet just as there is an official culture, there is also a hidden one in each city, and in those days, as ever, one should have listened to the silent one.

When one says that the time after a war is the right time to start over again and change society, this is not necessarily wrong, but the urge to return to the time before the war always ends up the stronger. One has to realize that there is no consciousness of the present, otherwise the present wouldn't always be so completely bungled, as is this one, but instead would be relegated to the past. Men in their sixties asked the young in good faith to look inward, part of them at least trying to involve themselves in things that were not their concern. As people tried to patch together the buildings, so others latched onto thoughts prevalent in the years before Hitler but that were no longer prevalent.

Yet how thoughts and ideas can become defunct after only seven years is still hard to understand. The biggest change in public matters involved a "currency reform," and thus those are the kinds of changes one speaks of as part of a "Year Zero" in world history when referring to 1946 or 1949, which in fact is what those years are often called. Hot water and plumbing, the first heat, the extermination of Viennese rats, these came hand in hand with the ballpoint pen and the replacement of ersatz goods with genuine quality products that turned saccharin into sugar and thin people into fat people until they went on their first diet, longing for their weight in the 1940s.

The loss of close ties that only needed seven years to be turned into lines drawn in the dirt also were mourned fourteen years later, as if those had been the best of times, living without light or water, wrapped in a blanket while drinking coffee found in a CARE package.

For Fanny Goldmann, who was a little older, things appeared different, though on the other hand she didn't quite know the difference between what was native to Vienna and what was native to Austria as a whole. What she did know she had learned from Harry Goldmann, who had maintained or created a precise memory of it while in Hollywood, and thus succeeded in creating from a somewhat colorless Fanny the essence of a Viennese lady by teaching her to hit the right pauses, as well as a way of speaking that was lazy, vague, and affected, and through which she could achieve perfection.

He could not appreciate Fanny as his work, however, for as he reached his goal he was no longer Fanny's husband. Fanny's other lovers were certainly bowled over by the effects learned at the Goldmann School, but there was no way they could know that one didn't learn such things at the Reinhardt Seminar, and therefore did not receive the latter's certified blessing.

Yet everything about Fanny seemed so natural and attached to the core of her being that no one could have imagined her as an antiaircraft gun helper or believed that a word like "flak" would have ever come out of her mouth. Instead, one could only imagine her saying something like, Lord, what did they call that back then, you know what I mean, what they used to try to take down the planes, that's what I mean.

You mean that kind of thing is still around? Where?

At the time no one knew that this same Harry Goldmann, whom Malina saw get off an El Al plane at Frankfurt airport, at one time didn't want to know anything about Israel, and that words like "kibbutz" were painful for him to hear, the entire heroism behind the country's existence not inspiring him at all. It was only as an older man that he began to resemble his father and that he finally came to realize that he was a Jew and that the paradise of Vienna and having the most beautiful woman in Vienna at his side could not make up for the incredible emptiness built up from an endless line of premieres and parties for premieres.

If Fanny hadn't felt so helpless and sad when she met her ex-husband for the last time, his name now having to be carried on only through her, she might have perhaps realized that not only was she twenty years older and an altogether different person, but also this glowing U.S. officer and ladies man, whom she had once been jealous of because of Maria Malina, had fallen out of the theater world, just as she had, and no longer felt "at home" in Vienna.

Instead, he was only going into exile now because none of us fulfills his fate in the bright light of history, such as among refugees or in war, but rather when no one talks about it anymore or pays attention. Goldmann's exile in America was something that one might expect to read about in his biography, but his real exile began after everything went wrong with a play he directed at the Habimah Theater* in Tel Aviv. Although everything there was wrong just as he imagined it would be, the young Israelis puzzled him more than meeting up with his former schoolmates from Vienna who had once been mean to him and not allowed him into their clubs. Since he wasn't welcome here for completely different reasons having to do with him being a man of the old world here among a young world, he began to get interested in it. Though he had never known anything of the history of Israel or the feeling that "these are my people," but rather the biographies of Austrian actors such as Bassermann or Kainz or Thimig,* he began to think about the Red Sea and the diaspora, about God's own country, about synagogues and pogroms. Now, however, there was nothing he could say to Fanny about it, nor that he was suffering and that every book, every document, seemed so monstrous since they only made people forget even more and made Israel seem like just another country. Why are you doing this to yourself? asked Fanny, who had a momentary insight when she looked at his desk. He shrugged his shoulders and tried to smile like he used to when she had asked him, Does it bother you when I do something silly?

I don't understand you, said Fanny quietly as she thought, He doesn't understand me. He has no idea why I've come to him, and to whom should I go if not him? Our marriage is indissoluble, that's what she wanted to say to him, but since she and Harry never thought about marriage or talked about it in that way, he wouldn't know what she meant. She smiled vaguely as she said, The feeling of being married to you, or of having been so, that is all that has lasted. Did you know that?

Look, Fanny, you were always free. I never tied you down.

Yes, unfortunately not, she said. It would have been better if you had.

But Fanny.

Yes, it would have been.

That's sweet of you, but let's not talk about it anymore. I'm sorry, but I don't have the time, for there's someone else who is stopping by, and then I have to go straight to the airport. Let me know if you need anything.

Fanny began to cry silently. I feel all right, she said, I'm fine.

Is there something wrong with young Marek? he asked sympathetically. Of course I know about it.

Fanny replied, Indeed something is wrong, but it's not important. I'll be all right.

Goldmann thought that as well, for he could not imagine Fanny not straightening things out with young Herr Marek, for she remained to him someone who was above it all and wonderfully carefree.

Are your mother and sister doing well? he asked. Aunt Aida died, she said, but that was to be expected.

One could hardly say that she died, for it was more that she simply was no longer there, just as Aunt Paulette and Aunt Lilli were no longer there, even though they were the ones who had once criticized all of Fanny's admirers and commented on Fanny's underwear and knitted and crocheted and did petit point on Fanny's purse.

Good Aunt Aida, said Goldmann, unable to suppress a little laugh. He had seen the young Fanny resurrect herself while surrounded by those ridiculous aunts and the colonel's wife who was now living with Maria Pilar and taking care of her grandchildren.

Mama is still the same, said Fanny, she always asks about you. I'll tell her you said hello if you want me to. To this day I have not told her about the divorce. Strange, don't you think?

Are you acting these days?

Ah, said Fanny, as the doorbell rang. She then stood and picked up her purse and set it in her lap. I'm supposed to be doing a television movie, something new. It's so experimental that I hardly understand a word of it. It's supposed to be very progressive, an interesting role, if one can call it a role.

How are you for money?

Oh, I'm fine, said Fanny. I'm supposed to make a film as well. I need to call Edelmann. She's such a pain, really a cross I've had to bear. Every three months she has a film for me, but then nothing comes of it. Today I'm no longer typecast, but neither was I earlier. Strange, you said back then that I wasn't today's "type." I don't know, though, just what or when "today" is for me. Back then I was too Greek and now I'm too mature, but not yet old enough for the older roles, and there are loads of them.

What do you mean by "today"?

Malina was of her day, with her burning ambition and her trembling presence onstage, which could make everyone as far back as the last row hold his breath. All of them looked up at her, mesmerized, and said, God, what a woman, she is simply beautiful.

I was never really an actress, you always knew that. Because of that I also understand what you saw in Malina. It was not her, it was something inside her, and that's why you always helped her. You believed in her and you were fond of me.

What then should I have wished for, her life or mine? Each was a sad case, nor would I have liked to live her life. And yes, the shark. There's a shark waiting for each of us, only for her it was perhaps painful and quick. For us the shark is not so obviously our murderer. It goes more slowly and he comes dressed and is more horrible, for the sharks in disguise do something to us that takes more time. Who your shark is, that I don't know. Hopefully I was not it. I never did anything to you, or perhaps I did now and then, but that was only to set the stage for what I didn't do.

Goldmann was the only man who had been good to her. Because of that, before she was even married to him, she had used his name for her debut performance, something which at the time struck everyone as strange, for people could not understand why she had to call herself Goldmann and use the name of her lover and protector. Some even said that it was nothing but some kind of pseudo-Semitism, for at the time many people wanted to have a Jewish name and no longer be called Huber or Moser. But for Fanny it was completely different. She hoped it would bring her luck.

Many years later, when no one spoke of Harry Goldmann anymore, but rather Fanny Goldmann, people who did not know the story or mixed it up were convinced that she was a Jew. She allowed the majority to believe what they wanted to believe. Meanwhile, Mama found it simply outrageous and on top of that a slight against the Wischnewskis. In any case, it was the whim of an actress daughter, and the three aunts, Aida and Paulette and Lilli, who had not gotten used to the latest vocabulary, said to their friends that our "niece Wischnewski" is not an Israelite, not in the least. She had simply gazed into the eyes of this man and one thing led to another. Involved in the theater, sleeping until noon, staying out until 3 A.M. and drinking, alas, this Goldmann was a type about whom nothing good could be said, a kind of con man, in the eyes of Fanny's aunts, who had a chauffeur.

And as far as what the Goldmanns used to be, they knew well enough. The elder Goldmann had run a yarn factory in lower Austria. Meanwhile, Fanny was the daughter of a colonel who had been a patriot and had met a tragic end with the German invasion. Because there had been Austrian officers who after Schuschnigg's last speech titled "Long Live Austria" knew what consequences would follow, he had not wanted to endanger his people, so he had sacrificed himself.

In reality, Colonel Wischnewski, as well as Fey, were neither victims nor indeed great patriots, but instead had played a dubious role in the murder of Dollfuss. His suicide was not that of a hero but rather an act of fear and doubt, a diversion so that it would never be known just what kind of double or triple role people like him had played in the first republic.

Heroic suicides are like most suicides except they are considered to be something more than merely justified, because people like Wischnewski, despite their dubious roles (which are also overestimated), are sensitive and ready to shoot themselves for what they consider to be a scandal, if it becomes known, but which is not a scandal if it remains secret.

It's a sublime cowardice that is not too far away from a sublime pride. Anyone who thinks about suicide (like his daughter would later, about suicide under quite different and ridiculous circumstances, and without the conjunction of important historical dates) does it because he thinks a scandal cannot be overcome and he has to live with it, or with what he has to confront through his own awareness and that of others, so much so that it is like living beneath a dangling sword. When Fanny Goldmann thought herself on the verge of an open scandal, although it was something that would have been forgotten after a short while and which she should have made nothing of (especially if she were not Fanny but someone else), Fanny Goldmann was her father's daughter, even though she had hardly known him.

What she could not ignore in the final analysis and what caused her to become deathly ill was the fact that she had let her guard down amid her own circle, revealing some things to an ambitious social climber from Mattersburg, her own happiness having caused her to be stupid and talkative, saying some things she should not have said. That she had made a couple of jokes about Harry and told the fellow how she had met him, this was what she couldn't get over after she had read what he made out of it.

Goldmann said to her, Tell me, your Rosenkavalier,' will he publish a book?

Fanny said, Oh yes, he's very talented.

Goldmann, who had accompanied her that day and kissed her hand, smiled and said sadly, Let's hope he has talent. That would be good for you. People will say that you did a lot for him. Quite frankly, I would never expect it of him, though I've only met him once and can't really judge.

That was the last time Fanny saw Goldmann. Goldmann suspected that he would not see her again because he felt like he was drifting toward some final destination as she walked away and he listened to her footsteps. But the fact that he would not see Fanny again and would live on, and that he would be too late for her funeral, this he never suspected during that final hour.

Later people said, Goldmann has changed entirely since the death of Fanny. He must have loved her tremendously, but she was always with other men and then finally with that little Marek, which must have been the last straw for him. In any case, she had always cheated on him left and right, and Marek apparently was also devastated. Other people said, Ah, poor Fanny, she always had bad luck. First this Goldmann, who constantly betrayed her, and then the affair with Marek, who left her for the little Krause woman. It's hard to believe, but the most beautiful women often have the most unbelievably bad luck and always with the most idiotic men.

Such were the observations from afar made by people who lived very close to one another and in such moments thought they could see quite clearly, despite being incredibly far from the truth. Not once did one of them hit on the truth of Fanny and Goldmann and Marek and so much that lay between them, nor did all of them together even come near it whatsoever. For people only notice when people get together or separate, but not the reasons behind such events, which are sometimes cheerful and sometimes tragic and unfathomable, each life being just as unfathomable as Fanny Goldmann's, making it seem impossible that any psychologist, behaviorist, or statistician could ever grasp the truth of any life for all of its monstrous depths and apparent folly.

The open lies which each person surrounds himself with, as well as the open admissions, these also make it all the harder for others to see things as separate and clear. Barely holding these lives together and allowing them to operate in darkness, essentially allowing only the final act to be played out in public under the lights, the force that directs these lives is something other, something in no way noble, but rather unseen, lying within humankind itself and its damnation.

The fact that, until the end, Fanny could not say to Goldmann what she wanted from him, just as she couldn't say to Marek what she expected of him, or that Goldmann could no longer call Fanny whenever he needed her, or that it took so long for Marek to shake her off, all of this is such a long and dark and untellable story (untellable as all stories are). Meanwhile, one can only hold onto what is tangible and look at one's fingers, try to look into someone's eyes, and write down the sentences that are spoken, so that something is said by which one can begin to glimpse what really happened.

notes

The source for a number of the notes below is Monika Albrecht and Dirk Göttsche's five-volume "Todesarten"-Projekt (Munich: Piper, 1995). Such notes will be followed by the designation AG with the appropriate volume and page number.

the book of franza

p. 7—"Champollion": Jean-François Champollion (1790–1832), who discovered the system of hieroglyphs by decoding the Rosetta Stone (AG 2:478).

p. 11—"imperial-royal order": Known in Austria as the "Kaiserlich und Königlich" brotherhood, or the K.u.K. These are young students who swear lifelong allegiance to one another and the Austro-Hungarian empire, often by scarring their cheek with a sword.

p. 19—"Among a hundred brothers": Quoted from a poem by Robert Musil titled "Isis und Osiris" (AG 2:478).

p. 20—"vulgo Tobai": In rural Austria families used to be strongly identified with their farms and estates, so much so that individuals were often referred to by the name of the estate on which they were raised. Hence, Franza is referred to here in Latin terms as an offspring of the farm of Tobai.

p. 20—"Nona" and "Neni": These are the Italian words for grandma and grandpa.

p. 21—"Windish": A Slovenian dialect spoken in Carinthia and the regions just beyond the southern border of Austria.

p. 34—"V Jezusu Kristusu Je Življenje In Vstajenje": Slovenian for "In Jesus Christ is the life and the resurrection" (AG 2:479).

p. 36—"Breasted": A reference to James Henry Breasted's History of Egypt, a copy of which Bachmann owned in German (AG 2:479).

p. 37—"Croatian rebels": The "Ustasa" was a nationalist and fascist movement founded in Croatia in 1929, which fought against the Serbs until 1945. Under Ante Pavelic, the rebels terrorized Serbs, Muslims, and Jews while protected by the Germans and Italians and partially supported by the Catholic Church. After 1945, the movement maintained an underground organization outside of Tito's Yugoslavia (AG 2:479).

p. 37—"Vlassov's hopeless band": Andrei Andreivich Vlassov (1901–46), a Soviet general who, while a German prisoner in 1942, offered to organize a pro-German army consisting of war prisoners and deserters and who founded the Smolensk Committee in the same year. In 1944, after the founding of the Committee for the Liberation of the Russian People, Vlassov was called upon to organize an anti-Soviet army consisting of war prisoners, deserters, civilians, Cossacks, and Georgians. After being sent back to the Soviet Union by the U.S. government in 1945, he was executed there in 1946 (AG 2:479–80).

p. 38 — "And 'rape,' that was another word": Franza does not realize what this English word means.

p. 41 — "therefore I declare all of my servants free": The last verse in Friedrich Schiller's play Wilhelm Tell (AG 2:480).

p. 41 — "for man is born free, is free": Quoted from Schiller's poem "Die Worte des Glaubens" (AG 2:480).

p. 46 — "Lord Percival Glyde": A character from Wilkie Collins's 1860 novel The Woman in White (AG 2:480).

p. 62 — "the marriage with Bluebeard": A reference to the fable "Barbe-bleu" ("Bluebeard") by Charles Perrault (AG 2:472).

p. 69 — "Everyman": Hugo von Hofmannsthal's adaptation of the mystery play Everyman, which traditionally opens the Salzburg Festival each summer (AG 2:481).

p. 69 — "But what is evil, what is it?": A reference to Konrad Lorenz's book Das sogenannte Böse (The Nature of Evil), published 1963 (AG 2:481).

p. 79 — "I am from a lower race": Bachmann echoes here a line from Arthur Rimbaud's "Une saison en enfer": "Je suis de race inférieure de toute éternité" (AG 2:481).

p. 81 — "Landru": The Landru case is one of the most famous murder cases in French history and was made into a film titled Landru by Claude Chabrol in 1962 (AG 2:472).

p. 81 — "the battle of the Mohács": A reference to the battle that took place at Mohács on August 29, 1526, in which the Hungarians under Ludwig II were defeated by the Turks under Suleiman II. The Turks later lay siege to Vienna in 1529 (AG 2:471).

p. 83—"neither of us got much out of victims": Franza makes a revealing verbal slip here in German by substituting the dative case plural for "opera" (Opern) with that for "victims" (Opfern). Unfortunately, there seems to be no way to capture this important nuance in English.

p. 86—"Those others also cried at Nuremberg": A reference to the witnesses who testified against Nazi war criminals at the trials held in Nuremberg after World War II.

p. 90—"Suez . . . a past war": A reference to the Suez crisis of 1956, during which the United States and Great Britain withdrew financial support for the building of the Aswan High Dam to protest the arming of Egypt by the East Block. Egypt's president responded by imposing high tolls on ships using the Suez Canal, which soon led to an attack on Egypt by Israel with the support of British and French aerial bombardment. After intense diplomatic pressure by the United States and the Soviet Union, a cease-fire was declared after seven days of fighting; eventually the Israeli, British, and French troops withdrew under the watchful eye of United Nations peacekeepers (AG 2:482).

p. 94—"for then I'll be able to eat it": A reference to Robert Musil's poem "Isis und Osiris" (AG 2:483).

p. 101—"a state visit": On May 13, 1964, the intial construction phase of the Aswan High Dam was completed. In celebration, the president of Iraq, Abd As Salam Arif, the president of

Yemen, Abdullah As-Sallal, the president of Egypt, Gamal Abd el Nasser, and the head of the Soviet Union, Nikita Khruschev, opened the first gates of the dam, diverting the Nile into the newly completed canal (AG 2:484–85).

p. 108—"the shadowy years during which no star hung in my mouth": Compare stanza 4 of Bachmann's poem "Prague, January 1964."

p. 109—"Thutmose": The successor to Queen Hatshepsut, Thutmose III hated his predecessor so much that he obliterated her carved image wherever he found it, including in her own mortuary temple.

p. 111—"Where is the Gulf of Aqaba!": A reference to T. E. Lawrence's Seven Pillars of Wisdom.

p. 112—"The whites are coming. The whites are landing.": Once again Bachmann echoes lines from Rimbaud's "Une saison en enfer": "Je ne vois même pas l'heure où, les blancs débarquent, je tomberai au néant, / . . . Les blancs débarquent. Le canon! Il faut se soumettre au baptême, s'habiller, travailler." In addition, Monika Albrecht and Dirk Göttsche comment that Bachmann's notion of how the whites will "resurrect themselves in a brown or black brain" can be linked to the postcolonial theory of Frantz Fanon, found in his books Black Skin, White Masks (1952) and The Wretched of the Earth (1961) (AG 2:485).

p. 114—"Hashish, hashinin, assassin": The word "hashish" derives from the Arabic word hashinin, which refers to assassins who carried out missions for Egyptian rulers. In preparation they would smoke the drug in order to give themselves courage (AG 2:69).

p. 119 — "The Arabian desert is surrounded by shattered visions of God.": See T. E. Lawrence, The Seven Pillars of Wisdom (1936) (AG 2:486–87).

p. 121 — "Cairo, the Victorious": The Arabic name for Cairo, "El Qahira," means "The Victorious."

p. 128 — "The sulfonamide and phlegmone experiments": Experiments carried out by Nazi doctors on prisoners in the concentration camps and later documented by Alexander Mitscherlich in his 1960 book Medizin ohne Menschlichkeit (AG 2:487).

p. 130 — "Prosecutor MacHaney": James MacHaney was the name of the prosecutor in the trial of the Nazi doctors (AG 2:487).

p. 131 — "Akhenaton's daughter": Akhenaton was the husband of Nefertiti.

p. 144 — "It was only a matter of time before Wadi Halfa would be destroyed.": After the completion of the Aswan High Dam, hundreds of miles of Nubian lands were flooded to the south as part of the creation of Lake Nasser, the world's largest artificial lake. Bachmann refers here to the expectation that eventually Wadi Halfa in Sudan would also fall victim to this flooding.

p. 146 — "a military coup caused all of the paintings of General Abboud to fall from Sudanese walls": In 1964, the military rule established by General Abboud in the Sudan in 1958 was overthrown and parlimentary government was restored.

requiem for fanny goldmann

p. 149—"Malina": One of the three principal characters in Bachmann's novel Malina.

p. 151—"the woman in the wheelchair": This woman is Eka Rottwitz, the central character of a fourth "Todesarten" novel planned by Bachmann. A successful journalist, she throws herself out of a window when jilted by her lover and thus ends up in a wheelchair.

p. 153—"Rossegger": Peter Rossegger (1843–1918), Austrian novelist born in the province of Styria and considered to be only a local talent.

p. 157—"Hofmannsthal's Everyman": A play by Hugo von Hofmannsthal that traditionally opens the Salzburg festival each June.

p. 159—"Duse": Famed nineteenth-century Italian actress whose real name was Olga Signorelli (AG 1:594).

p. 160—"Thank You for the Roses": No such play exists (AG 1:598).

p. 161—"Minister Fey": Emil Fey (1886–1938), army leader and, from 1933 to 1935, the vice-chancellor and interior minister of the Austria's first republic. When the German army entered Austria, he and his family committed suicide (AG 1:598).

p. 161—"Dollfuss": Engelbert Dollfuss (1892–1934), chancellor of Austria (1932–34), murdered by the Nazis (AG 1:598).

p. 161—"Planetta": Otto Planetta, the man charged with and convicted of the murder of Dollfuss, though his guilt was later questioned (AG 1:598).

p. 168—"Nussdorf": An outlying district of Vienna.

p. 169—"Siedler": Annerose Siedler, one of the stars of the 1949 Austrian film The Murder Trial of Dr. Jordan (AG 1:598).

p. 169—"Holzmeister": The actress Judith Holzmeister, wife of Curd Jürgens (AG 1:599).

p. 171—"St. Wolfgang": Popular lakeside town outside of Salzburg.

p. 172—"Burgtor": An arch located in the Burggarten park in the heart of Vienna.

p. 172—"Burgenland": A province to the east of Vienna whose inhabitants are often the target of jokes.

p. 178—"upper or lower Magdeburg or Taunus": Backwater regions and towns in Germany meant to serve as symbols of bleak provincial life.

p. 182—"Kohlmarkt" and "Graben": Well-known streets in Vienna's central first district.

p. 182—"Kärtnerstrasse": Vienna's main shopping street and tourist center.

p. 182—"St. Michael's": A church located across the street from the Hofburg Palace.

p. 186—"Stock im Eisen": A famed tree trunk in the middle of Vienna covered with nails that people have hammered into it.

p. 186—"Karlskirche": A Baroque church located in Vienna and built by Johann Bernard Fischer von Erlach.

pp. 187–88—"If, in order to examine her soul, one were to have brought Fanny before the Inquisition": An allusion to "La vengeance d'une femme," a short story by J. A. Barbey d'Aurevilly (AG 1:600).

p. 205—"Fanny died in December": When Fanny initially vows to live six months more, it is actually midsummer. Thus her death in December should not violate her earlier vow, though the narrative voice makes it seem that she has. Most likely this is due to an error in chronology on the part of Bachmann while drafting the novel.

p. 207—"Degischer": Vilma Degischer, a famous actress of Vienna (AG 1:595).

p. 208—"Neustift-am-Wald": An outlying district of Vienna.

p. 209—"Horváth and Nestroy": Ödön von Horváth (1901–39) and Johann Nestroy (1801–62), Austrian playwrights.

p. 209—"St. Teresa of Avila": Sixteenth-century founder of the Carmelite order of nuns (AG 1:606).

p. 209—"Heidegger": Martin Heidegger (1889–1976), German philosopher on whom Bachmann wrote her master's thesis in philosophy.

p. 209—"Jünger": Ernst Jünger (1895–1998), German novelist.

p. 209—"Claudel": Paul Claudel (1868–1955), French poet and playwright.

p. 211—"Reinhardt Seminar": A renowned acting school in Vienna, founded by Max Reinhardt in 1929.

p. 212—"Habimah Theater": A theater troupe founded in Russia in 1917, moved to Israel in 1928, and since 1958 the national theater of Israel (AG 1:607).

p. 212—"Bassermann or Kainz or Thimig": Albert Bassermann (1867–1952), German actor; Josef Kainz (1858–1910), Austrian actor; Helene Thimig (1889–1974), Austrian actress and member of a renowned family of actors (AG 1:608).

p. 216—"Schusschnigg's last speech": Kurt Schusschnigg (1897–1977) was the Austrian prime minister who in 1938 resigned his position to protest Hitler's annexation of Austria.

p. 217—"your Rosenkavalier": A reference to the ceremonial bearer of a rose between a wooer and his beloved in an opera by Richard Strauss.

ingeborg bachmann: a chronology

1926
Born on June 25 in Klagenfurt, Austria.

1945–50
Studies law and philosophy at the Universities of Innsbruck, Graz, and Vienna. Degree awarded by the University of Vienna in 1950 for a dissertation titled "The Critical Reception of Martin Heidgegger's Existential Philosophy."

1948–49
First poems published in Lynkeus. Dichtung, Kunst, Kritik, edited by Hermann Hakel.

1951–53
Scriptwriter at Radio Rot-Weiss-Rot in Vienna. Begins work on the first stories and drafts of what would later develop into the "Todesarten" novels.

1952
First reading at the Gruppe 47 gathering. Libretto for the ballet pantomime The Idiot, with music by Hans Werner Henze.

1953
Receives the Gruppe 47 Prize. Die gestundete Zeit, poems, published by Frankfurter Verlaganstalt.

1953–57
Lives in Italy on the island of Ischia, in Naples, and in Rome.

1955
Die Zikaden, radio play, produced in Hamburg. Takes part in the international seminar at Harvard Summer School of Arts and Sciences, led by Henry Kissinger.

1956
Anrufung des Grossen Bären, poems, published by R. Piper Verlag, Munich.

1957
Awarded the Bremen Literature Prize.

1958–62
Lives in Zurich, Munich, and Rome. Involved with the Swiss writer Max Frisch until 1962, after which her primary residence is in Rome until her death.

1959
Awarded the Radio Play Prize of the War Blind. Delivers acceptance speech titled "Die Wahrheit ist dem Menschen zumutbar."

1959–60
Delivers the first lectures for the Poetry Chair at Frankfurt University titled "Fragen zeitgenössischer Dichtung."

1960
Libretto for Hans Werner Henze's opera Der Prinz von Homburg.

1961

Das dreissigste Jahr, stories, published by R. Piper Verlag, Munich. Awarded the Berlin Critics Prize. Translations of Giuseppe Ungaretti published by Suhrkamp, Frankfurt.

1963

Residence in Berlin with support of Ford Foundation.

1964

Travels to Egypt. Awarded Georg Büchner Prize and writes her acceptance speech, "Eine Ort für Zufälle."

1965

Libretto for Hans Werner Henze's opera Der junge Lord.

1968

Awarded the Austrian State Prize for Literature.

1971

Malina, a novel, published by Suhrkamp, Frankfurt.

1972

Simultan, stories, published by R. Piper Verlag, Munich. Awarded Anton Wildgans Prize of Society of Austrian Industrialists.

1973

On September 26, severely burned in a fire in her Rome apartment. Death in Rome on October 17. Burial in Klagenfurt.